BEAUTIFUL LIES

Even Angels Have Their Demons

Josiyah Martin

Copyright © 2024 by Josiyah Martin.

All rights reserved. No part of this book may be used or reproduced in any form whatsoever without written permission except in the case of brief quotations in critical articles or reviews.

This book is a work of fiction. Names, characters, businesses, organizations, places, events and incidents either are the product of the author's imagination or are used fictitiously. Any resemblance to actual persons, living or dead, events, or locales is entirely coincidental.

Printed in the United States of America.

1

Hello, Darkness

Ariana awoke, coughing and disoriented. Her eyes blinked open, the air was heavy with the smell of dampness and decay, causing her to wrinkle her nose in disgust. She could feel the cold, hard ground beneath her, sending a shiver up her spine. *Where am I?* Panic surged through her as she struggled to piece together the fragments of her memory.

Slowly sitting up, Ariana pushed aside the heavy curtain of confusion. Shadows danced mockingly in the corners of her mind, elusive and foreboding. She was in a forest, that much was clear. But as to what she was doing here, that was a mystery. She could

Beautiful Lies

hear the sounds of birds chirping, and a faint breeze rustled the leaves of the trees above her.

Ariana surveyed her surroundings, trying to make sense of it all. The woods were large and towering, devoid of any personal touches or signs of life. It felt like she had stepped into a nightmare.

Memories began trickling back, fragments floating to the surface like forgotten whispers. She strained to recall the events that led her here but they remained tantalizingly out of reach. The last thing she remembered was being in Eclipse with Lexi and Madison.

Speaking of which, *where were they?* Ariana's heart quickened as she realized she was not alone in this eerie place. She turned her head slowly, anxiety gnawing at her gut.

Beside her lay two figures—Lexi and Madison—also awakening from their mysterious slumber. Their disoriented expressions mirrored Ariana's own bewilderment. It reminded her of those wild nights in high school when they would let loose after football games, drowning their teenage angst in reckless abandon. But this was different. This was something dark and unsettling.

Ariana felt a chill run down her spine as she looked closer at the two of them. They were both covered in dirt and dried blood, and Ariana had no recollection of how she had come to be here with them.

Her eyes then fell on a bright red light in the distance. The strange light seemed to shimmer and pulse, almost like a heartbeat. It was faint at first, but it grew brighter as she watched.

"Ariana," Lexi whispered cautiously, her voice filled with both fear and concern. "Are you okay?" She struggled to steady herself, her hand brushing against Ariana's arm for support.

Ariana tried to speak, but her words came out as a mere murmur. "I'm... okay." Her head throbbed with intensity, her thoughts still spinning in a disorienting haze. "Do either of you remember what happened? I can't recall anything," she confessed, desperately searching their faces for any sign of recognition.

Lexi and Madison exchanged a look of confusion before shaking their heads in unison. Silence settled over them, interrupted only by the distant rustling of leaves and the haunting melody of birdsong.

"It's like we all just blacked out and woke up here," Madison finally spoke up, her voice trembling with uncertainty.

Ariana sighed and glanced at her two friends warily. It was strange seeing the two of them together again after so much time apart. They all seemed so different from who they used to be - not only in appearance but also in attitude and demeanor - yet they were still undeniably the same people deep down inside that had bonded over secrets that also drove them apart.

Ariana slowly got up, her legs shaking beneath her as she moved towards the light. She quickly felt Madison grab her hand as they hesitantly approached the bright red light, the girls could now make out that it belonged to a silver Volvo with its trunk open from afar. Fear and confusion raced through their mind as they slowly moved closer to the trunk. The girls gave each other one final look of assurance before moving forward. Ariana let out a bone chilling shriek as she sees the silhouette of a man's body inside the trunk.

"F-Fuck," Ariana stuttered, unable to tear her gaze away from the gruesome sight. Her legs threatened to give way beneath her, but Lexi caught her before she crumbled to the floor.

"Is he...," Madison whispered. The girls stare silently as no one's brave enough to speak.

Despite her trembling limbs and racing heart, Ariana found herself inexplicably drawn back to the trunk. Curiosity mingled with dread as she crawled toward it, momentarily ignoring the throbbing pain in her head. She had to know the truth.

Gazing into the trunk, her stomach dropped as she recognized the face of the man inside. His eyes were wide open and his skin was coated with red smears that could only be described as blood. It was Jason Fanburg, one of the wealthiest men in River Creek. She met with his wife earlier that day to help handle her divorce settlement. She felt paralyzed by fear, unable to move or do anything but stare at the lifeless body.

The girls shared a look of disbelief before slowly getting up and away from the car. They were all too afraid to say anything as they tried to piece together what had happened that night. As they looked around, it was clear that they were in some sort of remote clearing surrounded by trees on all sides with no sign of civilization anywhere.

Ariana walked back towards the car one last time, her legs shaking beneath her as she stared at Jason's lifeless body one last time.

"Who could have done this" Ariana whispered, trying to hold back tears. Terror clenched Ariana's throat, rendering her almost voiceless. She felt an invisible weight pressing down on her chest, suffocating every breath she struggled to take. The boundaries between nightmare and reality began to blur, leaving her trapped in a waking hell.

"We can't just leave him here. We have to call the police," Madison said, her voice shaking.

Lexi anxiously scoffed, "But what if they think we did it? We woke up here with no memory of how we got here with a body of a man we don't even know."

Ariana's heart sank as Lexi spoke. She knew that Lexi was right. Going to the police could very well incriminate them if there's more to all of this. But leaving the body here was also not an option. They needed to find out what had happened to them and how they ended up in this forest with Jason.

"I have an idea," Ariana said, trying to sound confident. "We need to find out what happened to us and who did this. Right now our alibi is shaky, and none of us remember tonight making us the only prime suspects. We can't trust anyone else with this, not even the police."

The other girls looked at her skeptically, but they were also desperate for answers.

"What's your plan?" Madison asked, her voice trembling.

"We need to investigate," Ariana declared, her voice steady despite the nervous tremor in her hands. "We need to retrace our steps from last night, find out what happened to us. Only then can we uncover the truth." Her gaze swept over Lexi and Madison, silently pleading for their trust as they stood on the precipice of an abyss.

Madison stared at Ariana, her face a combination of puzzlement and disbelief. "This is madness," she said, shaking her head. "You want to play Nancy Drew while our lives are literally falling apart? You're a divorce lawyer for Christ's sake, not a detective Ari!"

Desperate for an escape, Madison started pacing back and forth across the clearing, her mind racing in every direction imaginable. She couldn't help but feel like this was all some sick joke– like someone had purposely put them in this situation for their own twisted amusement. But at the same time, a part of her wanted to believe that maybe she had actually stumbled upon something bigger than herself.

Lexi hesitated, her gaze distant as she wrestled with her own demons. Slowly, she met Ariana's unwavering stare. "We can't involve the police," she finally uttered, her voice filled with a mixture of fear and determination. "There's someone else who might be able to help us. Someone I'd rather not involve, but it might be our only choice."

Lexi glanced away, her face pale as she hesitated before continuing. "My mother has some... connections in the city," she said reluctantly as if admitting it was difficult for her. "She knows people who can help us with this kind of stuff, plus they'll know what to do with the body." She paused and looked at Ariana and Madison, her eyes filled with worry as she continued speaking slowly, "But if we ask for her help, she's going to want something in return. She always does."

Ariana and Madison looked at each other in shock - Lexi rarely talked about her family and especially not about her mother. But in moments like this she felt like her last name was branded onto her back.

"Lexi...," Madison hesitated.

"Don't," Lexi muttered.

Madison looked away, feeling guilty and powerless to help.

Ariana opened her mouth to speak but she couldn't force the

words to form. Ariana's mind was filled with a flurry of images - the dead man's terrified face, Lexi's solemn expression as she talked about her mother, and the darkness of the forest that surrounded them - it was too much for her to take in. Her legs suddenly felt weak and she stumbled backwards onto the floor, her breath coming in short gasps as if she were suffocating. She could feel her heart pounding against her chest and dozens of thoughts raced through her head all at once.

One image stood out from all the others - it was Jason's, his eyes begging for help as he laid there lifelessly. His face burned into Ariana's memory like a searing brand and it felt like it took over every inch of her being until she thought she would explode from panic. With effort, Ariana forced herself back into reality and looked up at Lexi and Madison who were both staring.

"We don't have any other choice," Ariana finally spoke up. "We need to figure out what happened to us and why we were all here with this man's dead body. Lexi, call your mother and see what she can do for us."

Lexi nodded, her expression grave as she pulled out her phone and dialed her mother's number. As she spoke to her mother, Ariana and Madison exchanged worried glances. They knew that this was only the beginning of a nightmare they couldn't wake up from. They were all in too deep and there was no going back. But they were determined to find out what happened and to clear their names. They would stop at nothing to uncover the truth, even if it meant going against the law and taking matters into their own hands. For better or for worse, they were in this together, and they would do whatever it takes.

The girls waited anxiously as the minutes stretched into what felt like an eternity. Finally, the distant hum of engines broke through the silence, heralding the arrival of four sleek black trucks. Ariana's heart pounded in her chest as she exchanged nervous glances with Lexi and Madison.

As the trucks rolled to a stop, a sense of foreboding settled over the clearing like a heavy fog. Figures clad in dark suits emerged from the vehicles, moving with purpose and precision. These were the cleaners, Ariana realized with a sinking feeling in her gut. The ones who made sure that incidents like this disappeared without a trace.

Leading the group was a woman who exuded authority with every step. Her sharp gaze swept over the three girls, assessing them with keen scrutiny. Ariana felt a shiver run down her spine as their eyes met, sensing the weight of unspoken questions hanging in the air.

"Rebecca," Lexi's voice cut through the tension, her tone tinged with a mixture of relief and apprehension.

The woman nodded in acknowledgment; her expression unreadable. "Lexi Montalvo," she replied curtly. "What do we have here? From my sources I heard you retired, no?"

"Something like that," Lexi shifted uncomfortably. "But this is something different."

"Of course," Rebecca said as her eyes moved to Madison's. "You must be Madison Bennett?"

Madison watched Rebecca, her heart pounding in her chest. She nodded, swallowing hard before responding. "Yes, I am."

"Your father was a great man. I hope you enjoyed your time in New York city. I hear you've been pretty busy up there." Rebecca's gaze lingered on Madison for a moment longer before turning to Ariana. "And last but not least, Ariana Bennett. Your father, Chief Bennett, must be so proud that you're following in his footsteps." Ariana grimaced, as the words hung heavily in the air like a dark cloud. Ariana could feel a sharp pang of self-recrimination.

"Enough with the introductions," Lexi interjected, her voice edgy. She was visibly uncomfortable with the situation.

Lexi took a deep breath, steeling herself for what was to come. "We... we found a body," she admitted, her voice barely above a whisper. "In the trunk of that car."

Rebecca's brow furrowed as she turned her attention to the silver Volvo, her eyes narrowing in contemplation. "And you three just happened to stumble upon it?" she asked, her voice laced with skepticism.

Ariana exchanged a wary glance with Madison, both of them acutely aware of the precarious situation they found themselves in. They couldn't afford to slip up now, not with their lives hanging in the balance.

"We... we don't remember how we got here," Ariana confessed, her voice trembling with uncertainty. "We woke up in this forest with no recollection of the events leading up to it."

Rebecca's gaze hardened as she studied them, as if trying to discern the truth from their words. "Convenient," she muttered under her breath, her lips pressing into a thin line. "And what were you doing in this forest in the first place?"

Before any of them could respond, Lexi stepped forward, her jaw set with determination. "That's none of your business," she retorted, her tone defiant. "We need your help, Rebecca. Not your interrogation."

A tense silence hung in the air as the two women locked eyes, each refusing to back down. Finally, Rebecca relented with a sigh, conceding to Lexi's demand.

"Fine," she conceded, her voice clipped. "But don't think for a second that you're off the hook. We'll need to debrief you properly once we get back."

With that, Rebecca turned on her heel, signaling for her team to take charge of the situation. As the cleaners set to work, Ariana couldn't shake the feeling of unease that settled over her like a heavy cloak.

Even as the forest was methodically scrubbed of their presence, the weight of the unremembered past seemed to cling to her like a stubborn shadow, tainting the crisp woodland air with a bitter tang of unresolved questions. Her gaze flickered to the now-empty car trunk, the sight of Jason's lifeless body burnt into her memory.

Lexi stood apart from them, her dark eyes hardened with resolve. She appeared unfazed by Rebecca's stern orders, but Ariana saw how she clutched her phone tighter, a silent testament to an internal storm. There was no doubt in her mind that Lexi's conversation with Catalina hadn't been easy.

As the drivers arrived and Rebecca began doling out alibis and a change of clothes to each woman, Madison stared at the ground, her long wavy hair casting shadows over her downcast face. Ariana felt a sudden pang of sympathy for her. For all of them really; trapped within their pasts, ensnared in events beyond their control.

One by one, they were whisked away until only Lexi remained. Her defiant gaze locked onto Rebecca's retreating figure and she steeled herself for what lay ahead. Ariana watched from afar as Lexi was led away towards another car headed to where Lexi's mother awaited. She felt an unexpected chill run down her spine as the car disappeared into the bleak night.

* * *

Several hours had gone by. The car was waning softly from the early morning light, and Ariana squinted to check her phone – only to remember it had gone missing along with all of her memories of the night before. Judging by the sun's rays streaming through the window she assumed it must be around 7am.

A sudden voice from the front of the car interrupted her thoughts as the driver informed her about the traffic ahead. Ariana peered through the window and by the familiar cityscape she knew she was close enough to walk home. As she stepped out of the car she looked down to remember she had been given an oversized band t-shirt and a pair of old shorts to change into. It was strange how even fully clothed she felt so naked. It was as if she was made out of glass and the only thing you could see was fear.

Ariana hesitantly made her way through the fog-shrouded street toward her apartment building. The atmosphere was oppressive, as if the very air was thick with secrets. Her footsteps echoed eerily on the damp pavement, and the world around her seemed distorted, like a haunting dream.

The high-rise, she had often called home, loomed like a sinister monolith against the gray morning sky, its glass facade resembling a fortress. The metallic accents, usually gleaming, now appeared tarnished and tainted. The shadows beneath the ornamental trees and potted plants seemed to writhe and twist.

Ariana's heart pounded in her chest, and the weight of what felt like the world bore down on her as she kept moving. She couldn't help but feel as though the city itself was closing in on her, the fog concealing her as she moved closer to the building, while also wrapping her in its eerie cloak.

Ariana lurched back to her apartment building, her pretty brunette hair disheveled and sticking to the sweat on her forehead. Her mascara had smudged from the tears that streamed down her face as she tried to make sense of the chaos around her. The weight of exhaustion hung heavily on her shoulders and it was clear she was mentally drained, struggling to keep it together. She felt like she had been hit by a train without any warning. And to make matters worse, the aftertaste of last night's drinks lingered in her mouth, refusing to fade away. She had barely processed what happened earlier that morning in the woods and all she wanted was a hot shower and a good night's sleep. But as she got closer to her building, an eerie feeling began to wash over her. Something didn't feel right - the air seemed thick with dread, like it was warning her of something bad about to happen. And then she saw it – police cars parked outside of the building, as if they were guarding it from something or someone. What if they knew, she thought. It was all over, her reputation, her career, her life. Gone.

As Ariana reached closer to her building, she was met with a chilling sight – a stark line of bright yellow crime scene tape, like a forbidden barrier marking a boundary between the living and the dead. It flapped ominously in the breeze, its color in stark contrast to the desaturated surroundings. The tape, pulled taut, barred her way with an unspoken warning.

Ariana felt her throat tighten as she tried to move forward.

The thought of what might be waiting for her beyond the barrier made her breath catch in her throat. She was about to turn and run when she heard a familiar voice call across the morning air.

"Ariana, wait!"

Ariana jumped back at the sound of Chase's voice calling out to her in the darkness. She spun around, startled at seeing him standing there silhouetted by the yellow crime tape, his face illuminated by the streetlights. Chase stood in front of her with his hands shoved in his pockets as he stood a few steps away from her. His normally perfectly combed black hair is now unruly and tousled, and his clothes are an amalgamation of the suit he wore to work the previous day.

He stepped closer and took hold of Ariana's arm, his grip strong yet gentle at the same time - like he was trying to protect her from something that lurked just beyond their sight. "Hey I came as quick as I heard," he said softly with a somber smile on his lips, "we'll figure this out together".

Confused, Ariana looked back at him. "What's going on?" she asked with a shaky voice, "why are there police cars here?".

Chase sighed heavily as he ran his hands through his hair. "I'm sorry I didn't answer you earlier," he said regretfully, "one of my friends on the force called me this morning about an incident in your building and I wasn't able to get to the phone in time...." He trailed off, looking away for a moment before turning back to her again. His gaze was full of concern as he spoke again. "From what I can tell so far, it seems like there's some sort of accident".

The sudden noise from a forming crowd broke her attention as people surrounded an area on the street, including paramedics with a stretcher. They were clearly trying to secure the scene and

Beautiful Lies

avoid further contamination from passersbyers.

Ariana bolted towards the crowd, she could feel her heart drop as she pushed through the crowd and tried to get a better look at the victim. With each step closer, Ariana felt fear coursing through her veins until finally, she got a clear view of the person on the stretcher. Her stomach dropped as she recognized the face – it was Scott, her younger brother. Tears pooled in her eyes and her body trembling as she saw his lifeless form being carried away by paramedics. The moment felt like an eternity as she stared in shock. How could this have happened? Why?

The questions raced through Ariana's mind as tears began streaming down her face uncontrollably. Chase quickly wrapped his arm around her shoulders and held tightly, reassuringly reminding Ariana that he was there for her no matter what.

Through blurry eyes, Ariana slowly began to process what had happened as the reality of the situation hit her. Scott was gone and all she could feel was this aching pain in her chest as she realized that he was never coming back. He was her light, her way out of the darkness that she had known to be her family. Darkness that has now swallowed her whole.

Chase noticed how lost Ariana looked and pulled her gently into him, holding her tightly as he tried his best to comfort her, all the while swallowing his own feelings of grief. They stood there for a few minutes until Chase slowly let go of Ariana, giving her one last gentle glance before turning away giving her a moment to come to terms with everything.

Ariana stared off into nowhere, unable to believe what had happened and wishing more than anything that this wasn't real. But no matter how much she wished it away or tried to deny it -

Scott was gone.

Ariana jolted back to reality at the sound of her name.

"Excuse me," a voice called from behind.

When she spun around, a tall, sullen officer stood before them. His badge read Detective Penbrooke; he had a stern expression plastered over his chiseled face. A handful of greying hair sat atop his head, and the wrinkles around his eyes suggested years of facing the darkness that humanity often concealed behind closed doors.

"We found something on the surveillance tapes we thought you should see," he said, his voice gruff as if every word was dragged from a well of reluctance. He activated a tablet device in his hand and passed it to Ariana. It was a black and white video footage, timestamped around the exact hour Scott's death might have occurred.

On the small screen, Scott appeared on the balcony. He was talking to someone, a figure shrouded in darkness whose face was obscured by an unfortunate camera angle. A sudden movement, a shove, and then Scott... was no longer in the frame, swallowed by the cruel void below.

Ariana let out a choked sob, her heart pounding like a drum against her ribs. The reality of it all crashed onto her like a monstrous tsunami wave threatening to drag her under its cold current. She blinked back bitter tears, her knuckles white as she gripped the tablet.

"Who is that?" Ariana's voice emerged as an anguished whisper.

"That's what we're trying to figure out," Officer Penbrooke replied with a sigh, running a hand over his weary face. "No one should have had access to your apartment... but clearly someone did."

"No... no, it's not possible," Ariana murmured, her gaze fixed on the grainy footage of her brother's last moments.

Suddenly a uniformed officer approached the detective with a somber expression, whispering something urgently into his ear. The detective's brows furrowed as he listened intently, his eyes flicking briefly to Ariana before focusing on the officer.

"What is it?" Ariana asked, her voice filled with apprehension as she watched the exchange.

Detective Penbrooke hesitated for a moment before turning back to Ariana, his expression grim. "We found something," he said, his voice grave. "Something that might shed some light on what happened to your brother."

Ariana's heart skipped a beat as she waited for him to continue, her mind racing with a thousand possibilities.

"It appears that Scott's cell phone was recovered from the scene," Detective Penbrooke explained, his tone measured. "And on it, we found a message from you, asking him to meet you at your apartment last night."

Ariana froze in terror as the officer stepped closer, suspiciously examining her every move.

Realization finally came crashing down on Ariana's shoulders like a ton of bricks. Her phone had been missing since she woke up in the woods and she had assumed it was just lost. But now that she put the pieces together, she knew this had been a setup from the start. Someone had gone to great lengths to get Scott alone. But why? The thought made her feel sick and it was hard to breathe as the realization set in.

"Have I done something wrong detective?"

Penbrooke studied Ariana, his eyes giving away nothing. "It's simple procedure. I do have to ask, where you were last night?"

Chase stepped in quickly, seeing the fear that had settled on Ariana. He could tell the detective was trying to get her into a corner and he wasn't about to let that happen. "Detective, I'm Chase Smith, lawyer and partner at Smiths and Associates. She answered your question already and has nothing else to say until we hear evidence that she is somehow linked or involved with Scott's death."

"Ariana," Detective Penbrooke began, his voice tinged with caution, "I know that your father is the Chief. I need to make it clear that this investigation will be impartial and thorough."

The weight of suspicion bore down on her like a heavy burden, threatening to crush her under its oppressive force.

"I understand, Detective," Ariana replied, her voice trembling slightly.

Chase shot her a reassuring glance, silently urging her to remain composed. "Ariana has nothing to hide," he interjected firmly. "And until there is concrete evidence linking her to Scott's death, she is under no obligation to answer any further questions."

The officer looked at them both for a moment before slowly nodding his head and leaving them with one final piece of advice - "Don't be a hero kid. This town has a thing for spitting those out." Chase scoffed as the officer walked away, and Ariana crumbled.

As tears streamed down her cheeks, she could feel Chase's firm hand patting her back gently as he silently promised her that he would do everything in his power to make sure justice was served. But what was justice after all? This wasn't some mere accident. Someone actually wanted to hurt her brother and make it look like she was involved. Fury raged within her, but it was quickly replaced by fear. Whoever had done this could still be out there somewhere, and what is their correlation to this horrid night?

"Ariana..." Chase whispered. His fingers trace her face guiding her to look up at his sterling blue eyes. He took a breath as he chose his next words carefully. "You know you can tell me anything, right? I can help you-"

"Stop." Ariana sighed. "It's been a long night and the last thing I need to do right now is be questioned from you of all people." Ariana's eyes fell to the ground. She hated that she had to keep this secret from him. She couldn't bear the thought of this poison affecting him too.

"I'm just trying to make sense of it all. See it from my perspective, your girlfriend calls you in a drunken panic and completely goes off the grid for hours the night before your big deposition. But you love her so much that you go stop by her apartment to not just find her here completely a mess but also her younger brother pushed out of a fucking balcony." Chase sighs knowing he said too much. "I'm sorry, I'm just worried."

"I know." Ariana grabs Chase's hands, squeezing them tight. "We'll figure it out together," Ariana smiled, pasting the lie across her lips. She knew she couldn't risk getting Chase caught up in this.

"Can you at least do one thing for me?" Ariana asked.

Chase nodded in response, "Anything."

"Go back to your apartment and try to get some rest, I'll be there soon. I think I'm just going to stay here and grab a few things," Ariana lied.

Chase looked at her hesitantly, not wanting to leave her side. But he knew that she was right. This was a situation that needed to be handled delicately and there wasn't much he could do to help her at the moment so he relented and kissed her goodbye before leaving.

Ariana watched Chase walk away until she couldn't see him anymore, tears filling her eyes as she thought about what this night had brought them. She wanted to go back and rewind the clock, erase this entire nightmare from existence. But the harsh reality of their situation settled in with a heavy weight on her heart. As Ariana looked away from the balcony, determined to find out what really happened that night, she steeled herself against the fear of an uncertain future with one promise – there would be no peace.

✷ ✷ ✷

Vines crept along the walls of the abandoned building as it loomed towards Lexi as she entered. It was almost impressive how this fortress hid amidst the sprawling industrial district on the outskirts of the city. The air was heavy with the acrid scent of oil and the distant rumble of machinery. Flickering fluorescent lights hung from the high ceiling, casting eerie, intermittent shadows on the cold, concrete floor.

Lexi's footsteps echoed off the walls as the guards led her further into the warehouse. The air became more and more oppressive, a sense of dread looming heavy in the air. Stacks of wooden crates and metal barrels, each labeled in indecipherable code, lined the narrow aisles. The hum of generators provided power to a network of surveillance cameras that blanketed the space, reminding all who entered that there was no escape.

Towering men, hidden behind black helmets and heavily-armored boots, appeared before her like a plague of locusts. The only color she saw was the vile stain emblazoned on their arms - one that was painfully familiar to her. A tattoo of a pair of eagle wings on their forearm.

The warehouse itself was a cavernous expanse of secrecy. Shelves lined with packages of various sizes and colors, tightly sealed and tagged, hinted at the illicit activities hidden within these walls. Lexi couldn't help but wonder what lay concealed in those packages—drugs, weapons. What has she gotten herself into?

At the far end of the warehouse, a raised platform served as the throne for the cartel's boss. Her mother, Catalina Montalvo. Behind a grand desk adorned with ivory inlays, Catalina sat, her presence cold . Her mother was a striking woman who, at one time, could've been called beautiful. Her dark hair, though streaked with gray, was still thick and luxurious. She had high cheekbones, a slender nose, full lips, and wide, dark eyes with long lashes. She was still tall and slender, but her skin had taken on a worn, tired look.

"Mi hija,"Catalina sighed, her voice laden with disappointment. She stepped down to approach her daughter. Her eyes studied her shape as she walked closer.

Lexi felt a familiar knot of tension forming in her stomach, and the weight of guilt pressed down on her. She had distanced herself from this for a reason, hoping to build a life away from family that had defined her upbringing. Yet, she found herself standing here, needing her mother's help.

Catalina continued, her words dripping with disdain, "You

thought you could just walk away from family? You've become soft, my dear, forgetting your roots. But this is why we need mothers. Mothers, we get a bad rap. We provide for our children and one day they turn their backs on us to seek... mediocrity."

Lexi braced herself as she knew her mother's words were a trap laced with manipulation.

"We didn't kill him," she whispered. The words felt foreign as they slipped her lips. Catalina chuckled.

Catalina's gaze remained unyielding, and she closed the distance between them. "You know, hija, there's something I can't ignore. You've come back to me in your time of need, despite your disloyalty." Catalina looked around the room as if she was collecting an audience. "But as a mother, I come to save you. Bring you home."

Lexi clenched her jaw, realizing that her mother was using this moment to bring her back into the family's web she tried so hard to run from. She needed her mother's help, but at what cost will she have to pay?

"Do you know anything about the man you killed?"

"We didn't-" Lexi stopped realizing the futility of her words.

"Right. Well that dead man is a Fanburg. His family had long history in gun trades with the La Conchas, the southsiders... those pirates," Catalina spat in disdain.

Lexi's brows furrowed in confusion. "What are you saying?"

"Mi hija, men just don't appear in car trunks. How well do you trust these girls."

As Catalina's words hung in the air, Lexi couldn't help but feel a growing sense of doubt about Ariana and Madison. They had been distant from her life since high school, and now they had suddenly reappeared.

The memories of their past were hazy now, and they had all walked separate paths. Lexi questioned whether she truly knew Ariana and Madison anymore or maybe ever at all. It seemed like it was all a different life now.

"Ma, you know these girls. You know these girls, we're practically sisters." Catalina sneered.

"Oh, so Ariana told you? She was repping his wife in his divorce. My sources say this was more like a shakedown poor thing. His wife realized he was into some things way over his head and threatened to leak everything she could find on his black book dealings. Let's just say inquiring minds would do anything they can to stay hidden."

Lexi's mind raced as she tried to piece together what Catalina was saying. Ariana, who had always been the responsible one, was involved in this mess too? And Madison, who had disappeared for years without a trace, showed up right when all of this went down.

"I don't know anything about this," Lexi said, trying to keep her voice steady.

Catalina's expression softened slightly. "I believe you, love. But you have to be careful. There are people out there who are trying to bring us down, and we can't let them. But don't worry hija, I've got it under control. You just need to do something for me in return."

Lexi's heart sank as she realized that her mother was going to use this as an opportunity to bring her back into the fold. She knew that there was no way out of this now.

"What do you need me to do?" she asked, resigned to her fate.

"There's a shipment coming in from Mexico next week. We

need you to oversee the transfer and make sure that everything goes smoothly."

Lexi nodded, knowing that she had no choice but to agree. "I'll do it," she said, her voice barely above a whisper. Deep inside, Lexi was struggling. Questions loomed over her brain and she realized she was surrounded. She knew that if she followed through with the task of her mother, she couldn't run again.

Catalina placed a hand on her daughter's shoulder. "That's my girl," she said, before turning to walk back to her desk. "Oh, and Lexi," she added, turning back to face her daughter, "make sure you keep an eye on those girls. We can't afford any loose ends."

With that, she sat back down at her desk, dismissing Lexi with a wave of her hand. As Lexi walked out of the warehouse, she couldn't shake the feeling of dread that had settled in her stomach. She knew that she was in too deep, and that her life would never be the same. She had to find a way out of this situation, but she didn't know how.

As she walked through the empty streets, her mind raced with thoughts of Ariana and Madison. She couldn't believe that they had been involved in something so dangerous, and she couldn't help but wonder what else they were hiding from her.

Lexi lit a cigarette, inhaling deeply as she tried to calm her nerves. She knew that she needed to figure out what happened the night before and how she got involved in all of this. She needed the help of Ariana and Madison, but she couldn't shake off the feeling that they were involved in this mess too.

Lexi had to reach out to her old friends and get to the bottom of this. She took a deep drag from her cigarette, the smoke swirling around her as she resolved to find Ariana and Madison, hoping they held the key to unraveling the web of deception and danger that had entangled them all.

* * *

As Madison walked through the wrought-iron gates of the graveyard, the air was heavy with the scent of flowers; a mix of sorrow and remembrance. Headstones stood like silent sentinels, each bearing the weight of someone's story.

The sky above was a canvas of muted grays, mirroring the storm within her. The gravestones cast long shadows, stretching towards the horizon. The wind whispered through the trees, carrying echoes of memories. And then, there it was—the true resting place of her family. The headstones, hidden in the shadows, held the names she etched into heart: Mary, Richard, and Jake. The realization struck like a thunderbolt, unraveling the mystery that had veiled her family's final resting place.

Fresh flowers adorned the landscape, a vivid contrast to the fading autumn leaves that crunched beneath her boots. Madison's breath hitched, caught in the ache of grief that had become her constant companion.

The gravestones stood in silent testimony to the car crash that had torn her family apart. The tragedy, still fresh, marked a wound that refused to heal. She knelt by the graves, fingers lingering on the cold marble. Tears welled in her eyes, threatening to spill over, but she fought to keep them at bay.

"Hey, Mom. Dad. Jake," she whispered, the words carried away by the wind. "I miss you guys so much." Madison's voice wavered, a fragile melody in the quiet cemetery.

The world seemed to hush in reverence as Madison struggled

to keep it together. The graveyard embraced her pain, offering solace in the silent communion between the living and the departed. Each step away felt like leaving a piece of herself behind, tangled in the roots of the memories that haunted her.

As she turned to go, a chill skittered up her spine, and Madison felt as if someone was watching her. She slowly spun around, searching the shadows for any sign of movement. Sure enough, off in the distance, she could just make out a figure standing silently in the shadows, observing her with an intensity that seemed almost predatory. As soon as their eyes met, the figure began to run away—the sound of their footsteps echoing like thunder over the cemetery grounds.

Madison's heart raced and her palms grew sweaty as she ran after the figure. She had no idea who it was or why they were here, but there was something familiar about them that tugged at the edges of her memory.

The figure darted between headstones and trees, leading her further into the graveyard. Madison's breath came in sharp gasps as she pushed herself to go faster, boots pounding against the earth in pursuit of her mystery target.

But try as she might, the figure seemed to always stay just out of reach—a ghostly apparition that melted away into nothingness with every step closer. Eventually, Madison stumbled to a halt near a large mausoleum, chest heaving from exhaustion. The figure had vanished without a trace.

Madison felt deflated and defeated until she heard someone calling out from behind. "Madison? Is that you?"

She spun around to find an older woman standing there—her face etched with lines of concern. It was Helen, an old family friend whom Madison hadn't seen since childhood. Helen quickly wrapped her in a warm embrace before pulling back and studying her intently.

"What are you doing here all alone? Are you alright?" Helen asked gently, brushing away an errant strand of hair from Madison's face.

"I'm fine," Madison replied softly before turning away with a heavy sigh. She had so many questions and yet being here brought back so much pain and sadness, that she wasn't sure if she could bear it any longer.

Helen seemed to sense this and put an arm around Madison's shoulders in comfort before guiding them both over towards a nearby bench where they could sit.

As they settled onto the bench, Madison felt a sense of relief wash over her, grateful for Helen's comforting presence. She glanced around the graveyard once more, the shadows seeming less ominous now in the light of day.

"I didn't expect to see anyone I knew here," Madison admitted, her voice tinged with a mixture of surprise and gratitude.

Helen offered her a sympathetic smile. "I come here often to visit my own loved ones," she explained, gesturing towards a nearby plot of graves adorned with flowers. "It's a peaceful place to reflect and remember."

Madison nodded, feeling a pang of empathy for Helen's loss. She knew all too well the pain of losing someone dear.

"I just... needed to be here," Madison confessed, her voice barely above a whisper. "Sometimes it feels like the only way to keep their memory alive."

Helen's eyes held a knowing look as she asked Madison what

had brought her back home after all these years away. Madison opened her mouth to explain when Helen waved away the question and pulled something from beneath her coat: A necklace with a locket in the shape of a butterfly.

As they sat on the bench, Helen reached into her pocket and pulled out a small velvet box. She hesitated for a moment before offering it to Madison with a gentle smile.

"Madison, I want you to have this," Helen said softly, her eyes filled with warmth and understanding.

Curious, Madison accepted the box and carefully opened it. Inside, nestled on a bed of soft fabric, was a delicate butterfly necklace, its wings adorned with shimmering crystals that caught the light.

"It's beautiful," Madison breathed, her fingers tracing the intricate design of the pendant.

Helen nodded, a wistful smile playing at the corners of her lips. "Butterflies have always been a symbol of hope for me," she explained. "They remind me that even in the darkest of times, there is still beauty and possibility waiting to emerge."

She reached out and took Madison's hand, placing the necklace gently in her palm. "Right now, it looks like you may need a little more hope."

Madison felt tears prickling at the corners of her eyes as she gazed down at the necklace, its delicate wings glinting in the sunlight. It was a simple gesture, but it carried with it a depth of meaning that touched her heart.

"Thank you, Helen," Madison whispered, her voice choked with emotion.

With a soft smile, Helen squeezed Madison's hand in

reassurance. "Remember dear, no matter how dark the night may seem, there is always the promise of a new dawn. And with hope in your heart, you can face whatever challenges lie ahead. So, tell me," Helen said with a smile. "What have you been up to since leaving River Creek? Are you still living in New York?"

Madison shifted uncomfortably at the mention of New York.

"You don't need to tell me if you don't want to," Helen said gently, giving Madison's arm an understanding squeeze before changing the subject. "But are you just here temporarily or do you plan on sticking around?"

Madison sighed heavily before finally answering. "I don't know, I originally came back here to say goodbye," she began slowly, voice trembling with emotion. "I think this town is much better off without me in it."

Helen's eyes widened in surprise. "But why would you say that? You belong here just as much as anyone else." She gently put her hand over Madison's and looked into her eyes with such warmth and understanding that Madison found herself spilling out the truth of what had happened since she had left River Creek. She talked about the struggles she had faced, the loneliness she felt in a new city, and how it seemed like no matter what she did, nothing could fill the emptiness inside her.

Helen listened patiently until Madison finished speaking before giving her a small smile. "It sounds to me like you've been through a lot these past few years," Helen said softly. She paused for a moment before continuing on. "You have so much potential, my dear, and so many opportunities ahead of you if you're willing to take them. Don't be afraid to reach out for help when things get tough—you'll find strength in numbers."

Madison nodded, she knew Helen was right—she had been through so much and had come out stronger than ever before. But Madison's heart sank as she said farewell to Helen.

Dread filled her veins as she walked through the cemetery back towards her family tombstone. Suddenly, a blood-curdling scream escaped her lips when she spotted a familiar face lying on the ground. It was an old family photo that had been defaced and destroyed--her face scratched out and the word "run" written in scarlet across it.

Just then, her phone buzzed with a group text from Lexi: "Hey, we need to talk NOW!"

2

Shadows of Promise

In the dim glow of the 24-hour diner, Lexi sat in a worn-out booth that had seen countless secrets exchanged over the years. The flickering neon sign outside cast a soft, nostalgic hue on the cracked vinyl seats and chipped Formica tabletop. This diner, once a refuge of shared confidences and late-night musings, now felt like a crossroads of trust and uncertainty.

The hum of the fluorescent lights above echoed the cadence of her thoughts as Lexi stirred her coffee absentmindedly. The aroma of stale coffee beans mixed with the distant sizzle of a late-night grill, created an ambiance that was both comforting and unnerved.

Lexi's gaze wandered to the empty seats across from her, where Ariana and Madison would often sit, their laughter harmonizing with the gentle clatter of cutlery. Tonight, those seats remained vacant, echoing the distance that had grown between them.

As she swirled the lukewarm coffee in her mug, Lexi grappled with the weight of uncertainty. These were the same walls that had heard her fears, dreams, and the whispered secrets of her heart. Now, she was here seeking answers, questioning the foundation of the trust that had once bound them together.

The morning unfolded with a slow, measured pace as Lexi waited for Ariana and Madison to arrive. The familiar cadence of footsteps approached, and Lexi's heart quickened.

Ariana and Madison entered the diner, they both looked tired and faces waned as they walked cautiously to the booth, exchanging wary glances as they took their seats.

"Look, I'm sorry for the 911 but I need to know, can I trust you," Lexi spoke as she studied her friends' faces.

"That's ridiculous Lex," Ariana said. "Of course you can trust us."

Lexi chuckled as the lie fell from Ariana's lips. "Is that what you said to Jason's wife too?" Lexi's sharp gaze focused on Ariana, her tone cutting through the air. "Ari, I think it's going to be a little hard with that trust thing without a little honesty. I had to find out from my mother that the guy in the trunk was your client's husband. A quick google search and a coffee and you have police at your door. Don't you think this is something you should have shared with the class?"

Ariana hesitated, her eyes betraying a flicker of unease. "Lexi, I... I didn't think it mattered in the chaos of what happened."

Lexi leaned forward, her frustration evident. "It matters. We woke up next to a damn car trunk, and you knew the guy inside. Not just any guy, a very bad guy Ari. What else aren't you telling us? Can we trust you?"

Madison's eyes darted between the two, sensing the growing tension. "Do you even hear yourselves? Like it or not we're in this mess together. We can't afford secrets right now and we can't fall apart."

Lexi's gaze remained fixed on Ariana. "This isn't just a secret. This is a lie. And it makes me question everything. Like what else are you hiding?"

Ariana took a deep breath, attempting to steady herself. "Look I'm just as lost as you are Lex. Before last night, I had what seemed like the perfect job, the perfect family, and now..." Ariana tried to hold it but a stream of loose tears fell from her eyes. "Scott's dead and I think someone is trying to set me up. I know that sounds crazy but I don't know why I can't remember what happened after the bar."

Lexi's eyes widen in shock, her anger dissipating. "What do you mean someone set you up?"

"Scott's dead," Madison said as her face drained of all color.

Ariana wiped away her tears, her voice trembling. "Someone pushed him off my apartment balcony. I don't know how he got there, but someone had my phone. I think someone drugged us or something. All I remember is the bar and then everything went black. Why don't any of us remember anything else?"

Madison's eyes widened as they filled with dread as she also remembered everything going dark. "Ari, I'm so sorry. But I can't help but to think that the same person who killed Jason also could have killed Scott? But that also means they are pretty capable of killing us. We need to go to your father Ari, tell him everything before it's too late."

Ariana shook her head, her expression fearful. "We can't, if someone really is behind all of this they kept us alive for a reason. Besides right now there's no body. No body, means no crime. Whoever did this obviously wanted to make sure we were caught so let's not give them what they want." Ariana and Madison's eyes shifted to Lexi.

"I have it handled," Lexi whispered. "But right now, we need to lay low. Whoever this is could be watching us." Lexi leaned back in her seat, her thoughts racing. "We also need to figure out what happened last night. We should retrace our steps, find out who we talked to, and if we left with anyone..."

Madison nodded in agreement; her eyes focused. "We'll do it together. We'll figure this out. For Scott."

The diner's door chimed as Lexi, Ariana, and Madison stepped out into the cool night air. The neon lights flickered overhead, casting an uneven glow on the empty streets. The city, normally bustling with life, now seemed hushed, as if holding its breath in anticipation of the unraveling mystery.

Silence enveloped them for a moment, broken only by the distant hum of traffic. Lexi felt the weight of the situation settling around them, and she knew that the path ahead would be treacherous. They needed answers, and time was not on their side.

Ariana wiped away the last traces of tears, her determination resurfacing. "Lex, you were right. We need to stick together," she insisted, her eyes meeting Lexi's. "No more secrets. We face whatever comes our way like old times."

Lexi nodded, acknowledging the unspoken pact forged in the diner. Madison, too, offered a determined expression, silently pledging her commitment to survival.

As they navigated the quiet streets, Lexi couldn't help but reflect on the irony of the situation. The 24-hour diner was once a haven for their shared secrets and their visual billboard of sisterhood; it now had become the starting point for a journey into the dark.

The trio made their way through the city, each step solidifying their resolve. The echoes of footsteps reverberated against the empty buildings, a symbolic march towards answers. The mysteries that lay ahead couldn't dampen the flicker of resistance that ignited within them.

Their destination was Eclipse, Lexi's bar. It had been a place of solace and pride for Lexi, a refuge from the chaos of the world. But as they turned the corner the facade, once welcoming and familiar, now stood as a skeletal structure, its windows shattered and its walls blackened by the unforgiving tongues of flames. Eclipse had been burnt down, reduced to a charred skeleton of memories and dreams.

Ariana's eyes widened, her hand covering her mouth in shock, while Madison stared in disbelief. Lexi, usually composed, felt a lump form in her throat as she surveyed the ruins of what was essentially her only home. The memories of Eclipse, now reduced to ashes, flooded her mind, and a profound sense of loss settled in.

Detective Penbrooke, with a gaze that betrayed an undercurrent of suspicion, approached the trio. His eyes, cold and calculating, scanned the devastated scene. Lexi braced herself for the questions she knew were coming.

"Lexi Montalvo?" the detective inquired, his tone measured as his eyes observed the women.

Lexi nodded, her voice steadier than she felt. "That's me. What happened here?"

Penbrooke studied her for a moment before responding. "Your bar caught fire last night. Arson, they say. We're investigating."

Ariana, her voice shaky, questioned, "Arson? Are you saying someone intentionally set fire to the bar?"

The detective's gaze lingered on Ariana, a flicker of suspicion in his eyes. "That's what it looks like. Montalvo, right? Any enemies you'd like to mention? We heard your family's got some connections."

Lexi met his stare with a steely resolve. "I run a bar, Detective. Also last time I checked, connections don't always translate to enemies."

Penbrooke's expression remained unreadable, but the unspoken acknowledgment hung heavy in the air. Turning to Ariana, he raised an eyebrow. "A lawyer like yourself should know when there's more to the story. First, your brother dies, and now this? You seem to be at the center of it all, Ms. Bennett."

Penbrooke handed Lexi his card, his gaze lingering for a moment longer before he walked away, leaving the trio amidst the ruins of Eclipse. Lexi felt the weight of everything come up all at once like a volcano erupting. She let out a scream as she kicked a piece of debris off the sidewalk. Ariana stared at the wreckage, her thoughts lost in the labyrinth of uncertainty. Madison, on the other hand, felt an unsettling wave of dizziness washing over her.

A sudden onslaught of nausea overcame Madison, her surroundings blurring as if the smoke had seeped into her very consciousness. She clutched her stomach, stumbling backward as fragmented memories clawed their way to the surface. Madison's surroundings begin to blur, as if she's viewing them through a haze or fog. The once sharp and vivid images around her become disjointed and distorted, making it difficult for her to make sense of her surroundings. The memories were like broken shards of glass, glinting dangerously in the dark corners of her mind and leaving her feeling unsteady and exposed, as if her very identity was being questioned and reshaped. She struggled to find her footing, but the shifting landscape of her past left her feeling dizzy and defenseless.

In the hazy recollection, Madison found herself back in the dimly lit confines of Eclipse Lounge. The pulsating beat of music and the chatter of patrons provided an auditory backdrop to the fragmented scenes. She felt the cool glass of a drink in her hand, condensation slipping through her fingers. A distant voice, distorted and muffled, asked, "Another drink for the pretty lady?"

Madison's heart quickened as the room swayed in her memory. The face of the man before her remained a featureless blur, his identity eluding her grasp. She could feel his breath on her neck, a disconcerting whisper that sent shivers down her spine.

The flashback ended as abruptly as it began, leaving Madison gasping for air, the remnants of the illusion dissipating like smoke in the wind. The reality of the burnt bar reasserted itself, and Madison found herself back in the present, her hands trembling.

Ariana and Lexi rushed to Madison's side, concern etched on their faces. "Madison, are you okay?" Ariana's voice cut through the haze of Madison's disoriented state.

"I... I don't know," Madison stammered, her attempt to make sense of the fragmented memory leaving her on shaky ground.

Madison's breaths came in ragged gasps as she struggled to articulate the fragments of her unsettling flashback. The words stumbled out of her, disjointed and laced with a palpable fear that mirrored the chaos within her mind.

"I... I was in the bar," Madison began, her eyes darting nervously between Lexi and Ariana. "I heard a voice, and I felt... I felt someone there. Asking if I wanted another drink. But I can't see his face. It's all a blur, and it's scaring the hell out of me."

Lexi and Ariana exchanged concerned glances, realizing the weight of Madison's words. The burnt remnants of Eclipse loomed in the background, a stark reminder of the mysteries entangled in the charred ruins.

As Madison's mind grappled with the intensity of her revelation, a sudden surge of panic gripped her. The pieces of the puzzle felt elusive, slipping through her fingers like smoke. The magnitude of the situation hit her with full force, and she recoiled from the weight of it all.

"I can't do this," Madison choked out, her voice trembling with uncertainty. "This is too much. I regret coming back here. I never should have..."

Tears welled up in Madison's eyes as the overwhelming emotions threatened to consume her. In a moment of desperate clarity, she turned away from her friends, running her hands through her disheveled hair.

"I want nothing to do with any of this," Madison declared, her voice wavering. "I'm sorry, but I can't stay here. I can't be a part of whatever this is."

With that, Madison turned, walking away without a second glance, leaving Lexi and Ariana standing in stunned silence amidst the remnants of their last memories. The echoes of Madison's footsteps faded into the night, leaving Lexi and Ariana to grapple with the fragments of their memories and the unraveling threads of the enigmatic night that continued to haunt them.

Lexi watched as Madison's figure disappeared into the night, her departure leaving behind a heavy silence that settled like a shroud over the ruins of Eclipse. The weight of Madison's words lingered in the air, carrying with them a sense of unraveling uncertainty.

Ariana turned to Lexi, her expression filled with concern. "What do we do now?" she asked, her voice laced with a mixture of fear and desperation.

Lexi exhaled slowly, trying to steady her nerves. "She needs time but we need to keep going," she replied, her voice resolute despite the tumultuous emotions swirling within her.

Just as Ariana was about to respond, the violent buzz of Lexi's phone cut through the ominous silence. A pang of apprehension filled the air as Lexi pulled it out, her fingers working swiftly over the screen as she unlocked it.

The message was from Rebecca. It read simply: "We need to talk. Meet me for lunch in an hour."

Lexi frowned at the text, her blood running cold at the thought of what information Rebecca might have for her. Their past encounters had been anything but pleasant and despite their complicated history, Lexi wasn't sure if she could trust Rebecca again.

"Do you trust her?" Ariana asked cautiously, a hint of trepidation in her voice. She watched as Lexi's brows knitted together in a pensive expression, her dark eyes reflecting the flickering nearby streetlight.

"Right now, we might not have a choice." Despite her strong demeanor, there was a hint of resignation in her voice. "We need answers," Lexi whispered, her voice steady despite the chaos surrounding them. "And if Rebecca has them... then we take whatever risk."

Ariana sighed heavily, nodding in agreement. The wind picked up around them, tossing their hair and bringing with it the faint scent of charred wood and old memories. Lexi turned her gaze back towards the remains of Eclipse bar, blinking away the tears that threatened to spill over.

"Alright," Ariana finally said, bracing herself for what was to come. "Go meet Rebecca, and in the meantime, I'll handle Detective Penbrooke, the last thing we need is him snooping around right now."

With that, they parted ways, the city wrapping them in its cold embrace as they disappeared into its shadows. Lexi's heart pounded in her chest as she walked toward her meeting place with Rebecca. Each step was punctuated by a flutter of unease. The last time she had seen Rebecca, things were complicated... That encounter still occasionally ran through Lexi's mind but right now none of that even mattered.

The meeting with Rebecca was set at an innocuous café on the outskirts of the city. The cool daylight did little to dispel the imprisoning atmosphere as Lexi walked in. Rebecca sat at a corner table, her face obscured by the sun glaring off the window behind her.

Rebecca sat across from Lexi in the cozy café, her demeanor a blend of professional composure and hidden emotion. The atmosphere between them crackled with unspoken tension, a reflection of the complicated history that lingered beneath the surface.

"Lexi," Rebecca began, her voice soft yet tinged with urgency. "Thanks for meeting me."

Lexi nodded; her expression guarded. "Of course, Rebecca. You mentioned you had some information for me?"

Rebecca's gaze lingered, her eyes betraying a flicker of emotion. "Yes, but before we get into that," she continued, her tone shifting slightly, "there are a few things I wanted to talk about."

Lexi's brow furrowed, sensing the underlying currents in Rebecca's words. "Go ahead," she replied cautiously.

Rebecca took a deep breath, her voice tinged with vulnerability. "Lexi, I... I've missed you," she confessed, her eyes searching for a reaction.

Lexi's expression softened, a mixture of surprise and hesitation crossing her features. "Rebecca, I..."

Rebecca interrupted, her words spilling out in a rush. "I know things ended badly between us, but I can't stop thinking about what we had. I've been hoping we could... reconnect."

Lexi's gaze faltered, caught off guard by Rebecca's unexpected confession. "Rebecca, I appreciate..."

Rebecca pressed on, her tone urgent. "Please, I've been thinking and maybe all of this happened for a reason, Lex. Maybe it's our time to finally get it right."

Lexi didn't know what to say; her eyes dropped to the floor. She didn't know how to tell Rebecca that she didn't feel the same way.

The silence was telling to Rebecca and she quickly began again. "I did some testing on Jason's body, and the results showed high levels of a street drug often referred to as Siren's Ambrosia."

Lexi's eyes widened in surprise, a chill creeping up her spine. "Siren's Ambrosia?" she echoed, her mind racing to process the implications.

"Yes," Rebecca confirmed, pushing forward a file she had brought with her. The afternoon sun cast a soft glow on the documents as Lexi scanned the contents quickly. "It's a dangerous drug on the streets right now, highly addictive, and it can lead to erratic behavior and even death. It's been linked to several deaths in the past few months alone."

Lexi's mind was spinning, the information hitting her like a wave. Siren's Ambrosia had been a blip on the radar of the underworld for some time now, but its ties to Jason's death could only mean that someone from the circles they moved in had a hand in it.

"It doesn't make sense..." Lexi said, rubbing her temples as she tried to piece together the puzzle before her. "We need to find out who is distributing this drug. Perhaps they can lead us to Jason's murderer."

Rebecca looked at Lexi with a solemn expression, her usual sarcasm absent. The golden sunbeam filtering through the blinds bathed her pale face, somehow making her look older and wearier. "I think," she began, her voice quiet, "we might already know who was distributing it."

Lexi's blood ran cold at the implication in Rebecca's words. She looked up from the documents, meeting Rebecca's gaze evenly. "Who?" she asked, bracing for the answer she was sure she didn't want to hear.

Rebecca took a deep breath before answering, seeming to take no pleasure in revealing what she knew. "Scott Bennett," she said finally.

The room seemed to fall into an unbearable silence as Lexi processed her words. Scott Bennett... The idea was preposterous, absurd. And yet there was an undeniable gravity in Rebecca's confession that demanded serious consideration.

"No..." Lexi said as though to convince herself more than Rebecca. "No, that can't be right." But even as she shook her head in denial, a part of her couldn't overlook the unsettling likelihood of its truth. Scott had access to all the right circles and importantly - to Siren's Ambrosia. "But... Scott is..."

"Dead," Rebecca finished her sentence with a grim nod. Rebecca softly sighed as she retrieved another document from her bag, sliding it across the table towards Lexi. "I wish it weren't true, but evidence doesn't lie."

As Lexi took in the harsh reality inked on paper - bank transactions, recordings of meetings - each piece added weight to the crushing revelation. Scott Bennett, Ariana's beloved brother and River Creek Police Chief's son, tangled up in this dangerous game...and paid the ultimate price.

"I am sorry, Lexi," Rebecca said softly. "It looks like Scott got mixed up with the wrong people."

Lexi swallowed hard, her mind spinning. Suddenly, Ariana's brother's death took a more sinister turn than she'd imagined. She felt herself draw inward, recoiling from the chilling reality that Scott may have been targeted by her own family's rivals.

"Thank you for telling me," Lexi murmured, her voice barely above a whisper. Her eyes bore into Rebecca's, an unspoken plea for truth reflected in their depths.

Rebecca nodded solemnly, returning Lexi's gaze with a steady one of her own. "I thought you should know..."

In that moment, despite the painful revelation about Scott's death, they shared a deeper connection; their tangled past and entwined present momentarily forgotten in the face of this grim discovery.

"Rebecca," Lexi began slowly, suddenly feeling weary. "We need to find out who did this to Scott...and why."

Rebecca stretched across the table, taking Lexi's hands into hers in an intimate gesture of solidarity. "I agree," she said earnestly. "I wish I can help more but..."

"I know. You're sworn to neutrality." Lexi looked down at their joined hands, feeling a momentary pang of guilt. She knew Rebecca was hoping for more between them; she could see it in the way Rebecca held her gaze, feel it in the warmth of her touch. But right now Lexi simply didn't share those feelings.

With Scott's mysterious death looming over them, Lexi steeled herself for the challenging path that lay ahead. She stood up abruptly, breaking their physical connection but nodding at Rebecca sympathetically. "I should go," she said, gathering her things quickly.

Rebecca too stood up with a worried look on her face. "Lexi," she said softly, "Please take care."

Lexi managed a small smile at Rebecca's concern. "I will. And you too." She turned then without another word and walked out of the café, leaving a silent and thoughtful Rebecca behind.

As the door to the cafe swung shut behind her, Lexi found herself lost in thought. Scott's death was no longer just a personal blow to Ariana; it was rapidly becoming a matter that threatened the very fabric of their lives in this city.

※ ※ ※

Ariana entered the police department, her heart racing with a mixture of apprehension and determination. The familiar scent of bureaucracy and faint echoes of ringing phones surrounded her as she made her way towards Detective Penbrooke's office.

Stepping into the office, Ariana saw Detective Penbrooke hunched over his desk, his eyes scanning a handful of documents. He looked up as she cleared her throat. "Ariana Bennett," he acknowledged in a gruff voice, "I wasn't expecting you."

"Detective Penbrooke," she nodded, her gaze unwavering. "You've been harassing my friends for information about my brother's death along with other crimes—information that I know you already have."

Penbrooke leaned back in his chair, a cynical smile playing on his lips. "And what makes you think I got any idea about your brother's death?"

Ariana's jaw clenched. She didn't like Penbrooke and his smug demeanor. But she had to play this carefully.

"Because my father is the Chief of River Creek police department," she said coolly. The room fell silent as Penbrooke's smile faded.

The weight of her lineage hung heavy in the air between them as Ariana continued, "My father wouldn't appreciate you treating his family or friends with such disregard for decency."

Penbrooke shifted uncomfortably under her gaze. She could see him calculating, perhaps reassessing how much leverage her surname carried around here.

Turning to leave, she paused by the door and added quietly, "I don't want to involve the higher-ups in this matter, Detective Penbrooke. But if this harassment continues...I will not hesitate."

"Is that a threat Ms. Bennett," Penbrooke asked, a hint of mockery in his voice.

"No, Detective." Ariana turned to him, her eyes glittering dangerously. "It's a promise."

She turned and walked out of the office, leaving Detective Penbrooke who was now visibly uncomfortable and frowning behind her.

Outside, Ariana let out a deep breath she didn't realize she'd been holding; she was playing with fire, going into the lion's den, so to speak. But it had to be done - not just for Scott's memory, but for Lexi and Madison too. Ariana knew that they were on borrowed time. The stakes were higher, the danger was looming around every corner. And yet, amidst all this, all Ariana could think about was a simple truth - it wasn't just their lives that had become intertwined with this mystery but their hearts as well.

3

Echoes

The autumn wind whispered through the branches of the ancient oak tree as Madison approached River Creek Elementary. As the school bell rang, echoing through the corridors of the school, Madison stood nervously outside the rusty gates of the school. Her heart raced as she scanned the bustling playground, seeking a familiar face among the children at recess. What was she even doing here, she thought as eyes finally found him.

Ethan Black, the embodiment of transformation, stood amidst the vibrant chaos of the playground. The leather jackets and rebellious attitude had been shed, replaced by a crisp button-down shirt that hugged his toned arms and broad chest. His dark hair fell in enticing tendrils across his chiseled features, giving a hint of the wild past he had left behind for this polished present.

Madison's gaze lingered on him, captivated by the way he effortlessly commanded attention even in the realm of energetic children. As she watched, guilt crept into her heart. She shouldn't have come here, uninvited and unexpected. It wasn't her place to intrude on the life he'd built after she left.

Deciding to retreat, Madison turned to leave. But before she could make her escape, a small voice interrupted her thoughts. A little girl, no older than six, stood in front of her, her eyes wide with innocence.

"Hi!" the girl chirped, her blonde pigtails bouncing with enthusiasm. "You're really pretty. Are you a princess?"

Caught off guard by the unexpected compliment, Madison managed a faint smile. "No, I'm not a princess. Just someone passing through."

The little girl's eyes sparkled with curiosity. "Why are you here? Are you a teacher?"

Madison hesitated, unsure how to answer. Before she could respond, a familiar voice approached.

"Emma, who do we have here?" Ethan asked, his eyes widening in surprise as he recognized Madison. A mix of emotions flickered across his face — surprise, confusion, and perhaps a hint of hurt.

Emma beamed. "This pretty lady says she's not a princess. I think she's hiding it."

Ethan chuckled, a bit of awkwardness in his laughter. "Well, Madison, it's been a while."

Madison couldn't meet his eyes, the weight of her past choices pressing down on her. "I didn't mean to intrude. I'll just—"

"Wait," Ethan interrupted, a mix of curiosity and concern in his gaze. "Why are you here, Madison? What brings you back after all this time?"

She hesitated, glancing at the children playing in the background. "I don't have a good reason. Just needed someone to talk to, I guess."

Emma tugged on Ethan's sleeve, whispering, "She seems sad, Mr. Ethan. Can we make her happy?"

Ethan exchanged a glance with Madison before smiling down at Emma. "I think that's a great idea, Emma. Maybe we can all be friends." He glanced over his shoulder at the children, who were now watching them with unabashed curiosity. "Madison, let me just tell the other teachers I'll be stepping away for a bit."

As Ethan disappeared inside the building, Madison found herself reflecting on their past. They had been inseparable once, in love and convinced that nothing could tear them apart. But life had other plans, and the weight of the world tore them apart.

"Alright," Ethan said as he returned, his expression serious yet gentle. "Let's find somewhere more private to talk."

Ethan guided her to an empty classroom, the walls adorned with colorful posters and children's artwork. The room smelled faintly of chalk and crayons, a scent that tugged at the corners of Madison's memory. She sat down in one of the small chairs, feeling her mind race as she tried to speak.

"Scott's gone," she blurted out, unable to contain her emotions any longer. "And I can't help but to think somehow this has something to do with me. Like I'm some angel of death... if maybe I hadn't come back none of this would be happening."

Ethan's face softened, and for a moment, it seemed as if he

was going to reach out to her. But he stopped himself, instead offering her a sympathetic smile. "It's natural to feel that way Maddie, you've been through a lot. But you can't blame yourself for something that was out of your control."

"Was it, though?" Madison whispered, her voice barely audible above the faint sound of the wind outside. "If I hadn't run away from my problems back then, maybe things would have turned out differently." Madison's eyes dropped to the floor.

"You can't keep blaming yourself for your parents. Sometimes, we have to make peace in hell. What's important now is you don't let this defeat you."

Madison looked into Ethan's eyes, searching for a hint of judgment or resentment. All she found was understanding – a reminder of why she had once loved him so deeply.

"Thank you, Ethan," she murmured.

"Always here for you, Madison," he replied, his eyes holding hers for a moment longer before they both turned towards the window, watching as the autumn leaves danced on the winds of change.

A gust of wind sent a whirlwind of orange and red leaves spiraling through the air, capturing Madison's attention as they danced past the window. She felt an odd sense of kinship with the leaves - both untethered, transient, at the mercy of each passing breeze. It was this very propensity for flight that had brought her to Ethan after all these years.

"Remember when we were kids?" she asked quietly, her gaze still fixed on the scene outside. "Whenever I got into trouble, I'd just... vanish. I'd run away and hide until everything blew over."

Ethan nodded, his eyes filled with a warmth that belied the

coolness of the day. "You were always good at disappearing," he agreed. "But life has a way of catching up with us, doesn't it?"

Madison tried to smile, but it felt more like a grimace. "Yeah," she admitted. "It does."

"Running away might provide temporary relief," Ethan said softly, leaning back against the wall and crossing his arms. "But in the end, it only prolongs the pain. You can't outrun your problems forever, Maddie. Sooner or later, you have to face them head-on."

"I know," she whispered, her voice cracking with emotion. "I'm just... I'm scared, Ethan. What if I just make everything worse?"

Ethan took a step closer to Madison, the distance between them narrowing until their bodies were almost touching. He could feel the tension radiating off her, the fear and uncertainty that gripped her heart. His hand reached out hesitantly, as if seeking permission, before resting gently on her arm.

"Madison," he whispered, his voice barely audible but filled with determination. "You've been running for far too long. It's time to stop, to face your demons and find the strength within you to overcome them."

Madison could feel her breath quickening, her heart pounding in her chest. There was a magnetic pull between them, an undeniable connection that had persisted even after all these years apart. She knew deep down that Ethan was right – it was time to confront her past and find closure.

In that moment of vulnerability, Madison's resolve wavered. Her mind flashed back to the vision she had earlier, the sensation of breath against her neck. Doubt crept in like a slithering serpent, whispering seductive lies of self-destruction. She hesitated, torn between the desire to surrender to Ethan's touch and the lingering fear that threatened to consume her.

But then Ethan leaned in closer, his lips barely brushing against her earlobe. His words caressed her senses like a gentle breeze, carrying with them an unspoken promise of healing and redemption.

"You are not an angel of death," he murmured against her skin, his warm breath sending shivers down her spine. "You are a survivor, Madison. A fighter, and I believe in you."

The room seemed to hold its breath as Ethan's words hung in the air, the tension between them palpable. She could feel the warmth of Ethan's breath against her earlobe, sending a sapid shiver down her spine.

Without hesitation, Ethan leaned in closer, his lips drawing closer to hers. The anticipation built between them, every passing second feeling like an eternity. And then their lips met – soft, tender, and electrifying. Their kiss deepened, igniting a flame that burned brighter with every tantalizing movement of their lips and tongues. It was a dance of longing and rediscovery, each tender caress unraveling the layers of pain and holding them both captive in a sweet surrender.

Madison pulled away from Ethan, her heart pounding in her chest as the weight of her actions settled over her like a shroud. The warmth of their kiss lingered in the air, but her mind was already racing with the cold reality of the situation. She couldn't let Ethan get entangled in the web of danger that seemed to encircle her.

"I'm so sorry, Ethan," she stammered, her eyes avoiding his. "This was a mistake. I shouldn't have come here."

Confusion clouded Ethan's expression as he searched her eyes for an explanation. "Madison, what's wrong? Don't shut me out please. We've both been through so much. "

Tears welled up in Madison's eyes, her heart aching as she got up and took a step back. "I can't, Ethan. I can't let you get caught up in all of this."

Ethan's brows furrowed in frustration, a mixture of hurt and concern etched on his face. "Madison, you're not alone in this. Let me help you."

But Madison shook her head, the weight of the unspoken dangers forcing her to push him away. "No, Ethan. Please, forget this happened."

She turned to leave, but Ethan's hand gently caught her arm. "Madison, I care about you. I can't just stand by and watch you go a second time."

Tears streamed down Madison's face as she pulled away from his touch. "You have to, Ethan. I won't be responsible for anything happening to you."

With those words hanging in the air, Madison fled the empty classroom, leaving behind the echo of a broken connection. She couldn't afford to let anyone else be dragged into the dangerous dance that had become her life.

※ ※ ※

The air hung heavy as Ariana glumly approached Chase's apartment building. Her footsteps echoed in the quiet hallway, a stark contrast to the chaos that had been unfolding. She couldn't shake the memories of Eclipse in ashes, it felt almost like a symbol of the unraveling enigma that had intruded into her life.

Chase's door loomed ahead, a portal to a realm where she could temporarily escape the haunting questions that tormented her. With a deep breath, Ariana raised her hand to knock realizing she had also lost the key to his place.

As the door creaked open, Ariana's gaze locked with Chase's concerned expression. His brows furrowed in worry, his lips pressed together in a thin line. She could see the flicker of uncertainty in his eyes as he took in her ratty appearance. His eyes scanned Ariana's face, searching for answers she was not ready to provide. She forced a weak smile, attempting to mask the turmoil within her.

"Hey," she greeted, her voice strained. "I'm sorry I've been out so long. This week has been a nightmare."

Ariana followed Chase into his apartment, the silence between them heavy with unspoken worries. She couldn't bear to look at him, knowing that he could see right through her.

But as she settled into the familiar living room, she noticed a subtle shift in his demeanor. The lines of concern on his face seemed to soften, replaced by something else. With a deep breath, he turned to face Ariana, his gaze steady and unwavering.

"I've been worried sick," Chase admitted, his gaze narrowing slightly. "But before we get into that, you should know your parents are in the kitchen."

"They are what," Ariana whispered as if the room got quieter. Her family meeting Chase was a significant step, one she hadn't anticipated on a day already fraught. It seemed as if protecting him had become a full-time responsibility. She had shielded Chase from the dysfunctionality of her family, and had shielded him from the second looks if the firm knew they were together. Fearing judgment and the potential fallout now looked trivial with everything else.

"I don't know, they just kind of appeared. What was I supposed to do, tell them to go away?" he exasperated

"Yes," Ariana said sharply. "Well no..." she sighed.

As they walked towards the kitchen, Ariana's thoughts raced. She had always presented her family as diplomatic, unified. Normal. The reality, however, was a tapestry of discord, hidden behind the polished lie her family had constructed for the outside world.

Upon entering the kitchen, the dissonance between Ariana's image of her family and the stark reality hit her like a tidal wave. Her mother, Freya usually poised and composed, sat with tear-streaked cheeks, cradling her cell. Beside her, her father, River Creek's Chief of police known for his intimidation, appeared unusually vulnerable.

The room felt heavy with unspoken grief as Ariana's parents turned their gaze towards her and Chase. Her father's eyes, normally sharp and discerning, were clouded with sorrow.

"Ariana," Freya whispered, her voice a fragile echo of its usual strength. "We called your office thinking you'd be there and your assistant gave us this address." Of course she did, Ariana dreadly thought.

Ariana felt a lump forming in her throat, but she pushed back the tears threatening to spill. "Mom, Dad, this is Chase."

Chase extended his hand in a gesture of greeting, attempting to diffuse the tension. "Mr. and Mrs. Bennett, it's a pleasure to officially meet you. Unfortunately, I wish it was under better circumstances."

Beautiful Lies

A strained smile touched her mother's lips, but her father remained scowly. The silence hung in the air, suffocating Ariana, who felt caught between two worlds.

Out of the corner of the kitchen, a figure emerged. Morgan, Ariana's sister, entered the room, her eyes sharply watching Ariana's. The two shared a striking resemblance, but where Ariana exudes warmth, Morgan emanated something colder.

"Chase, this is my sister, Morgan," Ariana introduced, her voice betraying a hint of discomfort.

Morgan's eyes flickered with an enigmatic gleam as she acknowledged Chase. "Nice to finally put a face to the name," she said, her tone revealing nothing of her thoughts.

Attempting to avoid any unpleasant conversations, Ariana cleared her throat, her voice trembling slightly. "Um, would anyone like some tea?" she offered, gesturing towards the untouched cups on the table.

Her mother nodded gratefully, her eyes brimming with unshed tears. "Yes, dear, that would be lovely."

As Ariana busied herself with preparing the tea, Chase exchanged a concerned glance with her. It was clear that her family was grappling with their own demons, their facades of strength crumbling under the weight of grief and uncertainty.

Chase, sensing the tension, tried to diffuse it with a casual comment. "Ariana's told me a lot about you."

Morgan's smile was cryptic, a prelude to the tumult that lay beneath the surface. As they gathered around the table, the room became a battleground of silence and lingering suspicions.

Chief Bennett finally broke the silence, his voice a stern echo. "Chase, why were you at my daughter's apartment last night?

Penbrooke mentioned you left quite a impression."

"Dad," Ariana interjected.

"It's a fair question Ari. Let him answer it," Morgan said, not even attempting to hide her enjoyment of this spectacle.

Ariana's heart raced as she braced herself for the impending confrontation. Her carefully crafted world was unraveling, exposing the fractures that lay beneath the surface.

Chase, caught off guard, stammered to find an explanation. "I—I was just checking in on Ariana. We've been dating, and with everything that's happened last night, I wanted to make sure she was okay."

Freya glanced at her, searching for confirmation. Ariana nodded, her eyes pleading with her parents to understand.

Her father's expression hardened. "Dating? You don't see the conflict of interest in dating one of your associates? Ariana, do you know what people will think?"

"For God sake, time and place James. Our son has just died." Ariana's mother, sitting at the kitchen table, looked up with a breathless expression. "Ariana, please, sit down. We need to talk."

Ariana felt a knot tighten in her stomach as she took a seat, Chase following suit. Her father glanced at Ariana with a mixture of disappointment and concern. The room fell into a heavy silence before her mother spoke.

"We got the call from Detective Penbrooke about Scott," her mother began, her voice trembling. "They said he's gone."

Ariana's heart sank, the weight of those words coming from her mother hit her like a ton of bricks. Chase's hand found hers under the table, a subtle reassurance. She looked at her parents, their grief etched across their faces, and realized that the

Beautiful Lies

unraveling mystery now extended to her own family.

"I didn't even know he was back in town," Ariana's father interjected, his frustration palpable. "What was he doing at your place, Ariana? Why didn't you tell us he was back?"

Ariana hesitated, choosing her words carefully. "I... I didn't know he was back. And last night, I woke up in the woods. I have no idea what happened or how Scott ended up..."

Her mother's eyes welled with tears. "In the woods? Ariana, what kind of life are you leading? First, your late-night escapades with your boss, and now this? We've lost one child, and I can't bear the thought of losing you too."

Ariana's chest tightened, guilt and sorrow flooding her. She glanced at Chase, whose grip on her hand tightened. "Mom, I swear, I don't know what happened. I'm just as lost as you are."

Morgan, seizing the opportunity to add fuel to the fire, chimed in. "Oh, she's lost, alright. Lost in her own self-absorbed world."

Chase shot Morgan a disapproving look, but Ariana's father couldn't hide his frustration. "Ariana, is this really the time for romantic entanglements? We're mourning the loss of your brother. Think of the family name."

Freya, overcome with emotion, broke down in tears again. Her shoulders shook as she struggled to speak through her sobs. "There's something you need to know," she managed to say between gasps for air. "Something about Scott."

The room fell into an even heavier silence, as all eyes turned to Freya, their curiosity piqued. With a trembling hand, she reached for a tissue and wiped away her tears before continuing.

"Scott... he wasn't always the person you knew," she

confessed, her voice barely above a whisper. "He had secrets, dark secrets that he couldn't escape from."

Chief Bennett furrowed his brow, a mix of confusion and anger crossing his face. "What do you mean, secrets? What are you talking about? Compose yourself."

Freya took a deep breath, steadying herself before revealing the truth that had haunted her for years. "Scott... he was involved with particular people he shouldn't have."

"What are you talking about?" Ariana's mind spun with disbelief. She had always seen her brother as the golden child, the one who had it all together. But now, her mother's words painted a picture of a different Scott.

"He owed them money," Freya continued, her voice heavy with regret. "And when he couldn't pay them back..."

Ariana felt a surge of anger rise within her chest. How could her parents keep this from her? How could they let Scott fall into such a dangerous situation without intervening?

"Why didn't you help him," Ariana yelled. "He's your son."

Ariana's words echoed in the room, her anger reverberating off the walls. Her parents flinched at the accusation, their faces clouded with guilt and sorrow. It was a painful realization that they had failed Scott in his time of need.

Ariana's mother reached out, tears streaming down her face. "Ariana, please understand. We tried to help him. We did everything we could, but he was deep in it. He didn't want us involved. He didn't want us to be put in danger."

"But he was your son!" Ariana's voice cracked with emotion. "How could you just stand by and watch him fall apart?"

The Chief's voice was heavy with regret as he spoke. "You

don't reason with the people he was dealing with Ariana. We were scared for ourselves, scared for you and Morgan. Your brother put this family at risk."

The weight of her parents' confession hit Ariana like a punch to the gut. The image of her once-perfect family shattered before her eyes, revealing the cracks that had festered beneath the surface for years.

"How can you be so self serving," Ariana whispered in non belief. "Your son is dead and you care about appearances more than anything else. How can you live with yourselves?"

Ariana's words hung heavy in the air, silence enveloping the room once again. Her parents looked at each other, their faces etched with shame and remorse. It was a truth they had long buried, an unspeakable secret that had eaten away at their souls.

Freya spoke, her voice trembling with raw emotion. "Ariana, we never wanted it to be like this. We thought we were protecting you, protecting our family. But we were wrong."

Tears welled up in Ariana's eyes as she realized the depth of her parents' pain. In their misguided attempts to shield their loved ones from harm, they had inadvertently caused more harm than they could ever imagine.

"I can't forgive you," Ariana whispered, her voice choked with sorrow and resentment. "Not now, not after everything that has happened."

Chase squeezed her hand tightly, offering his silent support. He understood the weight of the truth that had just been unveiled and knew that healing would take time. But he also knew that Ariana would need him by her side through it all.

Chief Bennett reached out for her hand across the table, his eyes pleading for understanding. "Ariana, please know that we love you. We made mistakes, but we did what we thought was best at the time."

Ariana pulled her hand away, tears streaming down her face. "Love isn't enough," she whispered brokenly. "I need more than empty words now."

The room fell into an abyss of sorrow as Ariana stood up from the table. "I refuse to be another person to fail Scott."

4

Ashes & Embers

The night clung to Lexi like a shroud as she stirred on the couch. The familiar scent of stale cigarettes and the low hum of a distant siren permeated the air, grounding her in the reality of unfamiliar surroundings. She blinked away the remnants of a restless sleep, her eyes adjusting to the dimly lit room.

As Lexi tried to make sense of her surroundings, the recent events flooded back – the fire, the chaos, and the gut-wrenching realization that Eclipse, and everything she's worked so hard to build, was now reduced to ashes. The couch beneath her was surprisingly comfortable, a stark contrast to the turmoil surrounding her.

"Morning," Emily's voice cut through the heaviness of the

room. She stood in the doorway, a cup of coffee in hand, concern etched across her face.

Lexi managed a half-smile, the weight of the night pressing down on her. "Morning. Thanks for... this." She gestured vaguely to the couch, her voice carrying the unspoken gratitude for a friend's refuge.

Emily joined her on the couch, the silence between them echoing the loss they both felt. Eclipse wasn't just a bar; it was a livelihood for those who worked there, a haven for many. Its ashes held more than memories – they cradled the livelihoods of those now displaced.

"You okay?" Emily asked, her gaze searching Lexi's eyes for a trace of stability.

Lexi let out a sigh, the heaviness of reality settling in. "I don't know. With the intensity of repairs we're looking at 3 months offline, maybe more?"

"Fuck," Emily swore under her breath, her frustration mirroring Lexi's. "What are we going to do Lex? The staff, the regulars, they're all in the dark. We can't just leave them hanging." Lexi ran a hand through her disheveled hair, her mind racing with the enormity of the situation. Emily could sense this as she closed the distance between them, offering a reassuring touch along Lexi's arm. "We'll have to keep them updated, and be transparent about what's happening. Maybe organize some events or fundraisers to support the staff during this downtime."

"Charity," Lexi chuckled bitterly, the sound devoid of humor. "Right when we needed it the least. But you're right, Emily. We can't let Eclipse's flame die out completely. We owe it to everyone who made it more than just a bar."

Emily nodded, her eyes reflecting determination. "We've faced challenges before, Lex. We'll get through this too. And about finding out who did this—"

Lexi's gaze hardened, a glint of resolve shining through the weariness. "I want answers too. But I don't want you or anyone else in the bar getting into any trouble."

Emily met Lexi's gaze; her expression serious. "Lex, we're a family, you know that. We stick together. If someone came after you or us, we need to know why."

Lexi's thoughts shifted to the events leading up to the fire and to everything before it. "Do you remember anything strange from last night? Anyone acting out of the ordinary or someone I was talking to?" Lexi's mind raced, recalling Madison's unsettling flashback.

Emily furrowed her brow, retracing the events in her mind. "It was a busy night. Lots of people coming in and out. But now that you mention it, there was this guy at the bar with a woman. Tall, dark hair, seemed a bit out of place. Definitely not regulars."

Lexi's attention sharpened. "What did he look like?"

"He had this intense look; he was covered in tattoos even on his hands. I asked if he needed a drink, but he declined. He did have an interest in your friend Madison," Emily explained, her brow furrowing with concern. "Why? You think he had something to do with all this?"

Lexi's heart sank at Emily's description. The pieces of the puzzle were starting to come together. "I don't know, Em, but Madison had a flashback earlier that might be the key to figuring this all out. We need to find out who he is and what he wants."

Emily's eyes widened, realization dawning on her. "I

remember now. Madison and the guy really started hitting it off. He invited the three of you to some afterparty happening on the West side and you left."

Lexi's stomach churned as the pieces fell into place. "An afterparty on the West side? That's not somewhere Madison would just go to willingly. We need to find him and figure out what the hell happened last night. There's more to this than just a fire at the bar."

Emily nodded, her concern deepening. "I agree, Lex. Maybe someone at the bar knows him or has seen him around."

"Just try to lay low. We don't want him to know we're looking for him, this guy could be dangerous," Lexi said.

Emily's eyes widened, realization and worry flickering across her face. "You're right, Lex. We can't ignore the possibility that he might be dangerous. But what if he's after your friend?"

Lexi's heart pounded in her chest as she pulled out her phone, dialing Madison's number. The seconds stretched into an agonizing wait, but the call went straight to voicemail.

"Fuck, no answer," Lexi muttered, her voice laced with anxiety. A pit formed in her stomach, a heavy sense of dread settling over her. "Emily, I need a gun."

* * *

The early rays of sunlight cast a melancholic glow over the sprawling estate, its once grand opulence now mere remnants of a bygone era. Memories lingered here like restless spirits, haunting the quiet corridors and hallways. Madison's footsteps echoed through the vast halls, a hesitant rhythm that seemed to awaken the whispers of the past. This was her family's legacy, a place frozen

Beautiful Lies

in time since the day tragedy struck. The walls were adorned with portraits of long-forgotten ancestors and antique furniture sat untouched, a constant reminder of what once was. As she walked, the air felt heavy with nostalgia and bittersweet longing for a different time.

As she wandered through the estate, a sense of emptiness enveloped her. The rooms, once filled with laughter and the warmth of family, now stood silent and still. It was a haunting tableau of memories, preserved in the amber of grief. Everything was left untouched, as if her family's presence still lingered within the walls.

Madison's fingers trailed along the ornate furniture, dust dancing in the sunbeams that filtered through heavy curtains. The weight of the past pressed on her, and the air seemed thick with the unspoken words that hung in the stillness.

A gust of wind rustled the curtains, and Madison felt a chill crawl up her spine. The estate, once a haven, now seemed to whisper tales of sorrow and loss. She questioned the wisdom of returning, of unearthing the ghosts that had been carefully tucked away in the recesses of her mind.

As she stepped into the study, the room where her father used to spend countless hours engrossed in his research, a shiver ran down Madison's spine. The musty smell of old books and fading ink filled her nostrils, triggering memories of long nights spent listening to her father's animated tales of adventure and discovery. But now, those stories seemed like distant echoes, drowned out by the weight of secrecy and uncertainty.

There was something off about this place today. The air crackled with an invisible tension, as if the walls themselves were holding secrets. Madison's gaze fell upon a worn-out leather chair in the corner, its seat sagging under the weight of years gone by. She hesitated for a moment before sinking into it, feeling as if the chair itself held fragments of forgotten truths.

Lost in her own thoughts, Madison's daydreams took a nightmarish turn. In the ethereal realm she conjured, the walls oozed with a sinister energy, and the laughter of her family twisted into anguished cries. The estate, once a sanctuary, now echoed with the ghastly resonance of a cursed history.

Abruptly, a gut-wrenching noise shattered the fragile illusion. Madison's eyes snapped open, and an oppressive darkness seemed to crawl across the room. The air crackled with an unseen malevolence, and her senses sharpened to an unsettling awareness.

There, at the end of the corridor, a figure draped in tattered black caught her eye. The murky shadows seemed to dance around the enigmatic silhouette. But this, was no ghost.

This was a person, wearing a mask that concealed their features. Madison's heart skipped a beat as an icy dread gripped her chest. The figure stood motionless for a moment, studying her with unseen eyes. She could feel the weight of their gaze, piercing through her soul and leaving her vulnerable.

In a sudden surge of fear, Madison turned to flee, her footsteps echoing off the marble floors. But the masked person was swift, closing the distance between them with each stride. Panic clawed at her throat as she realized escape was futile within the confines of this labyrinthine estate.

She darted into one room after another, desperately seeking refuge from this unknown assailant. The rooms blurred together in a dizzying whirlwind as she frantically searched for any means of

Beautiful Lies

defense. But the house seemed to conspire against her, providing no respite from the impending danger.

The masked person closed in, their presence suffocating Madison like a vise around her chest. She could hear them breathe, shallow and calculating. There was no doubt now that their intent was malicious, their purpose sinister.

Madison's heart pounded in her ears as the masked person finally cornered her in a dimly lit study. Her back pressed against a bookshelf, she could feel the cold, hard spines digging into her skin as she gasped for air. The room seemed to close in around her, its walls becoming a prison of fear.

The masked person stepped closer, their movements deliberate and predatory. In the faint light that filtered through the dusty windows, Madison caught a glimpse of glinting metal—a knife. A sickening realization washed over her, sending a wave of nausea through her already trembling body.

Her mind raced, desperately searching for a way out. Instinct urged her to fight back, to find some hidden strength within herself. But as the masked person lunged forward, their gloved hands finding purchase around her throat, Madison was overwhelmed by a force far greater than she could have ever anticipated.

As the masked person's grip tightened, Madison's vision began to blur at the edges. Darkness encroached upon her field of view, threatening to snatch away what little consciousness she clung to. Panic and despair mingled in her mind, an inferno that threatened to consume her whole.

But amidst the chaos and impending darkness, something unexpected happened.

Something far, almost a whisper floated through the air, permeating the suffocating tension. Madison strained to hear, her breaths shallow and ragged. The voice seemed to come from nowhere and everywhere at once, as if carried by the very winds that swept through the haunted halls of this cursed estate.

"Madison!" the voice screamed. Madison's eyes widened in disbelief. It was Lexi, clear and unmistakable. Her voice echoed from the front door.

The masked person faltered at the sound of Lexi's voice, their grip loosening slightly around Madison's throat allowing oxygen to reach her body. Their eyes darted around in panic, seeming to be searching for an exit strategy as they realized their advantage slipping away.

In that moment of hesitation, Madison took a gasping breath and summoned every ounce of strength within herself. The darkness that had threatened to consume her now fueled her resolve to fight back. With a surge of adrenaline coursing through her veins, she mustered her remaining energy and unleashed it upon the masked person.

In a blur of motion, Madison clawed at the assailant's gloved hands, desperately trying to pry them away from her throat. Every muscle in her body screamed with exertion as she fought for her life. Her fingers dug into the fabric of the mask, searching for any vulnerability, any weakness she could exploit.

The masked person, realizing their hold on Madison was slipping, unleashed a guttural growl of frustration and released her. Madison fell to the ground, her body gasping for air, her vision swimming with disorientation. The masked figure staggered back, realizing his opportunity for escape was thinning.

Lexi burst into the scene, her eyes widening in horror at the sight of Madison on the ground and the masked figure recoiling. "If I were you I wouldn't move!" Lexi shouted, revealing a shotgun aimed towards them.

The masked figure, panic etching the edges of their obscured features, made a desperate dash for the nearest exit. Lexi, swift and decisive, reacted instantaneously. She aimed the shotgun and squeezed the trigger, unleashing a thunderous blast that reverberated through the echoing corridors.

The blast tore through the air, but the figure moved with surprising agility, evading the lethal trajectory of the shot. Lexi's eyes widened in frustration as the figure disappeared into the shadows, the remnants of the estate's secrets cloaking their escape.

"Damn it!" Lexi cursed, her voice echoing through the empty halls. Madison, still recovering, looked at Lexi with a mix of fear and gratitude. The masked figure had slipped away, leaving behind more questions than answers.

Lexi lowered the shotgun, the adrenaline coursing through her veins gradually subsiding. "We need to find out who that was and what they wanted. I think there's more to that night than we thought."

Josiyah Martin

5

Shadows of Betrayal

Ariana's heels resonated in the hushed tones of the law firm's lobby; each click amplifying the nerves pulsating through her. The polished marble floor seemed to highlight her every step, intensifying her awareness of the professional facade she aimed to maintain. Her parents' words lingered in her mind, casting a shadow on the routine she yearned for.

Beside her, Chase walked with a supportive stride, concern etched in the lines of his face. "Ariana, are you sure about this? Maybe it's too soon to be back at work. You've been through so much."

Ariana forced a smile, her eyes revealing the inner turbulence that had been her mind. "Chase, I appreciate your concern, truly. But I need some semblance of normalcy right now."

Chase sighed, his worry palpable. "I understand, Ari, but you're not just an employee to me; you're my girlfriend. I can't help but worry about you."

Her grip tightened on his hand, seeking reassurance. "I know you worry, and I love you for it. But, I need to do this. I can't let my family get to me and undo everything I've worked so hard for."

Chase nodded reluctantly; concern etched in his features.

"Just promise me you'll take it easy, if it becomes overwhelming-"

Ariana nodded; gratitude evident in her eyes. "I promise. Now, let's face the day. We've got work to do."

Chase squeezed Ariana's hand before being pulled away as a client approached him, demanding his attention. Ariana took a deep breath and continued towards her office, trying to push away the unease.

Ariana's heart quickened its pace as she approached her office, the weight of recent events hanging heavy in the air. However, her strides faltered as she spotted Diane Fanburg seated inside through her office window, an unexpected presence that sent a jolt of anxiety through her.

Before Ariana could process the situation, her assistant, Rachel, intercepted her with a furrowed brow and a hushed urgency. "Ariana, wait. Diane Fanburg is in your office. She didn't have an appointment, and she insisted on speaking with you directly. I tried to redirect her, but she wouldn't listen."

Ariana's anxiety deepened, her mind racing to decipher the motive behind Diane's unannounced visit. Could she have already known about Jason? "Rachel, why is she here? Did she say anything?"

Rachel shook her head, her eyes reflecting a mix of concern and confusion. "No, she didn't disclose the purpose. Just insisted it was urgent and that she needed to speak with you immediately."

Ariana sighed, realizing the unexpected turn her day had already taken. "Alright, Rachel. Thank you for letting me know. I'll handle it from here. Please hold my calls and reschedule any appointments I have later."

Ariana entered her office, her eyes immediately drawn to

Beautiful Lies

Diane, a woman of striking beauty who seemed to possess an air of graceful poise. Before her marriage to Jason, Diane had carved her path as a ballet dancer, and the remnants of that elegance still lingered in the way she carried herself.

Diane sat in the plush chair, her posture upright, and her gaze, though composed, held a hint of intensity.

Ariana closed the door behind her, creating an isolated sanctuary within her office walls. She took a moment to compose herself, smoothing out the invisible creases in her demeanor before approaching Diane.

"Diane," Ariana said softly, taking a seat across from her. "It's been a while since we last spoke. Is everything okay?"

Diane's eyes flickered with a mix of relief and apprehension as she met Ariana's gaze. "I need to ask you something. Do you think me divorcing Jason is a mistake?" she replied, her voice filled with an underlying tremor.

Ariana glanced down at her hands, searching for the right words. "I can't say for certain, Diane," Ariana began cautiously, choosing her words with care. "Divorce is never an easy decision to make, and it's natural to question if it was the right one."

Diane sighed heavily, her shoulders slumping as though releasing a hidden burden. "I thought I knew him Ariana," she confessed, her voice barely above a whisper. "But... I've begun to doubt that. He's been acting strangely, now disappearing for days. How even in his absence, he finds a way to make everything about himself. Men...," Diane hissed.

Ariana leaned back, absorbing Diane's words. Diane didn't seem sad that Jason was missing, she seemed almost inconvenienced. Is this a case of love gone wrong or something else? "Disappearing for days? That's concerning. Have you tried reaching out to him, or is there any indication of where he might be?" Ariana's eyes met Diane's, her brows furrowing slightly. "Diane, it's understandable that you're feeling conflicted. Divorces can bring out unexpected emotions, especially when there's uncertainty about the other person's behavior."

Diane sighed, her eyes clouded with a mixture of anger and resignation. "It's not just about the divorce Ariana. I'm afraid his disappearance isn't just about avoiding the divorce; it's about escaping the consequences of his actions." Diane shook her head, frustration evident in her expression. "I've tried everything. It's like he's intentionally avoiding me. I don't know what to do anymore."

Ariana couldn't shake the guilt that gnawed at her conscience. She delicately probed further, trying to gather information without revealing her own motive. "Diane, when was the last time you saw him? Were there any clues about his state of mind or if something unusual happened?"

Diane sighed, her gaze distant as she recalled the last encounter with her estranged husband. "It's been a few days. He came by to pick up some belongings on Saturday, but he was acting strange, distant. I didn't think much of it at the time."

"Saturday," Ariana repeated, her voice steady but her mind racing. "And he hasn't been in touch since then?"

Diane shook her head, her eyes searching Ariana's for reassurance. "No, nothing. It's not like him to disappear like this. What if something terrible has happened?"

Ariana offered a reassuring smile, concealing the internal turmoil. "Diane, people can be unpredictable, especially in difficult situations like a divorce. Let me dig into this discreetly, see if I can find any leads on Jason's whereabouts. In the meantime, stay vigilant. If he contacts you or if you hear anything, don't hesitate to reach out. We'll figure this out together."

Ariana's attention wavered as she caught a glimpse of movement outside her office. The soft hum of voices reached her ears drawing her focus to Chase, engaged in an unusual conversation. It wasn't their typical high-profile client meeting; instead, a man covered in tattoos, a distinctive black flag etched on his neck, stood in the corridor. Ariana watched as Chase spoke intently with the tattooed man, his body language tense and guarded. She couldn't help but feel intrigued by their conversation.

"Diane, I cannot thank you enough for coming in today. I assure you nothing will get in the way of you getting your independence back. Please take care, and know that we will be in touch as soon as possible." The words rolled off Ariana's tongue smoothly, but her mind was consumed with questions and possibilities.

Once Diane left, Ariana entered the lobby and turned her attention to Chase. "What's going on, Chase? Who's our unexpected visitor?"

Chase met her gaze, his expression serious. "Ariana Bennet, meet Brayden Esposa. He's got some information that might be relevant to recent events. Thought it was better to discuss it discreetly."

Ariana studied Brayden; her intuition tingled at the sight of the black numerals on his wrist. "Information? About what?"

Chase hesitated, gesturing Ariana steps away from Brayden and earshot from others." There might be a connection with the burning down of Eclipse and the recent gang war in River Creek. Brayden has details. I thought it best to handle this quietly, considering the circumstances."

Ariana's heart pounded in her chest as the gravity of Chase's words sank in. The cartel families involved in the biggest gang war in town were notorious and ruthless. The infamous families, the Montalvos and the La Concha's, had been locked in a war for control over River Creek for years. It was a war that turned streets into battlefields, and had claimed too many lives. And now, Chase had stumbled upon a connection, a thread that could pull him into the bloodshed.

She glanced at Brayden once more, his tattooed arms crossed tightly over his chest. Ariana sensed that he was in over his head, just like Chase. The weight of the situation pressed upon her, threatening to suffocate her own sense of reason.

"Chase," she said, her voice barely above a whisper, "do you realize what we're getting ourselves into? These cartel families... they control everything. They have eyes and ears everywhere. If they catch wind of what we're doing..."

Chase nodded solemnly, acknowledging the danger they were both willingly stepping into. "I know, Ariana. But if we don't do something, who will? Innocent people like your brother are dying every day because of this war. We have a chance to make a difference, to bring justice to those who have been silenced."

Ariana felt a surge of conflicting emotions, torn between her desire for justice for her brother Scott and the realization that pursuing this path could endanger Lexi's family. The sudden image of Scott's lifeless body flashed before her eyes. How she tried to erase the thought of how broken he must have looked on

Beautiful Lies

the unforgiving pavement like a grotesque puppet abandoned by the puppeteer of life. However, the shadow of potential consequences loomed large, casting doubt on the choices she was about to make.

"Chase, I want justice for Scott more than anything, but we have to consider the risks," Ariana admitted, her voice a mixture of determination and concern. "You have to promise me Lexi will stay out of the crossfire. She has nothing to do with this outside of being born."

Chase met Ariana's gaze, a soft nod conveying his understanding. "I promise, Ariana. We'll do everything we can to keep Lexi safe. This is about justice, not revenge."

Ariana took a deep breath, her mind racing with thoughts of the dangers that lay ahead. She had always admired Chase for his unwavering determination and his relentless pursuit of justice. But now, as they stood on the precipice of something far more treacherous than either of them had ever encountered before, she couldn't help but question their decisions.

With her heart heavy with worry, Ariana followed Chase and Brayden into his office. The room was dimly lit, casting long shadows across the walls adorned with shelves of weathered books and trinkets collected from years of achievements and old mementos from cases. The air hung heavy with tension as Chase closed the door behind them, shutting out the outside world.

As they settled into their seats around the worn wooden desk, Ariana's eyes wandered across the room, landing on a faded photograph loosely tucked between two thick volumes. The weathered image depicted a younger Chase, his vibrant smile contrasting with the darkness that surrounded him. A pang of both fear and reassurance coursed through her veins—fear for what was to come, and reassurance knowing that Chase would stop at nothing to make things right.

Brayden cleared his throat, breaking Ariana from her thoughts. His eyes held a mixture of weariness and determination as he began to speak.

"Chase, Ariana," he began cautiously, "The feud between the Montalvos and the La Conchas has been escalating at an alarming rate lately. Rumors are spreading like wildfire that the families are forcing everyone to choose sides. You're either with them or against them. Turning your back on either family is akin to signing your own death certificate."

A shiver ran down Ariana's spine as Brayden' words sank in. The gravity of the situation became even more apparent. This wasn't just a matter of gathering information; it was stepping into a world where allegiances, meant survival and betrayal, equaled doom.

Chase leaned forward; his gaze unwavering. "So, they're tightening their grip on the city. But why now? What's their endgame?"

Brayden exhaled heavily; the weight of his revelations evident in the lines etched on his face. "It's a power play. The families want complete control over River Creek, and they're weeding out anyone who doesn't comply. Fear is their weapon, and loyalty is the price of admission. But there's something more going on, something they're not revealing. The streets are talking about an internal power struggle within the families, a struggle that's spilled out into the open."

Ariana's mind whirred with the implications. The pursuit of

Beautiful Lies

justice now entangled with a complex web of power dynamics and hidden agendas. The stakes were higher than ever, and the dangerous path they were about to tread seemed fraught with uncertainty.

Chase's eyes bore into Ariana's, a silent acknowledgment of the risks ahead. "Brayden, we need to get ahead of this. We need information, and we need to understand the bigger picture. Lives are at stake, innocent lives."

Brayden nodded, his gaze flickering between Ariana and Chase. "I can get you what you need, but you have to tread carefully. The families are watching, and they don't take kindly to interference."

As Brayden delved into the details of the perilous path they were about to embark on, Ariana's focus was abruptly shattered by a loud knocking on Chase's office window. Startled, she turned to see Rachel, her assistant, gesturing urgently to be let in.

Ariana sighed; irritation evident in her voice. "What is it, Rachel? Can't you see we're in the middle of something important," Ariana yelled through the door.

Rachel appeared in Chase's office, breathless and apologetic. She mouthed an apology before quickly gesturing to take a call. Without waiting for a response, she disappeared from view.

Ariana and Chase exchanged looks of confusion before turning their attention back to Brayden. He leaned forward, his voice low and intense. "The families have eyes everywhere. They'll be watching every move you make, every conversation you have."

Chase nodded grimly, his jaw clenched with determination. "We understand the risks, but we can't let fear dictate our actions."

Brayden' expression softened with admiration as he met Chase's unwavering gaze. "I like your spirit. But don't underestimate the families; they're ruthless and will stop at nothing to protect their interests."

Suddenly another loud wave of knocking flooded the office, drawing an annoyed response from Ariana. "I told you, Rachel, we're busy. Can it wait?"

Rachel's eyes widened as she held up her phone, conveying a sense of urgency. Understanding the gravity of her gestures, Ariana finally relented. She waved Rachel inside, her tone softened but impatient. "Fine, what is it?"

Rachel hesitated before speaking, her voice low and concerned. "Ariana, it's Madison. She says it's urgent, and she needs to talk to you right now."

Ariana's expression shifted from annoyance to genuine concern. Without another word, she excused herself from the meeting, signaling to Chase and Brayden that she needed to take this call. As she stepped outside Chase's office to answer Madison's call, a gnawing sense of dread lingered in the air.

The weight of the room hung heavy on her shoulders. She answered the call with a mix of concern and urgency, only to be met with an unexpected tone.

"Hello...Ari?" the voice trembled. The familiarity of Madison's voice sent a shiver down Ariana's spine. Before she could react, Madison continued, "We're in trouble, Ari. Lexi and I... we've been arrested."

* * *

The small interrogation room felt like a claustrophobic cage, its walls painted a dull shade of off-white that seemed to absorb any hint of warmth. Fluorescent lights hummed overhead, casting a harsh, unyielding glow that accentuated the starkness of the surroundings. The table, cold to the touch, stood at the room's center, its surface worn and marked by countless interrogations.

Lexi's chair, rigid and unforgiving, creaked beneath her weight as she shifted uncomfortably. The room held an air of sterile detachment, its ambiance devoid of anything that might offer solace. The sole window, high on the wall and barred, revealed nothing but a sliver of an indifferent sky.

A ticking clock on the wall mercilessly measured each passing second, its rhythmic sound amplifying the growing tension. The cadence of the clock seemed to synchronize with Lexi's racing thoughts, a constant reminder of the unknown that lay ahead. The room's silence, broken only by the ticking of the clock, wrapped around her like a suffocating shroud, intensifying the anxiety that gripped her.

The door swung open, revealing Detective Penbrooke and his partner, Detective Reynolds. The other detective was younger than Penbrooke, his eyes were a dark blue and his face checkered with freckles. Lexi's gaze locked onto Penbrooke's face as they both entered the room, noting the smug expression that seemed etched into his features. She quickly spewed out a facade of indifference, concealing the worry that threatened to surface.

"Alexis, we've got some questions, and I'm hoping you've got some answers. What were you doing at Madison's place? The Clark estate isn't exactly your casual hangout spot these days," Penbrooke spoke as he took a seat across from Lexi.

"Saving her life," Lexi scoffed. "This is ridiculous. We tell you that someone broke into her family's house and tried to kill her but you're in here interrogating us. I think police officer of the year is definitely in reach pal."

Penbrooke's partner, Detective Reynolds, leaned against the wall, his expression unreadable. "You expect us to believe there was an attempted murder, and you just happened to be the hero of the day?"

Lexi met Penbrooke's gaze with a cool stare. "Believe whatever you want. I don't owe you an explanation for being there for a friend."

Penbrooke leaned back, his smirk unfaltering. "Funny how the friend in question isn't saying much. Mind filling in the gaps, Lexi?"

Lexi sighed, her patience wearing thin. "I already told you, I was there to talk to Madison, things got really intense last time we talked. I wanted to clear the air. When I got to the house, I heard a noise and you know the rest. Now, if you're done playing detective, can I go? Or are you planning to arrest me for doing your job better than you do?"

Detective Penbrooke's expression shifted, the stern facade softening. "Lexi, I need you to understand. I'm not here to bust you. I think there's more going on than I realize, and I want to help. But I can't do that if you're not straight with me. You and your friends might be in danger, and I can't protect them if I don't know what's going on. Talk to me, and let's figure this out together."

Lexi leaned back in her chair, her eyes narrowing as she studied Detective Penbrooke. The room seemed to close in, and the ticking of the clock amplified the beating of her heart. Trust was a precious commodity, especially now, where alliances shifted

Beautiful Lies

like sand.

"I've heard a lot about trust, Detective. Usually ends up with someone dead, or stabbed in the back," Lexi replied, her voice laced with skepticism.

The door burst open, and Ariana stormed into the room, followed by Chase. "Enough of this nonsense," Ariana declared. "You're done. You can't keep questioning my client without proper cause, Detective. Lexi and Madison are leaving."

Detective Penbrooke begins to chuckle maliciously. "Ahh, Ariana Sinclair, the divorce attorney. Didn't I call it Reynolds," Penbrooke said, clapping his hands together. "You three are in the middle of something. Interwebbed but the nice thing about webs is that they always lead to the origin."

Ariana shot Penbrooke a challenging glare. "Save your theatrics for someone who cares. We know our rights, Detective. Lexi, we're leaving. Chase, go get Madison."

Chase nodded, and without a word, he left the room to retrieve Madison. Lexi rose from her chair, her gaze still fixed on Penbrooke. As she walked out of the room with Ariana, the ticking of the clock echoed in her mind.

As Ariana and Lexi entered the lobby of the police station, the air was heavy with tension. Madison sat on a worn-out couch, her face buried in her hands. Her hair was disheveled, strands sticking out at odd angles as if she had been running her fingers through them in frustration.

As they approached Madison, she lifted her tear-stained face, her red-rimmed eyes meeting theirs. Her trembling finger pointed towards the television screen mounted on the wall behind them. The news channel displayed an emergency news alert with a headline that sent chills down their spines: "Jason Fanburg Found Dead - Foul Play Suspected."

Ariana gasped, her hand flying to her mouth in shock. Chase's face hardened as he gritted his teeth and clenched his fists in anger. Lexi felt a wave of nausea wash over her as she stumbled backwards, struggling to process the news. How could this happen, there was supposed to be no body.

"No," she whispered, shaking her head in disbelief. "It can't be true."

Madison let out a sob, burying her face back into her hands. Ariana reached out to comfort her but stopped midway, frozen with shock. This was just the beginning.

Lexi's mind raced as she stood in the police station lobby, trying to make sense of everything. Her mother would never leave a loose end like this, unless she wanted to. This wasn't just a dead body; it was a symbol of war, and she had just handed her mother the perfect ammunition.

Ariana finally found her voice, breaking the silent tension in the room. "We need to leave. Now."

Chase and Madison nodded in agreement, still processing what they had just seen on the news. They quickly made their way out of the station, their minds racing with fear and confusion.

Ariana subtly gestured to Chase, silently indicating for him to pull the car around to the front of the police station. Chase nodded in understanding and left the three girls alone.

As the car engine hummed in the distance, Ariana turned to Lexi, her expression a mixture of concern and confusion. "We need to figure out our next move. With Jason's death hitting the news, there's going to be people looking for answers. We can't afford another misstep."

Lexi nodded, her eyes reflecting a mixture of fear and resolve. "My mother couldn't help herself. This wasn't just about Jason; it was about making a statement."

Ariana continued, her voice low and urgent. "She's orchestrating a war, Lex, and we're right in the middle of it. We have to stay ahead of her, anticipate her moves. The news might have only scratched the surface of her plan. We need to be prepared for anything."

Lexi clenched her fists, a fire burning in her eyes. "I can handle her. But what do we do about Madison? We've been targeted and who's to say this isn't the last attempt."

Ariana nodded, her mind racing with the weight of their predicament. "Madison, you're vulnerable right now. We need to keep you safe, but we can't make the police anymore suspicious. We have to find a way to navigate through this without ending up in prison."

"Or dead," Madison whispered.

Ariana acknowledged Madison's words with a solemn nod. "That's not going to happen. We won't let it."

Chase's car pulled up to the front of the police station, and he got out, his expression mirroring the gravity of the situation. Ariana turned to Lexi, "Take care of yourself Lex."

6

Shadows of Allegiance

Lexi paced nervously along the deserted docks, the rhythmic sound of lapping waves providing a disconcerting soundtrack to her impatience. Clutching her phone tightly, she stared out into the darkness, waiting for the unknown delivery her mother had orchestrated.

As the call connected, Lexi's frustration spilled into her words. "Seriously Mamá, you didn't think to tell me? It's all over the news."

Her mother's voice, soft but steely, resonated through the phone. "Lexi, mi amor, you need to trust. This was necessary, and you will understand in time."

Lexi's eyes scanned the area, searching for any sign of the impending delivery. "I don't like being kept in the dark. We're dealing with serious circumstances here, and I need to know what's going on."

Her mother's tone remained unwavering. "Lexi, mija, some things are better left unknown for now. Just trust that this was for the good of the family. You'll see," she said as she ended the call.

Lexi let out a frustrated sigh, her breath fogging up in the cool night air. Trust had never come easily to her, especially when it involved her mother.

As Lexi continued pacing along the docks, a sudden gust of wind rustled through the nearby trees. She shivered involuntarily, feeling a tingling sense of anticipation creep up her spine. Instinctively, she tightened her grip on her phone, waiting for any sign of the mysterious delivery.

Minutes turned into what felt like hours, but just as Lexi began to doubt whether anything would happen at all, a dim light flickered in the distance. Her eyes began to focus as she caught sight of a small boat emerging from the darkness, its engine humming softly.

The boat approached the dock with a quiet efficiency, its dark silhouette cutting through the still waters. Lexi's heartbeat quickened as the vessel neared, and she strained to see the details of the cargo it carried.

As Eric stepped off the boat, his dark brown eyes immediately locked with Lexi's. In that moment, it felt like time ceased to exist as they both stood frozen in shock and disbelief. It had been four years since they last saw each other.

Eric's presence on that desolate dock was both a blessing and a curse. Lexi's heart raced, torn between relief at seeing him again and the bitter reminder of the life they had left behind.

"What are you doing here," Lexi whispered her voice barely audible above the lapping of the waves against the boat.

"Lexi," Eric said, his voice coated with disbelieve. The weight of unsaid words hung heavily in the air between them.

Lexi's eyes were a tumultuous sea of emotions as she met Eric's gaze. She quickly remembered how translucent he made her feel. As if he could read the thoughts as she formed them.

"I could ask you the same question," Eric finally replied, his voice a mix of guarded vulnerability. He took a step closer, and the distance between them felt like a chasm filled with the echoes of their past. They had both been excommunicated from the Montalvo gang, stripped of their families' resources and dishonored for daring to defy their predetermined destinies.

Lexi's fists clenched at her sides. "I left all of that behind, Eric. Why are you here? It's not safe for us to both be here right now and you know this."

His eyes flickered with a mixture of hurt and something deeper. "You know when we were excommunicated together I thought things would be different. I've been trying to forget you ever since."

A bitter laugh escaped Lexi's lips. "Forget me? Or forget the life you lost because of me?"

Eric's expression tightened, and he took another step forward. "Lexi, it's not that simple. We both know how this works. We're bound by more than just our past."

Lexi turned away, facing the dark expanse of the water. The cool breeze carried the weight of their shared history, and she felt the burden of her choices pressing down on her.

"I didn't want you to be a part of this life, Eric. I left to protect you," Lexi admitted, her voice wavering with regret.

"And in doing so, you left me with nothing," Eric retorted, his tone heavy with resentment. "I've spent years surviving on the fringes, and all the while, you were building a new life for yourself."

Tears began to well in Lexi's face as she listened to the bitterness in Eric's voice. She ruined his life and he let her. Before she could speak, a voice from behind called out, "Eric, welcome back." The familiar came from her mother, Catalina.

Lexi turned to face her mother, her anger rising at the realization that this whole charade was orchestrated by her family. "What is this?" she demanded.

Her mother's gaze flickered between Lexi and Eric before settling on Lexi. "Mi hija, he is your Soar. I have arranged for him to return to us."

"Arranged?" Lexi finally managed to choke out, her voice laced with disbelief. "You arranged for Eric's return without telling me? What kind of game are you playing, Mother?"

Catalina's expression remained unreadable, a mask of stoicism covering any hint of emotion. "It was time for both of you to come back to where you belong. The family needs you, Lexi, and it's time to put aside your feelings."

Lexi's fists clenched at her sides, a surge of anger rising within her. She could see the chess piece move in front of her.

Eric, still standing beside her, looked torn between anger and resignation. The realization of being a pawn in this familial game seemed to weigh heavily on him.

"What do you want," Lexi whispered through gritted teeth, her voice trembling with a mixture of rage and betrayal. She could feel the weight of her mother's words bearing down on her, suffocating her with their expectations.

Catalina took a step closer, her dark eyes filled with a mix of urgency and desperation. "I need you both to investigate," she confessed, her voice barely audible over the crashing waves. "There are whispers, rumors among our network...someone is selling information that could tear us apart."

"You want us to investigate?" Lexi asked, her voice a mix of incredulity and skepticism.

Catalina nodded, her eyes scanning the darkness beyond the docks as if searching for unseen threats. "There are whispers of betrayal within our own ranks. Information is leaking, and I can't afford to have the family vulnerable. You both were once part of this world. I need you to navigate it once more, discreetly, and find out who is selling us out."

Eric's jaw tightened, a flicker of defiance in his eyes. "Fuck that. You expect us to waltz back into a den of vipers and play detective for you? We've left that life behind, and for good reason."

Catalina's gaze hardened. "You are still Montalvos. The ties that bind you to this family are bound by your life. This is not a request. It's an order."

Lexi felt a mix of emotions swirling inside her chest, a whirlwind of anger, betrayal, and a strange sense of duty. She had spent years trying to escape the suffocating grip of her family's world, only to be forcefully pulled back into its clutches. Yet, deep down, she knew that her mother was right. The Montalvos were not just a family; they were a powerful force in the city, and their influence reached far and wide.

As Catalina spoke of whispers and betrayal, Lexi's curiosity began to override her anger. If there were cracks within the Montalvo empire, she had to know. But it wasn't just the intrigue that enticed Lexi; it was the mention of a group called The Hawks. They were notorious for gathering information from every nook and cranny of the city. Known for their loyalty to those who crossed their palms with silver, The Hawks had an uncanny ability

Beautiful Lies

to uncover secrets that no one dared speak aloud. Maybe they could help uncover some of the mysteries that have been swirling around the last few days.

Catalina leaned in closer, her voice dropping to a whisper as she revealed more about The Hawks. "They are an enigmatic group," she murmured. "Their network spans across the city like an intricate web. They have informants in every corner, from street vendors to high-ranking officials. The Hawks are relentless when it comes to their pursuit of knowledge. The Hawks have been our eyes and ears for years, providing valuable information in exchange for amnesty within our territory," Catalina explained, her eyes narrowing with a mix of concern and suspicion. "But there are rumors that some Hawks have grown ambitious, selling information to the highest bidder."

Lexi's mind raced as she tried to grasp the gravity of the situation. The delicate balance of power within the city seemed to be teetering on the edge, and her mother was tasking them with the perilous mission of confronting this shadowy group.

Catalina's voice turned stern as she issued her command. "You will go to The Hawks and offer them a choice—pledge unwavering loyalty to the Montalvo family, or face the consequences of betraying us. Find out who among them is the snake in our midst."

Lexi exchanged a glance with Eric, the weight of their shared history and the dangerous task ahead settling over them like a dark cloud. The life they had tried to escape now demanded their return, and the fate of The Hawks would be a testament to their loyalty or defiance.

Josiyah Martin

* * *

Ariana's apartment, once a haven of comfort and familiarity, now bore the lingering echoes of the crime scene that had disrupted its tranquility. The air hung heavy with a sense of unease, casting shadows over the once-familiar spaces.

The living room, once adorned with plush furnishings and vibrant decor, now felt eerily muted. The crime scene investigators had left, but subtle traces of their presence remained – a faint chemical scent and the ghostly residue of fingerprint powder on surfaces. The curtains, once drawn back to invite sunlight, now hung closed, obscuring the outside world.

Madison anxiously clutched her phone as she spoke with her talent agent, Mark. The urgency in his voice resonated through the receiver, his concern evident. "Madison, where have you been? I've been trying to reach you for days. I've got a fantastic opportunity lined up for you, a chance to bounce back after that unfortunate incident. We need to discuss the details."

As Mark spoke, Madison's fingers gently traced the tender bruises around her neck, a painful reminder that there was no safe place. She swallowed hard, the gravity of her situation sinking in. Returning to New York now was out of the question; River Creek was holding her hostage.

"Mark, I appreciate your efforts, but I can't come back to New York right now," Madison confessed, her voice carrying a mix of vulnerability and somber. "I need some time, and I have things to take care of here."

Mark's tone shifted to a mixture of frustration and understanding. "Madison, you can't let one incident dictate your entire career. This opportunity could be a game-changer for you. You can't just disappear."

Before Madison could respond Ariana entered the living room, holding a steaming cup of tea in her hands. She noticed Madison's tense expression and gave her a soft smile. Madison, realizing the intrusion of the conversation, quickly wrapped up her call with Mark.

"Thanks for the tea," Madison muttered, her voice tight with a mix of emotions. "And for letting me stay here."

Ariana sat down beside her, concern etched across her face. "No, thank you for staying with me. I don't think I would have had the strength to come back here so soon after everything. You're not alone in any of this, Madison."

Madison managed a small smile, appreciating Ariana's understanding. Moments like this felt familiar; it reminded them both of a time when things were a lot simpler. How they both wish they could go back.

"Tell me, how's New York been? You were the only one of us to make it out of this place," Ariana inquired, attempting to steer the conversation away to something happier.

Madison's smile faded as she thought about her life in New York. "It's been a whirlwind, Ari. Glamorous on the outside, but a constant battle to meet everyone's expectations. I thought leaving here was my ticket to a better life, but sometimes, I wonder if it was just another kind of prison."

Ariana listened, her eyes reflecting a shared understanding. "I know what you mean. After you left I threw myself into my career and into building a name for myself. I guess in the process I kind of lost the point of it all."

Madison nodded in agreement. "I get it. But don't sell yourself short Ari, you have this place. You have an amazing boyfriend and a career ahead of you that most people could only dream of."

Ariana's gaze shifted, her eyes landing on a photograph on the nearby shelf. It was a photo of the girls captured during their senior prom. In the photo, Ariana, Lexi, and Madison stood together, smiles lighting up their faces. Ariana's attention focused on another detail-the presence of Ethan alongside Madison.

"Have you seen Ethan since you've been back in town," Ariana said with a pang of nostalgia and curiosity. Madison's eyes dropped down at the sound of Ethan's name. It was clear her feelings for Ethan hadn't dissipated.

"Maybe, well yes," Madison admitted, her voice tinged with a hint of uncertainty. "I didn't want to complicate things right after coming back. With everything recently I'm afraid getting close to him is just going to end up with him getting hurt."

Ariana's eyes politely observed the marks around Madison's neck. The unspoken truth lingered in the air, and Ariana could sense the weight of Madison's vulnerability. She placed a comforting hand on Madison's shoulder.

"There's something else I should probably tell you. Once we left the woods, I saw someone following me. Maybe the same person who attacked me this morning, I don't know. I just don't want to have to keep looking over my shoulder," Madison confessed.

Before Ariana could respond the doorbell rang unexpectedly. Ariana exchanged a puzzled glance with Madison as she got up to answer it, and when she opened the door, her sister Morgan stood on the other side. Ariana sighed as she contemplated pretending to not be home before making eye contact with the she-devil.

"Ari," Morgan said, her voice stoic. "We need to talk about Scott's funeral. Mom is overwhelmed, and she's asking for your help with the arrangements."

Ariana's expression shifted to one of silent acknowledgment. "Fine Morgan, come in."

Madison, sensing the tension in the air, gave Morgan a nod as they all moved towards the living room. The weight of recent events, combined with Morgan's presence, added a thick layer of tension to the apartment.

As they settled in the living room, Morgan remained composed, her steely gaze fixed on Ariana. Madison observed the scene quietly, realizing she is now witnessing a stand off between sisters.

"Mom wants a small, private service. She thinks it's what Scott would have wanted," Morgan stated matter-of-factly, her eyes avoiding direct contact with Ariana.

Ariana, her expression unreadable, nodded in acknowledgment. "Fine, I'll help with the arrangements. But don't expect me to play happy family after everything that's happened."

Morgan scoffed, "We're not expecting anything, Ariana. Just do what's necessary for the funeral, and then you can go back to your new life."

"That's not fair Morgan, your sister just lost her brother too," Madison said, finally unable to bite her tongue.

Morgan's cold gaze shifted to Madison, and for a moment, an unsettling silence enveloped the room. "You know what, how could I forget," Morgan chuckled. "Ariana and her little lap dogs.

How has New York been? I heard that the city never sleeps, much like you these days."

Madison, feeling the weight of Morgan's words, attempted to brush off the insinuation with a forced smile. "Oh, you know, the city is full of surprises. Keeps me on my toes."

Morgan's smirk deepened, as she leaned in slightly, her voice dropping to a sly whisper, "Speaking of surprises, I've heard you've developed a taste for something stronger than just the city lights. Is it true, Madison?"

Madison's eyes flickered with discomfort, but they maintained composure. "I have no idea what you're talking about, Morgan. You always had a vivid imagination."

Morgan raised an eyebrow, unimpressed. "Come on, Madison. I remember the days when our only vice was a shared bottle of wine. Now, it seems like you've upgraded to a more solo performance."

"Enough Morgan," Ariana shouted, her frustration evident. "This is about Scott. Show some respect."

Morgan straightened up, her facade of composure returning. "Fine. Let's focus on the funeral then. Ari, I'll expect your input on the arrangements. Don't disappoint Mom."

With that, Morgan left the apartment, leaving a lingering tension in her wake. Ariana sighed, running a hand through her hair, and Madison, feeling the weight of Morgan's insinuations, remained silent.

Ariana hesitated, wanting to address the uncomfortable remarks Morgan had made. She looked at Madison, concern etched on her face. "Madison, are you okay? What Morgan said was—"

Madison cut her off with a dismissive wave of her hand. "I've dealt with worse. Morgan's just trying to get under our skin like always. Let's focus on the funeral and staying alive."

Ariana nodded, still uneasy about the situation, but respecting Madison's desire to move on. "Alright, we'll handle this together. I just want you to know that if you need anything, I'm here."

"Thanks, Ari," Madison replied with a tired smile. "I think I just need some rest. It's been a long day."

As Madison headed towards the bedroom, Ariana watched her friend with concern lingering in her eyes. The weight of the past and the challenges ahead pressed on both of them, and as Madison closed the bedroom door, Ariana couldn't shake the feeling that the calm before the storm was merely an illusion.

7

Into the light

The bell above the coffee shop door jingled as Madison entered, the scent of freshly ground coffee beans enveloping her. The familiar hum of conversation and the soft jazz playing in the background provided a momentary distraction from the turmoil in her mind. She joined the line, her thoughts still echoing from the night before. She couldn't stand to face Ariana this morning so she snuck away moments before they were supposed to leave to meet Lexi at the diner.

As Madison waited for her turn at the register, her mind began reeling as if someone had rewinded an old tape. Memories of the masked figure's hands around her neck resurfaced. The crowded coffee shop seemed to close in on her, the low hum of chatter morphing into the distant echo of her own struggle for breath. She shook her head, trying to dispel the intrusive thoughts and refocus on the present. Suddenly, she felt a tap on her shoulder, and she turned to find a woman behind her, the woman met Madison with big dark expressive eyes, her style reflected a blend of vintage glamor and contemporary edge.

"Oh, excuse me darling, but those shoes are fabulous! Where did you get them?" the woman exclaimed, eying Madison's black ankle boots.

Madison, momentarily startled, managed a polite smile. "Thank you! I got them at a small boutique in New York."

The woman's eyes widened with recognition. "Wait a minute. Madison, right? From La Sombra? " The woman could see the confusion in Madison's eyes and she chuckled. "I'm Isabella Viento, we met at La Sombra Sunday night. I can't believe you don't remember. We had such a blast!"

Madison, now more intrigued than ever, tried to mask her confusion with a friendly demeanor. "Oh, Isabella! Right. It's all a bit of a blur, you know? La Sombra can do that to you."

Isabella nodded knowingly. "Oh, absolutely! It's like a different world in there. By the way, I heard some rumors about that night. You're a naughty girl," Isabella teased. "You really know how to make an entrance."

Madison forced a laugh, playing along with Isabella's teasing. "Oh, you know me, always leaving a lasting impression." If only that was an understatement Madison thought.

Isabella leaned; her tone conspiratorial. "So, spill the tea girl. What's the story behind you and Diego? He rarely interacts with newcomers and honey he couldn't keep his eyes off of you and your friends."

Madison's head begins attempting to fill in the blanks. After leaving Eclipse the girls must have gone there. With Diego? Could he be the man in the flashback, Madison thought as her mind began to spin.

"Diego? Oh, I'm sure he was just being friendly. We chatted a bit, but nothing too exciting," Madison replied, feigning nonchalance.

Isabella's eyes sparkled with curiosity. "Friendly, huh? You must have made quite an impression for him to break his usual routine. The man is like a fortress. It's a rare sight to see him engage with anyone, especially newcomers."

Madison inwardly sighed with relief, relieved that Isabella seemed more intrigued by the rare interaction than suspicious of Madison's lack of memory. She decided to probe further. "Diego's a man of mystery, it seems. What's his deal?"

Isabella chuckled, "Ah, the million-dollar question. No one really knows. Rumor has it that he's the owner, or maybe just a regular with a VIP status. Some even say he's connected to something bigger. Whatever the case, he's a tall drink of water, honey."

Madison forced a laugh, attempting to match Isabella's light tone while her mind raced with thoughts of Diego and the mysterious events at La Sombra. "A tall drink of water indeed. Do you think he'd be there tonight?"

Isabella's eyes twinkled with mischief. "Oh tonight is going to be a show. One thing about this voice honey, is it knows how to bring a crowd."

Madison's intrigue deepened, a mixture of apprehension and pure will bubbled within her. The idea of seeing Diego and getting more answers to finally move past that dreadful night held an undeniable allure.

As the line in the coffee shop advanced, Isabella glanced at her watch. "Well, I should get going. But seriously, consider coming to La Sombra tonight, be my guest. Who knows what mysteries await you this time?" She winked playfully before heading towards the exit.

Beautiful Lies

***

"You're kidding," Lexi exasperated. "That's like walking into a lion's den, Maddie. There's no way you're going there tonight."

Ariana, sipping her coffee, raised an eyebrow in agreement. "Lexi's right. La Sombra is not a place to play detective. It's dangerous, and we have enough on our plates already. It's too risky."

Madison leaned forward; her expression resolute. "I know it sounds crazy, but we need answers. There's something about that club, about Diego, that I can't shake off. It all feels connected somehow."

Lexi sighed, rubbing her temples. "Madison, we're dealing with a lot right now. Going to La Sombra is already risky on it's own. Now add in the fact that we're all missing time. What if you walk into a trap?"

"But what if I find something that can actually help us?" Madison pressed, her eyes pleading with Ariana for understanding. "I can't just sit here and wait in fear for another attack or for answers to just come to me."

Lexi exchanged a concerned glance with Ariana before relenting. "Fine but we're doing this my way. The smart way. You and Ariana will go tonight, if the three of us show up it brings too much attention. If this guy is involved, we need to be careful not to tip our hand. Keep your focus, Madison. We don't know what we're dealing with."

Ariana nodded in agreement. "Lexi's right. We stick to the shadows, observe, and gather information. These people are dangerous, no confrontations unless absolutely necessary. We need to be ghosts."

Madison agreed reluctantly, realizing the wisdom in their cautious approach. "Okay, I'll follow your lead. But we need to be prepared for anything. The moment we sense danger or something feels off, we abort the mission."

Lexi nodded, a determined look in her eyes. "Stick together and stay safe. We can't afford to fuck this up. While you guys are at the nightclub, I'll be handling our other issue." Lexi's eyes drifted out the diner window towards Eric, who was leaning against her car, smoking a cigarette.

"Can you trust him?" Ariana asked as she followed Lexi's gaze.

Lexi's expression tightened as she watched Eric in the distance. "I think trust is a little overrated, don't you? Like it or not, he's tied to all of this now."

Madison and Ariana exchanged a glance, understanding the weight of Lexi's words. They were all entangled in something bigger than themselves, with no clear way out. With a shared nod, they finished their lunch and made their way out of the diner.

The sun had set by the time Madison and Ariana arrived outside La Sombra. The neon lights bathed the streets in an ethereal glow, casting long shadows on the pavement. A line of eager club-goers snaked around the corner, waiting to be granted entrance into the club.

Taking a deep breath, Madison straightened her black leather jacket and adjusted her hair. She could feel her heart pounding in her chest, a mix of anticipation and trepidation coursing through her veins. This was it—the moment that could potentially unravel the secrets that had been haunting them all.

Beautiful Lies

With Ariana close behind, they approached the bouncer standing guard at the entrance. His imposing figure loomed in front of them, his arms crossed over his massive chest.

"IDs," he grumbled, his voice deep and unwelcoming.

Madison handed over their IDs, keeping her face composed. The bouncer studied them for a moment before returning their cards.

"Enjoy your night," he said curtly, allowing them to pass through the metal gates.

They stepped into another world. The thumping bass reverberated through the air, mingling with laughter and hushed conversations. Madison and Ariana made their way through the pulsating crowd, and as they approached the heart of La Sombra, the ambiance transformed into something more seductive. The dim, moody lighting cast sultry shadows on the velvet curtains and plush seating that adorned the intimate corners of the club.

The air was thick with anticipation as the girls neared the stage. Suddenly, the spotlight illuminated a figure in the center—a silhouette adorned in feathers and lace. Isabella Viento, the star of La Sombra, stood poised and confident, her voice a captivating melody that enraptured the audience.

Isabella's performance was a dance of seduction, each note resonating with a magnetic allure. The crowd was under her spell, lost in the enchantment of her presence. Madison and Ariana found themselves drawn into the mesmerizing performance, momentarily forgetting the purpose of their visit.

As Isabella's song reached its crescendo, she locked eyes with Madison, a glimmer of recognition passing between them. Madison's mind began racing, her focus shifting from the performance to the familiarity of this moment.

But before Madison could approach Isabella, a wave of bodies surged between them, separating them like an impenetrable barrier. Panic washed over Madison as she frantically scanned the crowd for Ariana. The only familiar face now merged into a sea of strangers, each lost in their own world of music and dancing.

"ARIANA!" Madison shouted, her voice drowned out by the pulsating beat. She weaved through the crowd, her desperation mounting with every passing second. It was as if time had slowed down, each second elongating into an eternity as fear clawed at her chest.

Madison's heart hammered in her ears as she reached the edge of the dance floor, scanning each corner of the club for any sign of Ariana. The colorful lights swirled around her, casting an eerie kaleidoscope on the walls. She felt her breath quicken, panic threatening to consume her.

Meanwhile, Ariana fought against the relentless tide of bodies, desperately trying to make her way back to Madison. Her eyes darted left and right, searching for any glimpse of her friend in this labyrinthine club. The air grew thick with sweat and perfume, making it hard to breathe as anxiety tightened its grip on Ariana's chest.

With each step she took, Ariana felt the suffocating intensity of the crowd pressing against her. The dimly lit room seemed to grow smaller, the walls closing in as if they held secrets meant to swallow her whole. She called out Madison's name again, her voice barely a whisper amidst the cacophony of music and chatter.

And then, just when Ariana's hope began to waver, a hand reached out from the shadows, its grip firm and unyielding.

Startled, she tried to pull away, but it was too late. Strong fingers closed around her wrist like a vise, pulling her towards an unmarked door tucked discreetly away from prying eyes.

Ariana's heart pounded against her ribcage as she was dragged into the private room, the heavy wooden door shutting behind her with a resounding thud. Her eyes struggled to adjust to the sudden change in lighting as she found herself face to face with Brayden, he was almost unrecognizable here.

"What the hell are you doing here?" Brayden demanded, his voice a low hiss, a mix of anger and trepidation.

Ariana's eyes narrowed as she pulled her hand free from Brayden's grip, a defiant glint in her gaze. "I could ask you the same question. What's going on, Brayden? What is this place?"

Brayden's expression remained guarded, but a flicker of something unreadable passed through his eyes. "It's not what you think. I'm just trying to figure things out, same as you?"

Ariana crossed her arms, a skeptical look on her face. "And how does La Sombra fit into all of this? Are you working for them?"

Brayden sighed, running a hand through his disheveled hair. "No, Ariana. I'm not working for them. I'm investigating them. There are things happening here—strange things. Things a divorce lawyer from the North side doesn't need to wrap herself in."

Before Ariana could respond, the door burst open, revealing a couple entangled in a passionate embrace. They froze, mid-kiss, as realization dawned on them that they were not alone.

"Oh, uh, sorry!" the man stammered, pulling away from the woman, both faces flushed with embarrassment.

Ariana seized the opportunity, her eyes narrowing at Brayden.

"This isn't over," she warned, before swiftly exiting the room, leaving Brayden with an apologetic smile from the couple and a sense of unresolved tension in the air.

Back in the pulsating heart of La Sombra, Ariana scanned the crowded dance floor for any sign of Madison. The colorful lights continued to dance, but Madison seemed to have vanished into the labyrinth of the club. Ariana's worry deepened as she navigated through the sea of bodies, calling out Madison's name.

✷ ✷ ✷

Lexi eyed the old library building with a mix of confusion and skepticism. The address her mother had provided seemed like an unlikely meeting place for the supposed leader of The Hawks. She exchanged a puzzled glance with Eric, who seemed equally perplexed.

"Are you sure this is the right place?" Lexi asked, her voice hushed.

Eric nodded, glancing around at the desolate surroundings. "This is what Catalina said. The leader of The Hawks wanted to meet us here."

Lexi tightened her grip on the strap of her bag, her senses on high alert. The air felt charged with uncertainty as they approached the entrance, the creaking sound of the library door echoing through the quiet street. As they stepped inside, the dim lighting revealed rows of dusty shelves and forgotten volumes, creating an eerie atmosphere.

"Hello, Lexi Montalvo," a unnerving voice echoed from the shadows. Out of the darkness emerged a figure, clad in a dark trench coat, their face partially concealed with a mask of a bird.

Beautiful Lies

Lexi's heart raced as the figure approached, the dim light reflecting off of their mask. She couldn't make out any features, making her feel even more unnerved.

"Who are you?" she asked, trying to keep her voice steady.

"I am known as the Observer," the figure declared, their voice firm. "I lead The Hawks, and I have been keeping an eye on your activities."

Lexi exchanged a wary glance with Eric, sensing that this encounter held greater significance than she initially thought.

"We've been informed of certain activities within the Montalvo family," the Observer continued. "There are whispers of betrayal, secrets, and power struggles. Your mother, Catalina, reached out to us for help. But with any great power, there has to be balanced. We will not be used to fight a war." The Observer's masked gaze held Lexi's, and in that intense moment, a silent understanding passed between them. "There is a storm on the horizon, Lexi Montalvo," the Observer whispered cryptically. "Choices must be made, alliances forged. The winds of change will not wait, and you will play a pivotal role I'm sure of it. Your mother seeks our assistance, but the path ahead is no man's land."

"Then help us," Eric pleaded. "If your allegiance is not to the Montalvo's they won't hesitate to eliminate your people."

The Observer's mask betrayed no emotion, but a sense of contemplation lingered in the air. "We walk a fine line, Eric. The balance must be maintained. I sense an impending war, and your family is at the center of it. We do not pledge allegiance lightly, but we offer guidance in tumultuous times."

Lexi's mind raced with the weight of the impending decisions. "If we refuse your help, what happens next?" she inquired, her eyes locked on the mysterious figure.

The Observer's response was enigmatic. "Then the storm will come, and chaos will reign."

Lexi absorbed the weight of the Observer's words, feeling the gravity of her choices pressing upon her like an invisible hand. She knew that her mother had sought help from The Hawks out of desperation, but now she understood that there was more at stake than just their family's survival.

The library seemed to shrink around her as she grappled with the enormity of the situation. Shadows flickered through the dusty air, whispering secrets that only she could decipher. Every step she had taken, every decision made, had led her to this pivotal moment. And now, confronted by the Observer, it was clear that there was no going back.

"What is it that you truly seek?" the Observer asked, their voice reminiscent of a haunting melody. "To find the answers behind the attacks on you and your friends, you must first know what to ask."

Lexi furrowed her brow, trying to make sense of the cryptic message. It felt as if time itself had slowed down, elongating the seconds into eternities as she pondered the Observer's words. She needed clarity, a singular question that would unravel the mysteries surrounding them.

A surge of determination flooded through Lexi's veins as she met the masked gaze of the Observer. "Who stands to gain from our downfall?" she asked, her voice steady and resolute.

A flicker of approval danced in the depths of the Observer's eyes. They nodded in acknowledgement before turning to a nearby bookshelf and lightly running gloved fingers along its worn spines.

Beautiful Lies

"The enemy you face is cloaked in layers of deception," the Observer revealed as they pulled a book from the shelf. Its cover was weathered and faded; the title barely legible. With a gentle tap, the Observer opened it to reveal a hidden compartment within its pages. Inside lay a map, intricate and detailed, marking out the various factions and alliances that existed in the city. "These are treacherous times," the Observer said, their voice laden with caution. "Power shifts like sand in the wind, and even the most trusted can turn against you."

Lexi's heart pounded in her chest as she took in the map before her. It was a labyrinth of intersecting lines and symbols, each representing a different faction vying for control.

"What do we do with this?" Eric asked, his voice filled with determination.

The Observer's mask turned towards him, analyzing him for a moment before replying. "You must navigate these alliances carefully. Seek out those who share your cause and walk alongside you in this fight against darkness."

Suddenly, before anyone could react, the doors of the library burst open with an explosive force. A group of armed men stormed into the library with guns, their faces twisted with malice. It was clear that they were not here for idle chatter or negotiation; they intended to eliminate any obstacles in their path.

Lexi's heart leaped into her throat as adrenaline surged through her veins. With instincts sharpened by necessity, she grabbed Eric's hand and pulled him towards an alcove hidden behind rows of towering bookshelves.

"We have no choice but to fight," Lexi whispered urgently to Eric, her eyes ablaze with determination. "Or die trying."

Eric nodded; his jaw set with unwavering resolve. Together, they took cover behind the tall bookshelves, their breaths coming in shallow bursts as they prepared for the imminent clash.

The library was a battlefield now, the air thick with tension and the scent of knowledge hanging on the precipice of destruction. The armed men moved with ruthless precision, unloading one bullet after the next, their heavy boots pounding against the marble floors as they closed in on their targets.

Lexi's heart hammered within her chest, each beat a thunderous battle cry urging her forward. Her palms were slick with sweat, but she couldn't afford to falter. Not now, when the stakes were higher than ever.

With a swift motion, Lexi unsheathed the knife she always kept hidden within her boot. Its blade glinted ominously under the dim light as if it hungered for vengeance. She tightened her grip around its hilt, drawing strength from its cold touch. Beside her, Eric readied his gun, fingers deftly pressing the trigger with practiced ease. His eyes gleamed with an intensity that matched Lexi's own as they locked gazes for a fleeting moment of silent understanding.

The first wave of attackers descended upon them like a tempest of fury and chaos. Lexi's body moved on instinct alone as she dodged and countered their relentless assault. The library was a blur of movement and sound, the echoes of gunfire and screams mingling with the scent of blood and gunpowder. Lexi and Eric fought with a fierce determination, their weapons becoming extensions of themselves in the heat of battle.

With each strike of her knife, Lexi felt a surge of energy coursing through her. It was a dance of steel and desperation as she spun, dodged, and lunged with deadly precision. The attackers were caught off guard by her agility and skill, some falling to the ground with permanent startled expressions as Lexi's blade found its mark.

Eric's gun roared alongside her as he picked off enemies from a distance, his sharpshooting skills proving invaluable in this chaotic showdown. Together, they fought side by side, their movements fluid and synchronized like a well-oiled machine.

But for every attacker they took down, it seemed like two more emerged to take their place. And despite their best efforts, they were slowly being pushed back towards the alcove where they had first taken cover.

Lexi gritted her teeth in frustration but refused to give up. She couldn't let these men win – not when her entire mission depended on it.

"Eric!" she called out between parries, "We need to get out of here!"

In the midst of the chaos, Lexi's mind raced. The attackers were relentless, and she couldn't help but wonder about the greater forces at play. The Observer's cryptic words echoed in her thoughts, urging her to seek the right questions for the elusive answers she sought.

As the skirmish unfolded, Lexi spotted a figure emerging from the shadows – a silhouette familiar yet shrouded in ambiguity. The Observer reappeared, watching the conflict unfold with a detached demeanor. Lexi's eyes locked onto his masked face, seeking answers in the midst of the battle.

"Why?" Lexi shouted above the tumult, her voice carrying the weight of frustration and urgency. "Why are we targeted? What is the purpose of all this ?"

The Observer's response was enigmatic, his words carrying through the cacophony like a haunting whisper. "The storm tests the strength of the tree." The Observer signaled towards a small gap between two bookcases, barely noticeable in the dim light of the library. Eric moved cautiously towards it, his weapon ready at his side. Lexi followed closely behind, her dagger at the ready.

With a collective breath, they quickly pushed the bookshelves aside, revealing a hidden doorway.

The hidden doorway led Lexi and Eric to a narrow alley behind the old library building. The cool night air rushed over them, providing a stark contrast to the heated chaos they had just escaped. Lexi's adrenaline began to wear off, and a sense of relief washed over her. She couldn't help but laugh, a nervous release of tension after the intense confrontation.

Turning to Eric, she expected to share the moment of realization and laughter, but her joy turned to dread. Eric walked slowly, his hand pressed against his side, where a dark stain was spreading across his shirt. Lexi's laughter died in her throat as she rushed to his side.

"Eric, you're hurt!" Lexi exclaimed, her voice filled with concern.

He tried to dismiss it with a weak smile, but the pain in his eyes betrayed the severity of the situation. "Careful, for a second it sounded like you actually cared about me," he teased.

Lexi's hands trembled as she assessed the wound. "We need to get you help. Hold on, Eric."

Lexi's heart raced as she struggled to keep her composure. She had always admired Eric's strength, both physically and emotionally, but now she feared that wasn't enough this time. She knew time was of the essence, and every second wasted brought them closer to losing him.

Supporting Eric's weakening body with all her might, Lexi guided him towards a deserted park nearby. The moon above cast an ethereal glow, illuminating their path as if guiding them. The sound of their hurried footsteps echoed through the empty streets, mingling with Lexi's desperate prayers for help.

Finally reaching a small bench nestled beneath a willow tree, Lexi carefully laid Eric down, cradling his head in her lap. The wound continued to bleed profusely, staining his shirt a deep crimson. Lexi's hands trembled as she pressed against it firmly, trying to stem the flow.

An overwhelming sense of fear washed over her. What if she couldn't save him? What if this was where their journey together would end? Lexi couldn't allow herself to entertain such thoughts. The night was far from over, and the secrets that surrounded them were bound to unravel this time.

8

V is for Vendetta

Lexi's hands trembled as she pressed them against the wound on Eric's side, the warmth of his blood seeping through her fingers. Panic threatened to consume her, but she fought to keep a clear head. With one hand, she reached for her phone and dialed the only person she felt she could trust in this moment — Emily.

As the phone rang, Lexi's mind raced with a million thoughts. How had everything spiraled into chaos so quickly? The encounter with The Observer, the library ambush, and now Eric's life hanging in the balance. Each moment felt like a step into a darker abyss.

"Lexi?" Emily's voice came through the phone, a mix of concern and curiosity.

"Emily, it's Eric. We're in trouble. I need your help," Lexi spoke rapidly, her words laced with urgency.

"What happened? Where are you?" Emily asked, her tone now edged with worry.

"We're near the old library building. I have no time to explain," Lexi snapped, her voice cracking with a mixture of fear and frustration.

As Lexi ended the call, she focused on Eric, trying to block

Beautiful Lies

out the chaos around her. The city streets seemed to blur into a disorienting backdrop, and Lexi felt a chilling vulnerability. Lexi focused on the task at hand, doing her best to stop the bleeding and keep Eric alert.

"Don't die on me you asshole," Lexi pleaded.

The distant wail of sirens grew nearer, a symphony of urgency that filled the air. Lexi's hands worked with a sense of determination, applying pressure to Eric's wound as if trying to defy the cruel twist of fate that had brought them to this point. Her pleas held a mixture of frustration and genuine concern.

"You're not allowed to die on me, you hear?" Lexi muttered, her voice a whispered vow against the turmoil of the city. The shadows seemed to dance around them, an intricate ballet of uncertainty, and Lexi couldn't shake the feeling that their lives had become entangled once more.

Time hung suspended, each second an eternity as they awaited the arrival of help. Lexi's eyes remained fixed on Eric's face, searching for any sign of consciousness, any flicker of the spirit that defined him. The city's heartbeat pulsed around them, a relentless rhythm that underscored the fragility of life in the face of unforeseen circumstances.

Eric's eyelids fluttered, the effort to open them evident on his pale face. Lexi held her breath, her eyes fixed on his, willing him to regain consciousness. A feeble smile played on Eric's lips as he struggled to focus on Lexi's face.

"I've never seen you cry before," he rasped, his voice barely audible above the city's dissonance.

Lexi's eyes glistened with unshed tears, her stoic facade momentarily cracked. "Save your strength, Eric. Help is on the way."

"No," Eric murmured, his hand weakly reaching for hers. "I hate it. I hate seeing you cry."

A bittersweet smile curved Lexi's lips as she squeezed his hand. "You're an idiot, you know that?"

Eric's eyes held a glint of humor despite the pain. "Always."

A few minutes later Emily's car quickly pull up to the nearby curb, and Lexi hurriedly ushered Eric into the backseat. Emily's eyes widened in shock as she took in the sight of Eric's pale face and the blood-soaked bandages.

"Lexi, what the hell happened?" Emily's voice was a mix of concern and disbelief.

"I'll explain on the way. We need to get him help, Em," Lexi replied, her tone urgent.

As Emily drove through the city streets, Lexi navigated her towards the only safe place she could think of. The neon lights of the city flickered in the distance, their glow casting an eerie ambiance inside the car. Emily, glancing at Lexi, furrowed her brows.

"Lexi, where are we going? This isn't the way to the hospital," Emily questioned, concern etched across her face.

Lexi took a deep breath, her eyes fixed on the unconscious figure of Eric in the backseat. "We can't take him to the hospital. Too many questions, too much risk."

Confusion shadowed Emily's expression as she continued driving. "What do you mean? Where are we taking him?"

Lexi hesitated for a moment, choosing her words carefully. "There's a place, an old preschool. It's a cover for something else. It's the only place he can get the help he needs, I just need you to

Beautiful Lies

trust me."

Emily gripped the steering wheel tightly, her knuckles turning white. She glanced back at Eric's pale, unconscious form and then over at Lexi's worried face. A million questions swirled in her mind, but she could sense the urgency in her friend's voice.

"Okay," Emily finally replied. "I trust you. Just tell me where to go."

As Emily turned down a side street, the neighborhoods became more run down, with boarded up windows and crumbling infrastructure. She shivered, feeling like they were venturing into the belly of the beast.

"We're close," Lexi said quietly. She pointed to an old building with peeling paint and a faded mural of rainbows. The sign above the door read "Happy Hearts Preschool" in chipped letters.

Emily pulled up to the curb, eyeing the building apprehensively. Though labeled a preschool, the structure had an ominous aura about it. Lexi stepped out and hurried to open the back door, gently pulling Eric's limp body from the car.

"Thank you Emily, for always having my back. Now lay low until you hear from me," Lexi said.

Emily nodded as Lexi adjusted her grip on Eric, a flood of memories rushed through her mind. This was no ordinary preschool - this was the training facility where she and Eric had spent their childhoods honing their combat skills. The rainbow mural was just a front to mask the rigorous martial arts practices that took place inside.

Lexi vividly recalled the grueling training sessions from her youth. Hours upon hours of technique drills, sparring matches, weapons handling - all designed to transform children into elite fighters. She had tried to forget those days, but now, carrying Eric's wounded body back to this place, the memories felt fresh and raw.

The interior was just as she remembered. Though faded, the walls still bore marks from thrown weapons, fragments of shooting target posters, stained fighting mats. As she laid Eric down, Lexi's mind drifted to their early training years together. They had been rivals then, competing to best one another's skills. There was no camaraderie, only a focus on becoming the top student.

How far they had come since those days. Now, Lexi would give anything to see Eric open his eyes again. Kneeling next to him, she brushed his hair back gently. "Just hold on," she whispered. "We're going to make it through this."

Lexi stood, taking in the surroundings that felt both foreign and familiar. This place held so many memories, yet now it felt almost like a different world.

Footsteps echoed down the hall and Lexi tensed, ready to defend Eric if needed. A figure emerged - a tall, muscular man with a stern face. Lexi's eyes widened in recognition.

"Professor?" she said in disbelief.

The man nodded, his harsh expression softening slightly. "It's been a long time, Lexi, since you and Eric disappeared after graduation."

Lexi lowered her head respectfully to her former teacher. "I'm sorry, Professor. We had our reasons for leaving."

The Professor gazed down at Eric's motionless form, his face grave. "What happened to him?"

Beautiful Lies

"He's badly injured. I didn't know where else to go."

The professor kneeled beside Eric, examining his wounds with a critical eye. "I see. We will do what we can for him." He called down the hall, "Kana! Daisuke! Come quickly!"

Two figures emerged, a man and woman, both carrying medical bags. Lexi stared in astonishment.

"We meet again, Lexi," Kana said with a smile.

Daisuke gave a short bow. "It's been too long."

Lexi could hardly believe it. Kana and Daisuke were the perfect examples of Nestlings. This phrase was often used to describe children born and raised in the Montalvo family. Just like all Nestlings, they had all shared the same dreams, aspirations, and the desire to become the best. But life had scattered them like autumn leaves, each drifting in a different direction.

As Kana and Daisuke labored over Eric, The Professor turned to Lexi with a solemn expression. "The world you left behind has changed, Lexi. There are forces at play, and your family is entangled in a dangerous game. You and Eric are not the only ones who have returned seeking refuge."

Lexi's brow furrowed in confusion. "Others have returned?"

The professor nodded. "The shadows are converging, and old alliances are being rekindled."

Kana exchanged a knowing glance with Daisuke before turning back to Lexi. "We owe you for our training days together. Your Soar is in good hands."

The professor, his hands busy with medical supplies, spoke without looking up. "We may have chosen different paths, but we share a history. We help our own."

The Professor nodded gravely. "Come, let us walk. There is

much to discuss."

He led Lexi down the familiar halls of the compound, past the training rooms and living quarters where they had all spent their childhoods together. Though the layout was unchanged, there was a somberness that hung in the air now.

"After you and Eric disappeared, things began shifting within the family," the Professor explained as they walked. "Your father and mother grew more paranoid, more controlling. They tightened their grip on the compound, forbidding us from leaving."

Lexi listened in dismay. She had hoped her parents would realize their authoritarian ways were wrong after she'd escaped with Eric. But it seemed they had only grown worse.

"Many couldn't take the restrictions anymore," the Professor continued. "They started to resist, to push back. It caused fractures, divisions among us."

He brought her to a window overlooking the grounds below. Several buildings showed signs of damage - scorch marks, broken windows, rubble. Evidence of the internal conflicts.

Lexi's heart ached at the sight. This had once been her home. She had never wanted to see it torn apart like this.

"And my mother?" she asked quietly. "Does she know what has happened to this place?"

The Professor's expression turned grave. "Your mother... she has changed. She is not the same woman you remember."

"She wasn't always like this," Lexi said, more to herself than anyone else.

The Professor nodded in understanding. "No, she wasn't. But after you and Eric were excommunicated, she became consumed with a need of control. And when she couldn't, she turned to darker means."

"Darker means?" Lexi repeated, unsure of what he meant.

"Yes," The Professor said gravely. "She started making deals to claim more territory in the city pushing other groups and families out.

The Professor led Lexi into a dimly lit room, its walls adorned with ancestral portraits and symbols of the Montalvo cartel. He motioned for her to sit, and as they faced each other, the weight of the revelations settled in the room.

"The city has become a battleground," the Professor explained. "Your mother's actions have drawn the attention of rival cartels, and The Hawks have become embroiled in the conflicts. The Observer believes that a storm is coming, and your family is at the center of it."

Lexi's eyes narrowed with determination. "Tell me everything. I need to understand what's at stake."

The Professor delved into the complex web of alliances and betrayals that had woven itself around the Montalvo family. Lexi listened intently, her mind absorbing every detail like a sponge. The city that had once seemed distant and detached now felt like a chessboard where powerful players moved their pieces with calculated precision.

As the Professor spoke, Lexi's thoughts turned to Madison and Ariana, unaware of the storm brewing in the shadows of their lives. The revelations about her family added another layer to the mysteries they faced, and Lexi knew that uncovering the truth was the only way to protect those she cared about.

Lexi absorbed the Professor's revelations, her mind racing to connect the threads. This web of deception went deeper than she could have imagined, threatening to ensnare all those close to her.

"There's one more thing you should know," the Professor said, his voice low. "We received word just before your arrival that someone has put a bounty on you and Eric's heads. They know you've returned."

Lexi tensed, her breath catching in her throat.

"How much?" she asked sharply.

"One million each."

The words dropped like stones in Lexi's stomach. Such a price would attract every lowlife and assassin in the city. Nowhere would be safe.

Lexi stood abruptly, her chair scraping against the floor.

As she strode from the room, the Professor called after her, "Be careful, Lexi. May the wind beneath your wings always guide you, and the shadows of our past never cast too long a shadow on your path."

Lexi said nothing, her face set with determination. The stakes were now higher than ever. One misstep could bring everything crashing down around them. She had to be ready.

The hunt was on.

✳ ✳ ✳

Madison's pulse quickened as she navigated the crowded dance floor of La Sombra, the pulsating beat of the music reverberating through her body. The neon lights painted the room in vibrant hues, casting an otherworldly glow on the eclectic mix of patrons lost in the rhythm.

Amidst the sea of faces, Madison's search for Ariana seemed futile. The air hung heavy with anticipation and the scent of various perfumes, creating a sensory overload that threatened to engulf her. The kaleidoscope of colors and undulating bodies triggered an unsettling feeling of déjà vu.

Suddenly, a surge of disorienting memories flooded Madison's mind. She was here, in this very spot before. The music, the lights, the energy—all of it was eerily familiar. It was a night fighting to rise in her subconscious, a night she struggled to remember.

As Madison weaved through the crowd, the memories coalesced into a vivid scene. The bass thumped in her chest, mirroring the rapid beats of her heart. A hand had gripped her shoulder, the touch both possessive and ominous. Panic surged through her veins as the flashback played out in her mind.

The faceless figure in the memory seemed to materialize in the shadows, a phantom presence that haunted her. Madison's breath caught in her throat as she grappled with the disconcerting sensation of being watched, the weight of an unseen gaze bearing down on her.

Madison's eyes darted around the club, searching for the source of her unease. But the faceless figure remained elusive, a lingering presence that seemed to slip through her grasp.

She pushed through the throng of dancers, her heart pounding with a mixture of fear and determination. She had to find Ariana, she had to tell her about the memory that had resurfaced. There was no time to lose.

As Madison reached the edge of the dance floor, she caught sight of Ariana's familiar silhouette near the bar. Relief flooded through her as she made her way towards her.

But before she could reach Ariana, a hand shot out from

behind her and grabbed Madison's arm in a bruising grip. She let out a cry of surprise as she was spun around to face her attacker.

It was him—the faceless figure from the memory. His features were still shrouded in darkness, but there was no mistaking those steel gray eyes that bore into hers.

"Madison," he hissed, his voice harsh and menacing. "You shouldn't have come back."

Madison's blood ran cold at the sound of the man's voice. Though his features remained obscured in shadow, there was something deeply unsettling about his presence. She tried to wrench her arm from his vice-like grip, but he only tightened his hold.

"Let me go," Madison demanded, summoning every ounce of courage she could muster.

The man leaned in close, his hot breath on her cheek. "You don't remember me, do you?" he asked, a sinister edge to his tone. "That night...this place..."

Flashes of memories pierced Madison's mind - the pulsing music, the crush of bodies on the dance floor, the feeling of a predator stalking his prey. She sucked in a sharp breath as it all came rushing back. The grip of Diego's hand on her shoulder. The panic surging through her as he pulled her towards the back exit. She had struggled against him, fought with all her might. And then...nothing. Only darkness.

"Diego," she whispered. "That night," Madison breathed, the color draining from her face. "You tried to take me."

Diego released his grip on her arm, holding up his hands imploringly. "No, you don't understand. I was trying to get you out of here, to safety. This place, La Sombra...it's dangerous.

Beautiful Lies

Madison took a cautious step back, her eyes narrowing as she studied Diego's face. "Why should I believe you?"

As Madison's eyes darted nervously around the club, she noticed the subtle movements of shadowy figures dressed in black, their gaze fixed on her. A chill ran down her spine, and instinctively, she clung to Diego's explanation.

Diego guided Madison to a dimly lit backroom, away from the pulsating beats and prying eyes. The muffled sounds of the music faded as the door swung shut, leaving them in a cocoon of relative silence.

"Those men in black are not here for the show," Diego began, his voice low and urgent. "They are after you and your friends."

Madison's eyes widened, the gravity of Diego's words sinking in. "Why? What do they want with us?"

Diego sighed, running a hand through his dark hair. "There's no time to explain."

Madison felt Diego's hand on her shoulder, guiding her further into the dimly lit backroom. She could hear the muffled thumping of the music from the dance floor, but back here it was quiet, the air thick with tension.

Diego moved swiftly, his eyes darting around. He slid open a panel in the wall, revealing a small hidden closet. "Get in," he whispered urgently.

Madison hesitated, uncertainty and fear etched on her face. Could she really trust this near stranger? But the look of earnest concern in Diego's eyes convinced her. She ducked inside the closet, Diego sliding the panel closed just as the door to the backroom swung open.

Madison held her breath, peering through a tiny slit in the

wood paneling. Two figures dressed in black entered, their faces obscured by hoods. Behind them strode a tall, imposing man with a scar across his cheek - clearly their leader. The man radiated menace and power.

"Where is she?" the scarred man demanded. His voice was like gravel, harsh and dangerous.

"I don't know who you mean," Diego replied evenly.

The man grabbed Diego by the shirt. "The girl. Madison. We know she came back here."

"All of this to impress some broad. Sounds a little desperate even for you Vic. She's using you can't you see that." Victor's fists clenched at his sides, his jaw tightening. "You always were the sellout. We were supposed to be different. The La Concha name means nothing now."

"You were always so weak brother," Victor retorted. "You wanted this life but never wanted to work for it."

"You and your self-righteous crap. You think you're better than me now?" Diego spat. "There's more to life than this!"

"Yeah? Like what? Digging ditches for a living? This is our birthright, Diego. And she's part of it."

Diego shook his head in disbelief. "She doesn't have to be a part of this, Vic."

Madison held her breath, listening intently as the voices of Diego and his brother, Victor, escalated in tension. She could feel the anger and frustration radiating from Victor's words, a palpable force that seemed to fill the room. Suddenly, she heard the distinctive click of a gun being cocked - her heart racing as she realized Victor had drawn a weapon. The closet smelled damp and musty; the cool wood pressing against her back as she strained to hear every word.

Diego took a step back, eyes wary. "You don't want to do this, Vic."

"Yes I do," Victor growled, finger tightening on the trigger. "You have exhausted my patience brother."

"We can leave all of this behind Victor - start over somewhere new."

But Victor shook his head vehemently. "No! We were born into this world! We belong here!" He took a menacing step forward, his eyes blazing with fury. "She's just another pawn in our game."

Before Diego could respond, Victor lunged forwards, slamming Diego against the wall and pushing the barrel of his gun up under his chin. "Tell me where she is!" he barked, voice harsh and commanding.

Diego winced as the cold metal pressed against his skin but he remained defiant. "I don't know!"

Victor sighed heavily, frustration clear, the room echoed with the deafening blast of a gunshot, a sharp and sudden punctuation that hung in the air. Madison's eyes widened in horror as she heard the sickening thud of a body hitting the floor. A heavy silence settled over the room, broken only by the soft, haunting notes of the distant music from the club.

Madison's breath caught in her throat as she pressed herself against the back of the closet, her eyes fixed on the closed door. The weight of the moment pressed upon her, and she struggled to comprehend the violence that had just unfolded.

Unable to stop herself from looking, Madison saw Victor standing over Diego's crumpled form. His expression was cold and unyielding.

"I told him he was too soft," Victor muttered, his eyes flickering over the lifeless body at his feet.

Madison could feel the blood pounding in her ears as she fought to control her ragged breathing, praying that the music would drown out any sound she made.

Victor glanced around the room once more, his eyes narrowing. "She couldn't have vanished into thin air," he growled, casting a menacing glare. "Search the building, tear it apart if you have to, but I want her found."

With a curt nod, the men fanned out, checking the room and one walking towards the hidden closet where Madison was hiding. She held her breath as one of them approached, convinced that her pounding heart would give her away. There was nowhere to run, nowhere to hide. The man pressed against the wall and Madison squeezed her eyes shut, preparing herself for the discovery that felt inevitable.

But then, as quickly as it had begun, it was over. The footsteps receded as she heard Victor barking orders into his earpiece. "She's somewhere in this damn building!"

Madison exhaled shakily as the adrenaline started to wear off, her entire body trembling. She couldn't believe what had just happened—Diego was dead and it was all because of her. Guilt weighed heavily on her heart as she huddled on the floor of the closet, listening to the footsteps getting fainter.

Madison held her breath, trying to calm her racing heart as the men's footsteps faded into the distance. She couldn't stay hidden in this closet forever, but the thought of leaving its relative safety made her stomach churn with anxiety.

Beautiful Lies

As she cautiously peered out into the dimly lit backstage area, a shadow suddenly fell across the door. Madison jumped back, stifling a yelp.

"It's okay, it's just me," came a hushed voice. Isabella, the singer from the club, was crouched outside the closet, concern etched on her face. "I don't have much time before they come back. We need to get you out of here."

Madison hesitated, wondering if she could trust the woman. But what choice did she have? She took Isabella's outstretched hand and slipped out of the closet.

Isabella led her through a maze of back hallways and side doors. Each time they passed an alcove or dark corner, Madison tensed, expecting one of Victor's men to leap out. But Isabella seemed to know the building well, and managed to evade the patrolling guards.

At last, they reached a door leading out to a back alley. Isabella unlatched it swiftly and waved Madison through. The cool night air was a relief after the stuffy, oppressive atmosphere inside.

"Thank you," Madison managed, her voice cracking. "But why are you helping me?"

Isabella gave a sad smile. "Let's just say I know what it's like to feel trapped here. What Victor did to his own brother... . Unforgivable." Her expression darkened for a moment before she shook her head.

"But we can't stay here, it's not safe," Isabella continued briskly. "I have an apartment a few blocks away. We'll figure out our next move there."

As they hurried down the alley, Isabella turned to Madison once more. "I'm trying to get my son out of this life. But Victor's reach is long, and I can't do it alone. If I help you, will you help me?" Her eyes were pleading.

Madison considered it for a moment before nodding. "Yes, I'll help in any way I can. You saved my life - it's the least I can do."

Isabella's shoulders sagged with relief. "Thank you," she whispered. "With Victor after us both now, we'll have a better chance sticking together."

Madison nodded, her mind racing as she followed Isabella down the dingy alleyway. Ariana was still inside that wretched club, at the mercy of Victor and his thugs. They had to get to her before it was too late.

As they emerged onto the main street, Madison froze. There, across the road, was the club's entrance. And walking out, flanked by two of Victor's men, was Ariana. Even from a distance, Madison could see her friend's eyes widen in shock and fear as she spotted them.

Madison's protective instincts flared. She moved to rush across the street, but Isabella held her back. "Wait," she urged under her breath.

Just then, the still night was shattered by the wail of sirens. Squad cars came screeching around the corner, red and blue lights flashing. Victor's men startled, then immediately began running down the alley to escape the approaching police.

In the commotion, Ariana broke free from her captors and raced across the street toward Madison and Isabella.

"Oh my god. I had it wrong. Diego's not the one we should be looking for," Madison said exasperated as if all the words were pouring out of her like water.

"I'm just glad you're safe," Ariana replied, relief washing over her.

Isabella looked around warily. "Come on, we need to get out of here. The police won't hold Victor's men for long. We can talk more at my place."

The sirens faded into the distance as the three women hurried off into the night.

9

A is for Allies

Madison's mind was filled with the weight of recent events, the images of the tragic scene in the club and the loss of Diego playing on a continuous loop. She couldn't shake off the feeling of guilt and responsibility for what had happened. As she looked over at Ariana, her normally hopeful demeanor now replaced by dread, Madison could see the fear and uncertainty in her friend's eyes. They were both caught in a dangerous situation and Madison couldn't help but question if there was a way out.

Inside the apartment, the soft glow of a single lamp illuminated the modest living space. Isabella gestured for them to take a seat while she brewed a pot of strong coffee, an anchor in the midst of chaos.

"So, someone named Victor is after us?" Ariana spoke, breaking the uneasy silence that enveloped them.

Madison nodded; her gaze fixed on the swirling steam rising from the coffee mug Isabella placed before her. "He's ruthless, Ariana. He killed his own brother without a second thought. And now he's after us."

Isabella took a seat, her eyes flickering with a mixture of fear and determination. "Victor and Diego ran the La Conchas together," she began. "It was no secret that recently Diego and Victor weren't seeing eye to eye. Victor liked the power and didn't want to share it with anyone, especially not his own brother."

Madison's mind raced as she tried to piece together the puzzle of their situation. She couldn't believe that someone would kill their own flesh and blood for power.

"Diego was more of a peacemaker," Isabella continued. "He wanted to keep things running smoothly at the club, but as tensions rose between him and Victor, he started to pull away from the business."

Ariana's brow furrowed in confusion. "But why would Victor be after us? We have nothing to do with their business."

"I don't know," Isabella said. "There's been whispers in the club that he's not working alone."

The three women sat in silence, their minds racing with the possibilities of who could be working with Victor. Madison couldn't shake off the feeling of unease, knowing that they were in danger and not knowing who to trust.

After a few moments, Isabella stood up and began pacing around the small living room. "I've been keeping my ears open at the club," she said. "There's been whispers that Victor has some new connections in the city. He's been building alliances as if he's preparing for something."

"This might be a long shot but have you seen a man by the name of Jason Fanburg recently at the club," Ariana said.

Isabella paused, her brows knitting in thought. After a moment, recognition sparked in her eyes. "Jason Fanburg, you say? Yeah, I've heard the name. He was there the same night as the both of you, talking to Victor. The conversation got pretty heated.

Why?"

"He's dead," Madison muttered. "And somehow he has something to do with all of this."

Isabella's expression darkened. "This is more complex than I thought. Diego and I had been secretly helping me gather evidence against Victor for his illegal activities. He knew how dangerous Victor could be and he wanted to put an end to it."

"Diego had planned on turning over all the evidence to the police tomorrow morning," Isabella continued. "But now that he's gone..." Her voice trailed off, tears welling up in her eyes.

"We have to get that evidence," Madison said firmly, determination flashing in her eyes.

Ariana nodded in agreement. "If Diego was trying to expose Victor's criminal activities, that evidence could be our ticket to exposing the truth and bringing justice."

Isabella wiped away a tear and composed herself. "I know where Diego kept his files. He had a secret compartment in his apartment, underneath a loose floorboard. But getting there won't be easy. Victor will likely have people watching, especially now."

Madison's mind raced as she considered their options. "We need a plan. We can't just walk into Diego's apartment and grab the evidence. We have to be strategic and avoid drawing attention."

Isabella thought for a moment. "There's an underground entrance to the apartment building. It's not commonly known, but Diego showed it to me once. It leads directly to the lower floors, away from the main lobby and potential prying eyes."

Ariana leaned forward. "That could work. If we can access the building discreetly, we might have a chance to retrieve the evidence without alerting Victor."

Isabella retrieved a set of keys from a drawer. "Diego gave me these for emergencies. There's one for the underground entrance, and another for his apartment. We need to move quickly, before Victor realizes what we're up to."

Suddenly a loud bang from the door echoed through the apartment. Isabella exchanged a wary glance with Madison and Ariana. The tension in the room heightened as Isabella cautiously approached the door and peered through the peephole.

"Ariana," the voice called out. The hard voice belonged to Chase. Usually his voice brought her comfort but not this time.

"Shit," Ariana whispered to herself. How do you even begin to explain any of this? Ariana slowly walked to the door as Isabella opened it.

The door opens, revealing Chase, his expression was a storm of conflicting emotions—anger, worry, and relief. His gaze darted between Isabella and the two girls.

"What the hell is going on, Ariana?" Chase's voice was stern, his jaw clenched.

Ariana's gaze fixated on Chase. "Chase, please try to understand that I know this looks bad, and I desperately wish I could explain everything," she implored, her voice cracking with emotion.

But before she could elaborate further, Chase's attention was diverted by the prying eyes surrounding them. "Excuse me?" he interjected, his eyes flickering towards Isabella for a brief moment before returning to Ariana. "Is there somewhere we can speak in private?" The tension in his voice hung thick in the air as he gestured towards a nearby room.

Isabella nodded as Chase led Ariana into Isabella's son's room. The room filled heavily with unspoken words. The walls, adorned with posters and memories of a teenager's life, felt both nostalgic and poignant.

"Are you trying to get yourself killed," Chase said. "Brayden said he saw you three leaving La Sombra. The same club where Diego La Concha was murdered by a Montalvo man."

"Is that what they're saying? Diego wasn't murdered by an Montalvo, he was murdered by his own brother Chase."

Chase's expression shifted from anger to concern as he absorbed Ariana's words. He took a step closer, his eyes searching hers for truth. "His own brother? Why would Victor do that?"

Ariana sighed, the weight of the situation pressing down on her. "There's a power struggle between them. Diego wanted to go legit, and Victor couldn't have that. But that's not the only issue. Somehow we're involved and Victor, and his men, will stop at nothing until we're dead.

Chase's eyes widened with a mix of disbelief and alarm. "Involved? What does that mean, Ariana? Why would they come after you?"

Ariana ran a hand through her hair, frustration evident on her face. "I don't know everything, I'm still trying to piece together the details. Diego had been investigating and he might have found something that could connect all of this together and put Victor away."

Chase's mind raced as he tried to make sense of everything Ariana was telling him. He couldn't believe that Victor would go so far as to kill his own brother, let alone involve innocent people like Ariana and Isabella.

Beautiful Lies

"Ariana, do you have any evidence or proof that Diego was murdered by his own brother?" Chase asked.

Ariana shook her head. "None that wouldn't endanger the safety of others. But I've been trying to get my hands on any information he might have had before he died. I know it sounds crazy, but I think Scott and Jason's deaths might be connected as well."

Chase's eyes narrowed as he processed this information. "What makes you think that?"

"Diego had been investigating something big, something that might have led to Scott and Jason's deaths," Ariana explained. "I don't know what it is exactly, but I think it has to do with the cartel war."

Chase nodded in agreement. "We need to find out what Diego was investigating," Chase said firmly. "And we need to find a way to take down Victor before he comes after you again."

As the weight of their conversation settled in the room, Ariana could see the gears turning in Chase's mind. He was processing the gravity of the situation, the danger they were facing, and the mysteries surrounding Diego's death.

Chase sighed; his expression determined. "We can't let Victor and whoever else is behind all this threaten us. Ariana, you need to be careful. Don't go at this alone. We need to work together, figure out what Diego knew, and expose these criminals for who they are."

Ariana nodded, gratitude filling her eyes. "I didn't want you involved in this mess, but now that you are, I'm glad to have you by my side."

Chase reached out, gently cupping Ariana's face in his hands.

"I'll always be by your side, Ariana. No matter what."

The tension in the room eased as they shared a brief, reassuring moment. Ariana knew the challenges ahead were formidable, but with Chase's support, they felt less insurmountable.

Meanwhile, Madison and Isabella, waiting in the living room, exchanged worried glances. The shadows of uncertainty still loomed over them.

As Ariana and Chase rejoined them, a spark gleamed in Chase's eyes. "We need to get that evidence from Diego's apartment and expose Victor's crimes. Isabella, do you know a safe way for us to get there without attracting attention?"

Isabella nodded, her resolve unwavering. "I have a key to an underground entrance that Diego showed me. It's discreet, away from prying eyes. It should give us a chance to get inside without being noticed."

Madison spoke up, her voice firm. "Let's not waste any time. We need to move quickly before Victor catches wind of our plans."

* * *

Lexi sat by Eric's side, her eyes filled with a mixture of relief and concern. The makeshift medical room in the preschool's hidden compound was dimly lit, and the air carried a lingering scent of antiseptic. The Professor, Kana, and Daisuke had done their best to treat Eric's gunshot wound, but the toll on his body was evident.

"How are you feeling?" Lexi asked, her voice soft as she reached for Eric's hand. His skin felt clammy, and his grip was weak.

Eric managed a weak smile. "Like I've been hit by a freight train," he replied hoarsely. "But I've had worse."

Lexi chuckled softly, a hint of tears glistening in her eyes. "You scared the hell out of me, you know that?"

He winced as he shifted on the makeshift bed. "I'm sorry, Lex. I didn't plan on catching a bullet tonight."

The Professor, having finished his work, approached them. His demeanor was calm, a stark contrast to the chaos unfolding outside the compound. "Eric, you're fortunate. The bullet passed through cleanly, and we were able to address the internal bleeding. However, you need rest and time to recover."

Eric nodded weakly, his gaze drifting to Lexi. "Thanks for patching me up, Professor. And thanks for bringing us here. I owe you."

The Professor inclined his head. "We have our own debts, Eric. Your presence here has already set events in motion."

Lexi furrowed her brow. "What do you mean?"

The Professor's cryptic words sent a chill down Lexi's spine. Before she could inquire further, a thunderous boom shook the walls of the compound, raining dust and debris down upon them. Eric tried to sit up, wincing against the pain.

"They've found us," the Professor said grimly. He strode to the window and peered out at the army of shadowy figures assembling outside. Each one was clad in dark, mottled armor that seemed to drink the light from the air. Their movements were stiff yet deliberate as they surrounded the compound, cutting off any hope of escape.

Lexi's heart pounded. "Who are they?"

"No ones. With this bounty on your head, mercenaries from all corners will come seeking the reward," the Professor explained, his gaze fixed on the encroaching threat. "You've brought a storm upon us."

Lexi's mind began to quickly run. This wasn't it, this wasn't the way things were going to end. "Can you walk?" Lexi asked Eric, determination flashing in her eyes.

Eric nodded, a grim determination matching hers. "I can do more than walk. I'm ready to kick some ass."

Lexi's lips curled into a determined smile. "Good, because I don't plan on going down without a fight."

The Professor, Kana, and Daisuke exchanged glances, silently acknowledging the gravity of the situation. The compound's defenses had been compromised, and the only option left was confrontation.

As Lexi helped Eric steady himself, the Professor spoke with a steely resolve, "We have weapons stored in the armory. Gather what you can, and we'll make our stand in the main hall. We might not have the element of surprise, but we'll show them that we're not easy prey."

The group moved with purpose, navigating the underground passages back to the compound's main hall. Lexi's mind raced with thoughts of survival, of protecting those who had become her unexpected allies.

The armory was a flurry of activity as Lexi and Eric hastily gathered whatever weapons were within reach. "Grab that shotgun," Lexi shouted, pointing to a corner of the room. Eric nodded, quickly grabbing the weapon and loading it with ammo.

As they armed themselves, the tension in the air became

almost palpable. Daisuke and Kana took up positions by the windows, their eyes scanning for any signs of movement outside. The Professor stood at the doorway, his hand gripping a rifle tightly.

"Everyone ready?" he asked gruffly, his voice betraying no fear.

Lexi checked her handgun one last time before nodding. Eric gave a firm nod as well, his eyes steeling for what was to come.

Suddenly, there was a loud crash from outside. They all froze, waiting for the next sound. "They're here," Lexi said through gritted teeth.

Without hesitation, they all sprang into action. The sound of gunfire rang out as they fought off the encroaching threat. Lexi and Eric fought side by side, their movements fluid and coordinated after years of training together.

But even as they fought, Lexi couldn't help but notice how Eric's usually calm demeanor had turned into something more primal. His eyes glinted with determination and his jaw was set in a hard line as he took down one enemy after another.

Shadows cast by the flickering emergency lights danced on the walls, creating an eerie backdrop to the imminent clash. The Professor barked orders, directing the defense. Shots rang out, echoing through the cavernous hall. Lexi's instincts kicked in as she fired at the advancing mercenaries, her focus unwavering.

The sound of gunfire and shouting echoed through the underground compound as Lexi, Eric, and the others fought for their lives. The once-peaceful sanctuary had been transformed into a warzone, and the battle showed no signs of slowing down.

Kana and Daisuke were a force to be reckoned with. Kana's

katana sliced through the air with lethal precision, her movements fluid and graceful. She twirled and leapt, her blade finding its mark every time as she took out enemy after enemy.

Daisuke stood at a distance, his sniper rifle steady as he picked off targets with deadly accuracy. His sharp eyes scanned the battlefield, finding weak points in the enemy lines and taking them down with precise shots.

Together, Kana and Daisuke made a formidable team. They moved in perfect synchrony, covering each other's backs and taking down anyone who dared to get in their way.

Lexi fought alongside them, her gun firing off rounds as she moved from one spot to another. Eric was a force on his own as well. His military training gave him an edge on the field, his movements swift and calculated as he took out opponents with ease. The battle raged on for what felt like hours before finally coming to an end. The sounds of gunfire died down until there was only silence left in its wake. Panting heavily, Lexi looked around at her companions. They were all covered in sweat and blood, but they were alive.

The Professor approached them with a grim expression on his face. "We need to regroup," he said firmly. "We can't stay here any longer. They'll come back with reinforcements."

They hurried to gather supplies and make preparations to move out. As they did, Lexi kept a close eye on Eric. Something was definitely off about him. His movements seemed jittery and erratic compared to his normal calm and controlled demeanor.

As they were packing up the last of their gear, Eric suddenly cried out in pain and collapsed to the ground, clutching his side. Blood was seeping through his fingers. He had been so aggressive and reckless; he must have left himself open and failed to notice that he had torn the stitches from a wound inflicted during the battle.

The others rushed over to him. Kana applied pressure to try and stop the bleeding while Daisuke examined the wound. It was deep and Eric was losing blood fast. This was bad, Eric needed medical attention urgently.

The Professor's face was grave as he regarded Eric's deteriorating condition. "This is worse than I feared," he murmured, almost to himself. Turning to the others, he said more loudly, "We cannot delay. Eric needs immediate care, but we also cannot lead those men back to the warehouse."

"We can lose them in the woods," Daisuke said, his voice determined. "Kana and I know these woods better than anyone. There's a path that leads us to the warehouse. Eric, can you make it?"

Eric gritted his teeth and nodded, struggling to get to his feet. Lexi and Kana each took one of his arms to help support him as they began their journey through the dense forest.

The terrain was rough and the trees provided little cover as they made their way deeper into the woods. Lexi could hear the sound of their pursuers getting closer, their shouts and commands echoing through the trees.

"Lexi, take point," The Professor ordered, breaking her out of her thoughts. "We need to move faster."

Without hesitation, Lexi took off running ahead, scanning for any signs of danger or obstacles in their path. She could hear Eric's heavy breathing behind her and knew he was struggling to keep up.

The woods around them seemed to come alive with the sound

of their pursuers. Shouts and heavy footfalls echoed through the trees as their pursuers closed in.

"We have to move, now!" Daisuke yelled.

Kana and The Professor supported Eric between them, his face pale and clammy. Blood continued to soak through his shirt from the jagged wound in his side. He stumbled along weakly between them as they plunged into the dense underbrush, branches whipping against their skin.

Somewhere close behind, a gunshot rang out, the bullet burying itself in a tree trunk just inches from Lexi's head. Her heart hammered against her ribs. Adrenaline flooded her system but she fought to keep control, focusing everything on supporting Eric as they pushed deeper into the ominous woods.

Lexi's breath burned in her lungs as she raced ahead, dodging between trees and vaulting over fallen logs. The sound of their pursuers was growing louder, closer. She risked a glance back and saw figures moving through the trees not thirty yards behind.

"We can't outrun them while carrying Eric," Daisuke said through gritted teeth.

The Professor's face was etched with tension, her eyes darting around for options. "We'll have to make a stand. Help me get Eric down."

They lowered Eric to the forest floor, propping him against a mossy boulder. He was barely conscious, head lolling to the side.

"Give me your gun," The Professor said to Lexi. Lexi hesitated only a moment before handing it over.

Crouching behind the thick trunk of an old oak, The Professor clicked off the safety and took aim at the oncoming figures. Lexi and Daisuke took cover behind nearby trees, hearts pounding.

Beautiful Lies

A shout rang out from their left. One of the gang members had circled around and now stood only twenty feet away, gun leveled right at Lexi.

"Drop your weapons!" he yelled. Blood pounded in Lexi's ears. This was it. After everything, it would end here in the shadows of the forest. She slowly raised her hands in surrender.

Daisuke closed his eyes for a brief moment, taking a slow breath. When he opened them again, his gaze was steady. With sudden speed, he grabbed a fallen branch from the forest floor. In a blur of movement, he snapped the branch across his knee, creating two sharp stakes. Gripping them tightly, he flung the stakes with deadly accuracy. One pierced the gun hand of the gang member threatening Lexi, while the other found its mark in the thigh of an approaching man.

The gang members stumbled in shock and pain. Daisuke pressed the advantage, leaping forward and dispatching two more with swift chops to the neck before they could react. The remaining pursuers hesitated, thrown off by his strength.

Lexi's eyes were wide, mouth agape. "Daisuke...how did you...?"

He gave a thin smile. "I guess you can say we all grew up Lex. Let's just say I've lived a few lives." With that, he grabbed Lexi's hand and pulled her into a run. Adrenaline flooded her veins as they sprinted through the trees. The Professor provided covering fire, dropping two more gang members before falling in behind them.

They had bought some time. But the core group still pursued, enraged by the resistance. As the footsteps crashed closer, Daisuke led them veering off the path to a rocky outcropping. Squeezing through a narrow gap, they found themselves in a small cave just big enough for the five of them. Chests heaving, they collapsed against the damp stone walls. Lexi stared at Daisuke and Kana, the children she knew had transformed into warriors before her eyes. There were hidden depths she had never guessed at. She shifted closer, a new spark lighting in her belly. The darkness enveloped them, but she had never felt more alive.

* * *

Isabella led the way, her eyes scanning their surroundings for any sign of danger. The group moved through the dimly lit underground entrance, the cool air carrying a hint of dampness. The narrow passage seemed to stretch endlessly before them, the distant echoes of their footsteps merging with their hushed conversations.

Ariana walked alongside Chase, her curiosity getting the better of her amidst the tension. "I've been meaning to ask. How did you know Brayden? You seemed to trust him, like you know each other well."

Chase glanced at Ariana, a mixture of emotions flickering in his eyes. "Brayden and I have a complicated history. We grew up in the same neighborhood. But the thing is, he wasn't always like this."

Ariana furrowed her brow, sensing there was more to Brayden's story than met the eye. "What do you mean?"

Chase took a deep breath. "Our town wasn't always plagued by cartels and crime. There was a time when it was a close-knit community, where people looked out for each other. But when the cartels took over, everything changed."

Ariana could see the weight of Chase's memories bearing down on him. "What happened?"

"Brayden's family got caught in the crossfire. They were good people, just trying to make a living. But to those people you're just collateral. One day, they became victims of a senseless act of violence. One day the Montalvo and The La Concha's had a turf war that resulted in Brayden losing his parents, and the town lost its sense of safety."

Ariana's eyes softened with understanding as she listened to Chase's painful revelation. "I'm so sorry, Chase. I had no idea."

Chase nodded, gratitude in his eyes for Ariana's empathy. "After that, I swore to do whatever it takes to protect this town and its people from the horrors of the cartels. That's why I practice law. But sometimes, it feels like I'm fighting an uphill battle."

Ariana placed a comforting hand on Chase's arm. "You're doing everything you can, Chase. And now, we're in this together. We'll find out what Diego was onto and expose the truth. We'll make things right."

As they continued down the underground passage, Madison and Isabella walked a few steps behind, giving Ariana and Chase a moment of privacy. Isabella cast a knowing glance at Madison, silently acknowledging the complexities of the situation.

The group continued down the dark passageway, their footsteps echoing off the cold concrete walls. Up ahead, a sliver of light crept underneath a closed door.

"This must be it," Chase whispered as they approached the door. He slowly turned the handle, the metal creaking softly as the door swung open.

They stepped cautiously into the apartment, eyes darting

around to take in their surroundings. The living room was modestly furnished, with a threadbare sofa and a small TV perched on a plastic crate. Stacks of newspapers and magazines were piled haphazardly around the room, gathering dust.

As they searched through the apartment, Ariana couldn't help but feel a sense of unease. It was clear that Diego had been living in this small, rundown apartment for quite some time. The walls were adorned with posters and articles about the cartels, evidence of his obsession with taking them down.

Suddenly, Madison let out a gasp from the other side of the room. "Guys, look at this!"

They all rushed over to where Madison was squatting and saw that she had pulled out a hidden box underneath the floorboard. Inside was a stack of papers and photographs.

Ariana picked up one of the photos and her heart sank. It was a picture of Madison's father, shaking hands with a well-known cartel leader, Don Raptor. She felt a wave of betrayal and confusion wash over her as she looked at the smiling faces in the photo.

"These are all incriminating evidence against powerful people," Isabella said solemnly as she flipped through some of the papers. "Diego must have been gathering information on them."

Ariana's hands trembled as she sifted through the stack of photos. She recognized politicians, police chiefs, judges - all posing with cartel members, exchanging handshakes and smiles. One photo in particular made her blood run cold. It was an image of her brother Scott, his arm wrapped fraternally around the shoulder of a young man she knew to be Diego.

"Scott..." she whispered, tears filling her eyes.

Beautiful Lies

Madison and Isabella exchanged worried glances. Ariana's reaction confirmed that the photo was indeed real.

"Why...why would he be involved with these monsters?" Ariana asked, her voice strained with anguish.

Isabella placed a gentle hand on her friend's shoulder. "I don't know. But now we understand why Diego was killed. He must have uncovered the truth about Scott and others working for the cartels. We have to bring this evidence to light."

Madison's mind raced as she thought about what they could do with this evidence. They could expose these criminals and finally bring justice to Scott's death.

But then she remembered - it wasn't just one cartel leader they were up against; it was an entire network of powerful and dangerous people. And now they had proof that her father was involved with them.

"We need to be careful with this," Madison said slowly, struggling to keep her emotions in check.

Isabella nodded grimly. "You're right. We can't risk anyone else getting hurt."

"Guys, in here," Chase called out. They gathered in the doorway of the bedroom, taking in the bizarre scene. The walls were covered in Diego's frenzied scribblings, phrases in Spanish scrawled repeatedly between sketches of skulls and other disturbing images.

"Looks like we found Diego's inner demons," Isabella said grimly. She ran her fingers over the unhinged ramblings, wondering what dark visions had possessed his mind.

Ariana's eyes landed on the unmade bed, zeroing in on a tattered notebook lying open. Kneeling down, she scanned the page filled with Diego's cramped handwriting. "Listen to this," she said. "'I saw her today, the woman with no heart. She was with La Concha's men by the docks. They are planning something big tonight.'"

"When was this," Madison demanded.

"Sunday. The night we can't remember."

"We need to get out of here," Chase said suddenly, his eyes darting around the room.

Madison froze, listening intently. In the distance she could hear the rumble of approaching engines. "They're coming," she whispered.

Isabella's eyes widened in alarm. She grabbed the notebook and tucked it into her bag. "Diego must have known too much. We need to move, now!"

The group raced outside just as two black SUVs came screeching around the corner. Masked men sprang from the vehicles, assault rifles aimed directly at them.

"Run!" Chase yelled. They sprinted down the alleyway, bullets ricocheting off the brick walls around them. One caught Chase in the shoulder, causing him to cry out in pain. Still, he kept running.

Madison's heart hammered violently in her chest. They ducked behind a dumpster, struggling to catch their breath. The sound of shouting voices and pounding footsteps grew louder.

"We're trapped," Isabella hissed. She ripped a strip of fabric from her shirt and quickly bandaged Chase's wound.

He grimaced, flexing his arm gingerly. "I'll live. But we need a way out." His eyes scanned the alley, finally landing on a fire escape ladder. "Up there, come on!"

Beautiful Lies

They scrambled up the rusty metal rungs just as their pursuers rounded the corner. Boots pounded on the pavement below as they climbed higher. At the third story landing, Chase pried open a window and they tumbled inside, pressing themselves flat against the wall. They held their breath, listening to the frustrated shouts below.

"They're getting away!" one man yelled in Spanish. "Fan out, search the area!"

Madison let out a shaky breath, her mind racing. What did La Concha want with them? And how had they found them so quickly? She glanced at her friends' tense faces, knowing they were all thinking the same thing. Their problems were just beginning.

Madison's breath caught in her throat as the sound of boots on metal rungs rang out below them.

"We have to move," Chase whispered harshly, clutching his bandaged arm.

Isabella's wide eyes met Madison's and she gave a slight nod. They crept out of the dingy room on the third floor and into a narrow hallway. The fading floral wallpaper was peeling and the carpet threadbare, but they moved silently on stockinged feet towards the far end.

Madison's heart dropped when she saw the hallway was a dead end. They were trapped. Again.

Heavy footsteps echoed up the stairwell, voices calling out in Spanish. The girls shrank back against the wall, Madison's hand finding Isabella's and squeezing tight.

Chase's jaw was set, his eyes burning with intensity. "Get behind me," he murmured.

Madison shook her head firmly. "No, we stand together."

As the first man appeared in the hallway, Chase launched himself forward with a guttural cry. He collided hard, throwing punches and elbows wildly. Two more men rushed to join the fight.

Isabella and Ariana trembled next to Madison. They weren't trained for this. But they had to do something.

With a scream, Isabella jumped onto one man's back, pummeling him with her fists. The man swiped at her, roaring in rage.

Adrenaline flooded Madison's veins. She grabbed the nearest object - a rickety wooden chair - and swung with all her strength. It splintered against her target's shoulder and he stumbled.

They had to fight. They had to escape. Madison swung again and again, her softness hardening into desperate survival. For her friends. For herself. They would get out of this alive.

Madison grabbed Ariana's hand and pulled her down the hallway, Isabella and Chase close behind. The men's shouts echoed after them as they sprinted up a narrow staircase.

"Where are we going?" Ariana cried.

"The roof!" Chase yelled back. "There's a fire escape on the east side."

Madison's lungs burned but she didn't slow down, taking the stairs two at a time. They burst through the heavy metal door onto the rooftop, the night air cool on their skin. In the distance, sirens wailed.

Chase was already halfway down the rusty fire escape. "Hurry!"

The girls scrambled down after him, the metal creaking and groaning under their weight. As their feet hit the pavement, the rooftop door slammed open above them.

"Go, go!" Chase urged.

They ran down the dark alley, the sound of their pursuers growing fainter. Madison's heart pounded wildly. They had made it. They were free. But they weren't safe, not yet. The real danger still lay ahead, cloaked in mystery and violence. She glanced back at her friends, their faces grim. They would see this through together, no matter where it led them. For now, they just had to keep running.

10

Blood Bonds

The journey through the shadowy woods had been perilous, but Lexi, Eric, and their new companions managed to reach the warehouse under the cover of darkness. The air was thick with tension as they approached the looming structure, its metal exterior blending seamlessly with the night.

As they approached, Lexi could feel the weight of the night's events pressing down on her. Eric, though weakened, had managed to keep pace with the group. The Professor, Kana, and Daisuke moved with a purpose that mirrored the urgency of the situation. The confrontation with the La Concha gang had left its mark on all of them.

Upon entering the warehouse, Lexi's eyes searched the dimly lit space until they landed on Catalina, her mother and the leader of the Montalvo cartel. Catalina stood near a table strewn with maps and documents, her posture regal and commanding.

The group hesitated for a moment, glancing at each other before Lexi took a step forward, determined to deliver the news.

"Mother," Lexi began, her voice steady, "the meeting with The Hawks didn't go as planned. The La Concha's were already aware of our intentions. We were ambushed, and it turned into a firefight."

The Professor stepped forward, acknowledging Catalina with a nod. "Their numbers are greater than we anticipated."

Catalina's face remained impassive as she absorbed this information. After a tense moment, she turned to fully face the group.

"It seems our enemies have grown bold while we've been in the shadows," she said, her voice low and controlled. She clasped her hands behind her back as she slowly paced.

"The time has come to remind those pirates who exactly holds the power in this city."

Lexi shifted uncomfortably. "Mother, open war will only lead to further bloodshed. Perhaps there is a more tactful solution-"

Catalina whirled to face her daughter, eyes flashing. "Diplomacy? After they dared to threaten what is mine?" She stepped closer to Lexi, who forced herself not to retreat.

"I understand you wish to avoid violence, but the choice is not ours to make. The La Conchas and the others must be burned from the rotted core in which they've grown."

Lexi met her mother's gaze unflinchingly. "And if we resort to their methods, how are we any better? More violence will only continue the cycle."

Catalina's expression hardened. "You question my leadership now, when lives... our lives hang in the balance?" Her voice was icy.

The tension in the warehouse grew suffocating as the two women stared each other down, neither willing to back down.

Catalina's eyes shifted to Eric, still weakened from the gunshot wound. "Eric," Catalina spoke, her voice measured.

"You've found yourself in the midst of a storm."

Eric nodded, acknowledging the gravity of the situation. "It seems we're all caught in it together."

Catalina waved for the professor to see Eric to the infirmary while Catalina took Lexi on a walk to discuss matters privately. As they headed down the dimly lit corridor, Catalina placed a gentle hand on Lexi's shoulder.

"I know you only wish to avoid more bloodshed," Catalina said softly. "But there are some things you have yet to understand, my fierce daughter. The roots of this conflict run deeper than you know."

Lexi tensed, ready to argue, but Catalina raised a hand. "Walk with me. Hear what I have to say before you judge."

Catalina led Lexi through a corridor adorned with photographs and artifacts, each telling a chapter of the Montalvo family's history. The walls displayed images of a humble bakery in the outskirts of the city, where the original Montalvos led a modest life. Lexi's gaze lingered on a picture of a smiling couple, Henry and Camila Montalvo, standing proudly in front of their small bakery.

"The Montalvos were content," Catalina began, her voice carrying a sense of nostalgia. "Your great-grandparents, Henry and Camila, were known for their warmth and generosity. Their only son, Alejandro, was the pride and joy of their lives."

The next photograph captured the innocence of a young Alejandro, a carefree boy with a bright future ahead. Lexi couldn't help but feel a pang of sorrow knowing the tragedy that awaited him.

"Tragedy struck," Catalina continued, her eyes flickering with a mixture of pain and anger. The tone shifted as the photographs depicted a devastating loss—the senseless violence that claimed Alejandro's life. A somber shadow fell over the room as the narrative unfolded. "Alejandro fell victim to the senseless violence that plagued the city. Camila, unable to cope with the loss of her only son, succumbed to the darkness that enveloped her heart."

As they moved through the corridor, Catalina stopped before an ornate door. Opening it, she revealed a room transformed into a personal museum, a tribute to the Montalvo family's journey.

The walls were adorned with murals depicting the town and intricate carvings that told a story of redemption. The centerpiece was a massive mahogany desk, a symbol of Henry Montalvo's transformation from a broken man to a revered patriarch.

"Left alone and consumed by sorrow, Henry made a solemn vow to transform his pain into purpose," Catalina continued, her fingers tracing the carvings on the desk. "He turned his attention to the community that had witnessed his family's tragedy—a community scarred by poverty, crime, and violence."

Lexi's eyes took in the images of Henry opening his home to orphans and those misunderstood souls living in the shadows of society. The Montalvo home became a sanctuary for those seeking refuge from the harsh realities of River Creek.

"Henry found solace and redemption in providing a haven for those who had nowhere else to turn," Catalina explained, her voice resonating with pride. "The Montalvo family, born out of tragedy, became a beacon of hope for the downtrodden."

Photographs displayed moments of joy and laughter, capturing the essence of a family that extended beyond blood ties. The Montalvos were now a diverse group of individuals brought together by circumstance.

"As the Montalvo family grew, so did their influence within the community," Catalina continued, leading Lexi to a wall adorned with newspaper clippings and commendations. "But in a city ran by corruption and crime, we found ourselves at odds with those who sought to exploit the weak."

Lexi's mind swirled with emotions as she took in the history of her family. Admiration for Henry's resilience and determination mixed with a sense of unease as she learned of their involvement in less-than-legal activities.

Catalina led her to a corner of the room where a large portrait hung, featuring Henry and his late wife Camila standing proudly with their children. Lexi couldn't help but notice that Alejandro's photograph was missing from the frame.

"Henry made sure that Alejandro was never forgotten," Catalina said softly, noticing Lexi's gaze. "He built this place to honor his memory and to continue his legacy."

Lexi nodded, understanding the importance of keeping loved ones close even after they were gone.

As they continued to explore the room, Catalina pointed out photographs of various community events organized by the Montalvos – from holiday celebrations to charity drives.

"We wanted to give back to the community that had given us so much," Catalina explained. "We may have started out as victims, but we refused to be defined by tragedy. We chose to use our pain as fuel for positive change."

Lexi admired their resilience and strength, but a question nagged at her.

"What about all the bloodshed?" she asked cautiously. "How

Beautiful Lies

does that fit into this narrative?"

Catalina's expression darkened slightly before she responded.

"We do what we have to do in order to protect our family and those we care about," she said firmly. "Sometimes that means making difficult decisions and engaging in activities some wouldn't understand. But I can assure you, it is always for a greater good."

Lexi nodded, not fully convinced but not wanting to push further on the subject.

As they made their way back through the corridors toward the entrance, Lexi couldn't help but feel conflicted. On one hand, she admired and respected what the Montalvos stood for and what they had accomplished. On the other hand, she knew everything came with a price.

Lexi's mind churned with conflicting emotions as she navigated the labyrinthine corridors of the Montalvo warehouse alone. The weight of her mother's revelations, the clandestine world she had unwittingly stepped into, bore down on her shoulders. As uncertainty clouded her thoughts, she sought her own solace.

In her wandering, Lexi stumbled upon a door slightly ajar, revealing a soft glow emanating from within. Curiosity piqued, she cautiously pushed the door open and found herself in a chamber adorned with Montalvo insignias, dimly lit by flickering candles. The air carried a palpable sense of reverence and anticipation.

Lexi watched in awe as the young boy and girl, both barely teenagers, stood before an altar adorned with Montalvo symbols. Their families and members of the clan surrounded them, creating a protective barrier around the sacred ceremony.

The atmosphere was charged with reverence and anticipation as a woman stepped forward to officiate the ceremony. She wore traditional garments embroidered with intricate designs and her face was solemn.

As she began to speak in Latin, the young girl and guy exchanged vows and promises to each other. They seemed confident and sure of their words, despite their young age. Watching this in front of her she couldn't help but remember her Soar ceremony with Eric. How young Lexi could never imagine the weight of her pact.

Suddenly, Lexi noticed that a man who she assumed to be the girl's father stepped forward from behind her. He carried a small dagger in his hand that glinted in the candlelight.

He made his way to the boy and held out the weapon for him to take. With trembling hands, the boy took it from him and then turned towards the young girl.

Lexi couldn't help but reflect on her own situation – still unsure of where she fit into this world, let alone who she could trust or rely on.

Lost in thought, Lexi didn't notice Kana approaching until she spoke.

"Quite a sight, isn't it?" Kana said softly, gesturing towards the altar.

Lexi nodded, still feeling a bit overwhelmed by everything she had witnessed since arriving at the Montalvo compound. "Do you ever think of what life would be like without all of this," Lexi said.

"Sometimes," Kana whispered. "Sometimes I wonder what

life would be like with parents and a hobby." Lexi giggled at the thought of Kana having a hobby, a concept that seemed almost foreign in their tumultuous world.

"Can you imagine me doing something normal?" Kana added with a wistful smile.

Lexi chuckled, picturing Kana engaged in a serene activity far removed from the chaos of their reality. "Maybe gardening or painting? Something completely unexpected."

Kana grinned. "I'd probably be terrible at it, but it's a nice thought."

As they continued to watch the ceremony unfold, Lexi's gaze was drawn back to the young couple at the altar. The exchange of vows had transitioned into a moment of profound symbolism. The young boy, now armed with the dagger, made a small incision on his palm, mirroring the girl's actions. Their blood mixed, a silent promise sealed with the ancient ritual.

Kana's voice brought Lexi back to the present. "You're still thinking about your Soar ceremony, aren't you?"

Lexi nodded, her thoughts a tangle of emotions. "I never realized how much it would shape my life. How the choices I made that day would lead me here."

Kana's gaze shifted from the ceremony to Lexi, her eyes filled with a quiet determination. She stepped closer, her movements graceful and calculated. "Lexi," she began, her voice low but carrying the weight of sincerity, "there's something we need to talk about."

Lexi turned to Kana, sensing a shift in the atmosphere. "What is it?"

Kana took a deep breath. "Daisuke and I, we want to help

you. We want to restore order to the family, to bring it back to what it once was."

Lexi studied Kana's expression, searching for any hint of deceit. "Why? What's in it for you?"

Kana's eyes locked onto Lexi's, unwavering. "Our family is falling apart, and we can't stand idly by. Daisuke and I believe in you, Lexi. We believe you can be the force of change that the Montalvos need."

Lexi's mind raced with conflicting thoughts. Trust had become a rare commodity, and yet, here were two individuals offering their allegiance.

"We know you have a bounty on your head," Kana continued. "We're willing to help you navigate through this chaos. But in return, we ask for your trust and a chance to rebuild what has been broken."

Lexi's mind was a whirlwind of conflicting thoughts as she pondered Kana's proposition. On one hand, the idea of having allies was alluring but on the other hand, the thought of putting her trust in someone else, especially in these uncertain times, filled her with a sense of unease. She couldn't help but feel torn between her desire for support and her instincts to keep her guard up at all times. And yet, as she looked into Kana's eyes, she couldn't deny the genuine sincerity shining through, making it even harder to make a decision.

After a moment of contemplation, Lexi nodded. "I can't promise blind trust, but if you're genuine about helping me and restoring the family, then I'm willing to work together."

Kana's face softened with gratitude. "Thank you, Lexi. We'll stand by you, every step of the way."

As they watched the Soar ceremony unfold, a silent understanding passed between them, binding their fates in ways that extended beyond the flickering candles and the ancient rituals of the Montalvo family.

***

Chase winced as a sharp pain shot through his shoulder. The wound, sustained in their narrow escape, was a nagging reminder of the danger that pursued them. Madison's focus shifted to him, a mix of concern and determination in her eyes.

The gravel crunched beneath Madison's sneakers as she led the group through the overgrown path that led to her family's estate. The moon cast an eerie glow on the sprawling estate, its grandeur standing in stark contrast to the chaos they had narrowly escaped in town.

Madison couldn't shake the unease that gripped her. The memories of the masked figure as their hands were against her neck reemerge, sending trembles down her spine. She stole a glance at Isabella and Ariana their faces etched with concern. They had all faced danger together, but the shadows of the past seemed to haunt their every step.

Ariana's voice cut through the silence. "I've been trying to reach Lexi, but there's no answer." She held up Chase's phone, frustration evident in her eyes.

Chase winced again, but his focus remained on the task at hand. "Keep trying. We need to know she's safe."

The mansion loomed ahead; its ornate façade cloaked in darkness. Madison's hands trembled as she fumbled for the keys in her pocket, the metallic jangle echoing in the stillness. She pushed open the heavy door, the creaking hinges protesting as if remembering the weight of secrets they held.

The grand foyer greeted them, memories of opulent gatherings and family celebrations now tainted by the looming threat that trailed them. Madison led the group through the winding corridors.

As they reached the study, Madison couldn't help but glance at the portrait of her father that hung on the wall—a stark reminder of the man she had believed to be a symbol of a good man. The same man whose image now flickered with doubt in her mind.

Isabella sensed Madison's turmoil and placed a comforting hand on her shoulder. "We'll get through this, Madison. We'll get you answers."

Ariana, still focused on the phone, finally let out a breath. "I got through to Lexi. She's okay, but she's facing some trouble of her own. The La Conchas are after her."

Madison's eyes widened, the gravity of the situation sinking in. "Lexi? Why would they be after her?"

Ariana shook her head. "I don't know, but she needs our help. She's at the Montalvo compound. We have to go."

Chase, ever the strategist, assessed the situation. "We can't afford to split up, especially with the cartel involved. Madison, we need to know everything. Is there anything in this place that can help us understand what's happening?"

DING DONG

The doorbell echoed through the grand foyer. Madison froze, her heart skipping a beat. She exchanged a wary glance with Isabella, Ariana, and Chase, who shared her concern.

Beautiful Lies

Ethan stood at the doorstep, his eyes searching for Madison. His face mirrored both relief and worry as he took in the group gathered in the surroundings.

"Madison, I heard about what happened. Your parents' home, the break-in. Are you okay?" Ethan's concern was genuine, but Madison's mind raced with conflicting emotions.

Before she could respond, Chase winced, his hand clutching his injured shoulder. "Ethan, we're in the middle of something, and it's not safe. Madison needs time to figure things out."

Ethan's gaze didn't waver from Madison's. "Madison, I know you. You've always tried to handle things on your own, but this time, let me be there for you."

Madison swallowed hard, her emotions in turmoil. She nodded reluctantly, knowing that pushing Ethan away might only drive him further into the danger she sought to shield him from. Her hands trembled as she reached out to take his. "Ethan, I..." Her voice faltered. How could she make him understand without putting him in harm's way?

Madison took a deep breath, steeling her nerves. She had to trust her instincts, as dangerous as it seemed. "Ethan, there are things I need to tell you. But you must know, once you step through this door, there's no going back. Are you willing to take that risk?"

Ethan met her gaze unwaveringly. "I'd follow you anywhere."

Madison nodded, blinking back tears. She led Ethan inside, Ariana and Chase trailing behind cautiously. The dim apartment was heavy with foreboding, shadows dancing across the sparse furnishings. Madison took a seat on the worn sofa, motioning for Ethan to join her.

Madison took a deep breath and began to explain the danger she was in - the cartel that was after them, and the secrets she had discovered that could bring them down. Ethan listened intently, his jaw tightening with concern.

As Madison immersed herself in the inner workings of everything, they knew about the La Concha's, a sudden and jarring noise erupted at the door. It was as if someone had slammed their fist against it with all their might, causing the entire room to shake. The sound echoed through the hallway like a gunshot, instantly grabbing Madison's attention and making her heart race with adrenaline.

They all jumped, heavy boots stomped down the hall outside, and a man's gruff voice called out, "Open up! We know she's in there!"

Madison shot to her feet, terror etched on her face. Ethan and Ariana moved in front of her protectively while Chase ran over to a display case holding a engraved pistol.

"We need to get out of here, now!" Ariana said urgently. She rushed to the window to check if they could escape that way.

Chase began to take off his bloody shirt wrapping it around his hand to smash the display grabbing the pistol. "I won't let them hurt any of you," he told Madison fiercely checking the gun for bullets to reveal three bullets in the chamber.

The intruder pounded on the door again. "Last chance! The girl dies if you don't open up!"

Madison trembled, her mind racing. She knew the cartel wasn't bluffing. But how could they get out? They were trapped, and Ethan was now in the crosshairs with her.

The pounding on the door intensified as Victor's men

prepared to burst through. "I'm giving you to the count of three before we shoot the lock and come in guns blazing!" Victor shouted from the hallway.

Madison's heart dropped into her stomach. This was it. After all they had struggled through, the cartel had finally tracked them down.

She turned to her friends, tears pooling in her eyes. "You need to get out of here. I have what he wants."

"We're not leaving you," Ethan said fiercely, gripping her hand.

Chase cocked the antique pistol, his jaw set. "Let them come. I've got three bullets with their names on them."

With an ear-splitting crack, the door splintered open. Half a dozen armed men swarmed inside, Victor at the front with his signature gold-plated pistol glinting.

"There's my girl," he purred, his eyes landing on Madison. "You've caused quite a lot of trouble. But it's over now."

Madison stepped forward, her chin raised defiantly. "Let my friends go, Victor. I have what you want."

Victor smiled slowly. "Loyalty. I admire that." He waved his men back. "I'll make you a deal. Come with me without a fight, and your friends can leave unharmed."

Madison hesitated, then nodded. This was the only way. She wouldn't gamble with her friends' lives.

As she moved toward Victor, the room filled with the sounds of a click- Chase had pulled the trigger of the antique pistol. But the decades-old ammunition merely clicked dully in the chamber.

Victor shook his head. "I tried to be reasonable." He raised his own pistol at Ethan.

"No!" Madison screamed. But the gunshot split the air, and Isabella collapsed.

Madison rushed to Isabella's side as she fell, blood blossoming from the gunshot wound in her chest.

"You monster!" Madison cried, glaring accusingly at Victor.

He shrugged, unrepentant. "I gave fair warning. The blame lies with your reckless friend."

Madison pressed her hands over Isabella's wound, staunching the flow of blood. Isabella was pale but conscious, gritting her teeth against the pain.

"Why?" Madison demanded, looking up at Victor with tear-filled eyes. "I'm here, just like you wanted. Why keep hurting them?"

Victor holstered his pistol and crouched down beside her. "You still don't understand, do you prima?" He used the Spanish term of endearment gently, tilting her chin up. "I'm not doing this to be cruel. I'm doing it to protect you."

Madison jerked back, confusion mingling with her anger and fear. "Protect me? From what?"

"From them," Victor said grimly. He stood and paced away from her, running a hand through his slicked-back hair.

"Madison, you're my blood. My family. My cousin." He turned back to her, his expression earnest. "You know nothing of your birth right. The thing these people are trying to rip from us."

Madison's mind spun, a whirlwind of confusion and disbelief. Isabella groaned in pain beside her. The revelation that Victor was her cousin sent shockwaves through her already tumultuous world.

Victor took a step closer, his eyes imploring her to understand. "The Montalvos—they're after something that rightfully belongs to us. Our family has a legacy, a power that runs through our veins. I won't let them take it from you."

Madison struggled to comprehend the gravity of Victor's words. The pain in Isabella's eyes mirrored her own inner turmoil. Chase, still holding the useless antique pistol, glared at Victor with a mixture of anger and betrayal.

"I don't believe you," Madison whispered, her voice strained. "What power? What legacy?"

Victor sighed, as if carrying the weight of centuries. "It's in the blood, Madison. It's a connection to something greater, something the outside world would exploit and destroy. I've been trying to protect you, to bring you back to where you belong."

Madison's head throbbed with conflicting emotions. The revelation felt surreal, and she struggled to reconcile the image of Victor as a ruthless cartel leader with the idea that he saw himself as a protector.

"Catalina," Victor said solemnly, his gaze unwavering, "she orchestrated the events that led to your parents' demise. It was a power play within the family, a move to consolidate control. Your mother and father were collateral damage in a much larger game."

Madison's breath caught, and her eyes locked onto Victor's, searching for any sign that he might be lying. Ariana and Chase's expressions mirrored her disbelief, their connection to Catalina making the revelation all the more shocking.

The room felt like it was closing in on Madison. The memories of her parents, the masked figure, the break-in—all of it connected to the mother of the very person she had believed to be a pillar of strength in her life, Lexi.

"Why?" Madison's voice trembled, anger and hurt bubbling to

the surface. "Why would she do that?"

Victor's gaze softened, but the gravity of his words remained. "Power, Madison. In our world, power is everything. Your parents stood in the way of what she believed was her birthright. And now she sees you as a threat."

A surge of conflicting emotions overwhelmed Madison. The person she had trusted, the matriarch of the Montalvo family, had played a role in the tragedy that shattered her world. The revelation shattered the last vestiges of trust in her life.

"Madison," Victor's voice was gentle, "I know this is hard to grasp, but you have a choice now. Stay with those who have deceived you, or come with me and reclaim what is rightfully yours."

Ariana gripped her arm, steadying her. "Madison, listen to me. I know you're in shock right now, but you can't trust Victor. We have no proof of what he's saying."

Chase nodded; his expression grim. "This could be a manipulation tactic. Don't let your emotions cloud your judgment."

Victor held up his hands. "I have no reason to lie to you, Madison. I'm trying to help you see the truth." His eyes bored into hers, willing her to believe him.

Madison's pulse pounded in her ears. She wanted to scream, to break something, to unleash the tempest building inside her. For so long she had blamed herself for her parents' deaths, carrying the weight of survivors' guilt. To learn it had all been part of Catalina's ruthless ambition was too much to bear.

"Come with me, Madison," Victor implored, his voice low and persuasive. "We can make this right, together."

Ariana gripped Madison's shoulders, forcing her to meet her gaze. "Don't listen to him. We're your family now, Maddie. We'll get justice for your parents, but we have to do this the right way."

Madison trembled, tears shining in her eyes. She had trusted Lexi, considered her a sister. To have that trust shattered so violently left her reeling. But Ariana and Chase had been by her side from the beginning. If she couldn't trust them, she couldn't trust anyone.

Slowly, she stepped back from Victor. "I...I need time," she stammered. "This is too much."

Victor's face flashed with frustration before smoothing into a look of sympathy. "I understand this is difficult," he said gently. "But we don't have much time. The longer you stay, the more danger you're in."

Madison shook her head, backing towards the door. The walls felt like they were closing in on her. She needed air.

"You'll never have to be scared again," Victor said, his voice low and smooth as velvet.

Madison hesitated, glancing back in her father's study where Ethan still crouched over Isabella's limp body. She couldn't tell if her friend was still breathing or not. This was all her fault. If only she had listened to her gut instead of letting her stubborn pride push them into this dangerous investigation. Now Isabella was paying the price.

Victor extended his hand, his dark eyes searching hers. "Come with me, Madison. I can protect you."

She wavered, tears blurring her vision. She was so tired of being lied to, so tired of being afraid. Chase had promised to keep them safe, but now Isabella hovered at death's door. What other choice did she have but to trust Victor?

Behind her, she heard Ethan's panicked voice saying Isabella's name over and over as he tried to stem the flow of blood from the bullet wound. Madison blinked back her tears. As much as it hurt to leave them, she knew she had to get away.

Slowly, she reached out and took Victor's hand. His fingers curled around hers, warm and steady. For the first time that night, her pounding heart began to slow. Victor guided her out of her family's estate toward the street where a sleek black car idled against the curb.

Madison tried to take one last look at Ariana, Ethan and Isabella, but their forms receded into shadows. She said a silent prayer for her friend, then turned away. Victor held the car door open for her, and she ducked inside, the leather seat still warm beneath her.

As Victor slid into the driver's seat, Madison felt the fear that had gripped her all night finally loosening its claws. Maybe Victor was right. Maybe with him she really could be safe.

11

The Funeral

Ariana stood in the small chapel bathroom, the dim light flickering above the mirror casting shadows on tear-streaked cheeks. The hushed sounds of mourning echoed through the chapel as she tried to catch her breath. The loss of her brother, Scott, was a wound that seemed too deep to ever fully heal.

As Ariana attempted to steady herself, the door creaked open, and Lexi stepped in. The heavy weight of grief hung between them, and without a word, Lexi embraced Ariana. Their silent hug conveyed more than words ever could, offering a momentary refuge from the pain that surrounded them.

In the confines of the bathroom, Ariana found solace in Lexi's presence. She closed her eyes, holding onto the embrace, as if trying to anchor herself in a world that seemed to be slipping away.

Lexi, breaking the silence, whispered, "I'm here for you, Ari."

Ariana nodded, her voice barely above a whisper, "Thank you, Lex."

As the two friends held onto each other, Ariana's mind began to wander. In the mirror's reflection, she silently counted to ten, each number a fleeting attempt to push away the overwhelming thoughts that threatened to drown her.

One. The pain of loss, fresh and raw.

Two. Memories of Scott, her brother who had shared her laughter and tears are now shrouded in questions as she wonders if she really knew him at all.

Three. The weight of responsibilities that now rested solely on her shoulders as she held onto Diego's secret arsenal of information.

Four. The aching sensation she felt as she knew her family was forever altered.

Five. The realization that life could change in an instant.

Six. A desire for strength to keep going.

Seven. The fear of being swallowed by the darkness.

Eight. Regrets, the unspoken words and moments that slipped away.

Nine. The uncertainty of what lay ahead.

Ten. The dreaded resolve to face whatever came next.

As Ariana released a steadying breath, she felt a warm reassurance in Lexi's embrace. The weight hadn't lifted, but for a brief moment, it felt shared.

"Madison", her voice gently said, "I've been worried, Lex. We haven't seen Madison in ten days. Do you think she's okay?"

Lexi's expression shifted, a mixture of concern and guilt. "I don't know, Ari. She's been dealing with a lot, especially after what we learned about her family."

Ariana's worry deepened. "Do you think your mother's involvement might have pushed her away for good? Could she have joined the La Conchas?"

"I'm unsure of most things these days, Ari." Lexi continued to hold onto Ariana, a silent support in the midst of sorrow. Trying to ease the tension, Lexi spoke, her voice soft and reassuring. "Ariana, I have to say, you've done an amazing job with everything. The funeral arrangements, the tributes—it's all so well put together. Your brother would be proud."

Ariana managed a small, appreciative smile, grateful for the distraction from the overwhelming emotions. "Thanks, Lexi. I just wanted it to be something he deserved."

"I think he would love it. You know I would say on the other hand, your family knows how to make a statement. The media coverage, the people attending—it's impressive how they can even make a funeral self serving. "

Ariana's smile faded as she processed Lexi's words. "Statement? What do you mean?"

Lexi hesitated, choosing her words carefully. "Well, your family invited the media and it seems to be every important figure from River Creek to the funeral. It's like they're making a statement about Scott and your family."

Ariana's eyes widened in disbelief. "What? I thought this was supposed to be a private, intimate ceremony. I didn't want all this attention. With everything else going on the last thing we need is more eyes on us."

Lexi nodded in understanding. "I figured you didn't plan for it to be this way. Maybe your family thought it would be a way to honor Scott in their own way, but I can see how it blindsided you."

Ariana took a deep breath, struggling to process the sudden shift in the funeral's tone. "I wanted a chance to grieve, damn it. We just saw a mother be shot in front of us Lexi. I just saw a 17-year-old boy become an orphan. And all I wanted was a moment. Even in war, soldiers allow their enemies to bury their dead."

Lexi tightened her grip on Ariana's shoulders, offering silent support. "It's a lot to handle, especially with everything else going on. Maybe after the funeral, you can talk to your family about how you feel. They might not have realized it would affect you this way."

Ariana nodded, a mix of frustration and hurt in her eyes. "I need to have a conversation with them, but it's hard. After finding out about Scott's life and that they knew he was in danger, it's been tough to forgive them."

Lexi squeezed Ariana's hand. "Take your time. Grieving and forgiveness don't have a set timeline. Do what feels right for you."

A gentle knock echoed on the bathroom door, and Chase's voice followed. "Ariana, Lexi, we should head out soon. The funeral is about to start, and your mom is looking for you, Ariana."

Ariana took a moment to compose herself, wiping away a stray tear. She glanced at Lexi, grateful for the support. "I'll be out in a minute," she called back to Chase.

As Lexi released her from the embrace, Ariana met her eyes, a mix of sadness and appreciation. "Thank you, Lexi. It means a lot that you're here."

Lexi managed a small, understanding smile. "Of course, Ariana. I'm here for you."

Ariana nodded, taking a deep breath as she prepared to face the mourners.

The atmosphere in the chapel was somber as Lexi joined Eric, Daisuke, and Kana, who were discreetly keeping watch for any signs of trouble. The rows of mourners, the hushed conversations, and the floral arrangements created a melancholy backdrop for the occasion.

Beautiful Lies

Lexi took a seat next to Eric, her gaze lingering on the casket at the front of the chapel. Eric nodded in acknowledgment, his eyes reflecting a mix of gratitude and concern.

"How are you holding up, Eric?" Lexi whispered, mindful of the solemn setting.

Eric offered a small, reassuring smile. "Recovering, thanks to The Professor and whatever shit he puts in those syringes. I'll be back on my feet soon enough."

Lexi couldn't help but feel a surge of guilt. "I'm sorry you got caught up in all this. If I had been more careful—"

Eric gently interrupted her. "Lexi, it's not your fault. We're all in this together, remember? Besides, I signed up for this when I chose to help you."

A heavy silence settled between them, and Lexi couldn't shake the weight of unspoken emotions. She stole a glance at Eric, his features etched with resilience, and a flicker of something more.

"I saw you back there," Eric began, his voice low and measured. "When you thought you might lose me... you looked terrified."

Lexi's heart skipped a beat. She averted her eyes, feeling exposed. "I can't afford to lose anyone else, Eric. Not after everything that's happened."

Eric reached out, gently turning her face toward him. "You don't have to face it all alone, Lexi. We're here for you, and I'm not just talking about the danger we're in. I care about you."

Lexi met his gaze, her expression guarded. "I appreciate the sentiment, Eric. But let's focus on getting through this mess. We don't have time for anything else."

The chapel fell into a hushed silence as Catalina made her entrance. Her presence demanded attention, and the air seemed to tighten with an unspoken tension. Ariana's father James, acknowledging Catalina's presence, gestured toward an empty seat in their aisle. The weight of unease settled upon Ariana and Lexi as their eyes met, a silent exchange revealing shared concern.

After the chapel filled, James rose and stood at the podium, his grief-laden eyes scanning the somber crowd gathered for Scott's funeral. The chapel was filled with mourners, their faces etched with sorrow, sharing in the collective grief of a life cut short. Ariana, seated alongside Lexi, clenched her fists, her emotions roiling beneath the surface.

As James began his speech, Ariana's anger simmered. Every word he spoke felt like a distortion, a falsification of the reality she had known. His tales of a close-knit relationship with Scott, filled with shared laughter and precious moments, grated against the truth she held dear. The charade of a perfect family, carefully constructed for the public eye, intensified Ariana's frustration.

The congregation nodded solemnly, absorbing the carefully crafted narrative of a father mourning his son. Ariana's jaw tightened, her knuckles turning white as she gripped the edge of her seat. The weight of unspoken truths and concealed pain pressed down on her, fueling the anger that simmered within.

Suddenly, James shifted the tone of his speech, catching everyone off guard. "In the face of this tragedy," he announced, his voice projecting with newfound determination, "I have made a commitment to our beloved town of River Creek. I believe that, as a community, we can overcome the darkness that has taken my son from us."

Beautiful Lies

Ariana's eyes widened, her anger momentarily replaced by shock. The unexpected revelation hung in the air. James continued, "I am running for mayor, and I am proud to announce that Catalina Montalvo will be joining me as deputy mayor. Together, we will protect the city's history and ensure the safety of our citizens."

The congregation buzzed with whispers, caught off guard by the sudden political announcement at a funeral. Catalina Montalvo, a name associated with shadows and secrets, now aligned with James in a bid for mayoral leadership. Ariana's gaze shifted to Lexi, a silent acknowledgment passing between them.

The air grew tense as Lexi's eyes followed Eric's gaze to the entrance of the chapel. Madison, flanked by Victor and an ominous group of hooded figures, walked in. The atmosphere shifted; the somber mourning disrupted by an unwelcome intrusion.

Kana and Daisuke, attuned to the undercurrents of danger, subtly began to prepare for any potential confrontation. Their eyes met briefly, a silent agreement passing between them. The Montalvo compound had seen enough conflict, but it seemed that trouble had followed them even to Scott's funeral.

Lexi's heart raced as she observed Madison. The distance between them felt like an unbridgeable chasm, filled with unanswered questions and the weight of betrayal. The hooded figures accompanying Madison raised suspicion, their identities concealed like shadows in the dimly lit chapel.

Eric, sensing the tension, leaned in close to Lexi. "Something's not right. Stay alert."

Lexi nodded, her eyes never leaving Madison. The funeral, once a moment for shared grief, now brimmed with an undercurrent of uncertainty. The La Concha's men moved with purpose, their presence casting a pall over the sacred space.

As Madison took her seat, the hooded figures dispersed, blending into the crowd. Kana and Daisuke, poised for action, exchanged a glance.

The somber ambiance of the funeral was shattered when Victor, a dark figure in his own right, stepped forward to take control of the ceremony. His voice, a chilling resonance, cut through the mourning crowd as he began to deliver a message that sent shivers down the spines of everyone present.

"Today, my friends, we stand at the precipice of change," Victor proclaimed, his words carrying a sinister weight. "The oppressors, the rich who have reveled in their decadence, and the Montalvo snakes who slither in the shadows—today, we declare war on them all. No longer will we cower in fear. Today marks the beginning of a cleansing, a reckoning for those who have ruled through terror and deceit."

As Victor spoke, realization dawned on the gathered mourners. The exits were being barricaded, and hooded figures were spreading throughout the chapel, pouring gasoline in a macabre preparation for something far more sinister than a mere speech.

Fear rippled through the crowd, a palpable wave of panic and confusion. The solemnity of the funeral had been twisted into a platform for Victor's malevolent agenda. In the eyes of those trapped within the chapel, the desperate need for escape mirrored the flames that threatened to consume them.

Lexi's pulse quickened, her gaze darting between the exits and the hooded figures. The air became thick with the acrid scent of gasoline, and a sense of impending doom hung over the chapel like a shroud.

Kana and Daisuke, poised for combat, exchanged a grim look. They understood the gravity of the situation—this wasn't just an attack on the Montalvos; it was an assault on everyone present. The flames of chaos had been ignited, and the only way out was through a storm of danger.

As Victor's fanatical speech reached its crescendo, the first flames flickered to life, casting dancing shadows on the walls. The funeral, once a solemn occasion, had transformed into a nightmarish stage for a war that threatened to engulf them all.

Chaos erupted as the fire began to spread. People scrambled over pews and stampeded towards the exits, desperate to escape the inferno. Ariana lunged towards Madison, trying to rescue her from Victor's grip, but her path was blocked by the panicked crowd.

"We have to get these people out!" Eric shouted over the screams. He kicked open a side door and began herding people to safety. Chase and Daisuke joined in, guiding the terrified mourners outside.

Amidst the smoke and confusion, Victor's men had surrounded the building, blocking the main exits. The only escape was through the side doors that Eric had opened. As Lexi ushered the last few stragglers out, she caught a glimpse of her mother near the pulpit as Victor approached her.

In the dimly lit chaos of the chapel, Victor and Catalina locked eyes for the first time, the air thick with tension and the weight of unresolved grievances. Victor, fueled by a simmering rage, approached Catalina with a menacing determination.

He reached out, fingers curling around her throat, his grip tightening. Catalina, unyielding and proud, met his gaze with a defiant glare. The corners of her lips curled into a taunting smile, refusing to show any sign of fear despite the pressure on her windpipe.

Victor's voice, low and seething, cut through the chaos. "You took everything from me, Catalina. You destroyed my family, and now it's time you pay for what you've done."

Catalina's response was a mocking laugh, her eyes gleaming with a mixture of arrogance and disdain. "Your family is rotten fruit. "

Victor's nostrils flared with fury, but before the confrontation could escalate further, Eric emerged from the shadows, his presence a silent threat. He approached with deliberate steps; a gun held firmly in his grasp.

"Let her go, Victor," Eric's voice was steady, the cold edge of authority cutting through the tension.

Victor's grip on Catalina tightened for a moment, a dangerous glint in his eyes. However, the appearance of the gun at his temple gave him pause. Reluctantly, he released Catalina, allowing her to step back, unfazed by the encounter.

As Victor turned to face Eric, the situation escalated in an instant. Victor, quick as a striking serpent, knocked the gun out of Eric's hand with a swift movement. The metallic clatter echoed through the chapel, drawing the attention of those nearby.

The acrid scent of gasoline lingered in the air as Madison's eyes fixated on the gun, its metallic surface reflecting the flickering flames that danced around the chapel. The ominous footsteps drawing nearer sent shivers down her spine, a dreadful prelude to what awaited her.

In that tense moment, Ariana finally caught up to Madison, her voice tinged with desperation. "Madison, please! You have to make the right decision. We can find another way out of this."

Madison's anger flared at Ariana's words, her frustration bubbling to the surface. "Right decision? What does that even mean, Ariana? Every 'right' decision I make seems to end in me losing. I've lost my family, my home, and now, I feel like I'm losing myself."

Ariana's eyes pleaded with Madison, fear beginning to creep into her heart. The flickering flames cast eerie shadows on Madison's face, highlighting the turmoil within. The Madison she knew seemed to be slipping away, replaced by a version tainted by darkness and anger.

"If you're going to shoot anyone it should be me Maddie." The chaos surrounding them, the crackling flames, and the distant sounds of the ongoing struggle faded into the background as Lexi's words cut through the air like a blade. Madison turned to face Lexi with Kana now straight behind, her eyes reflecting a turbulent mix of emotions – surprise, defiance, and a lingering pain.

Lexi's voice was steady, her gaze unwavering. "If you're going to shoot anyone, Maddie, it should be me."

Ariana watched the exchange, a knot tightening in her stomach. The weight of the situation bore down on them, and Madison's internal turmoil was palpable. The flickering light of the flames cast shadows that danced across their faces, emphasizing the gravity of the moment.

Madison's grip on the gun tightened, her jaw clenched.

Madison stared at the gun in her hand, her knuckles white

from grasping it so tightly. She had never imagined herself capable of violence, yet here she was, consumed by rage and betrayal.

Ariana and Lexi watched her warily, unsure of what she might do next. They had been friends once, as close as sisters.

Lexi let out a shaky breath, holding Madison's gaze. "Because I'm the reason we're in this mess. I'm the one who's family betrayed you, who led you down this dark path." Her voice broke. "If anyone deserves punishment, it's me."

Madison shook her head, blinking back tears. The gun felt impossibly heavy in her hand.

"I don't know if I can," she said, the admission paining her. She had come here wanting vengeance, had been prepared to spill blood. But now, confronted with the reality of it, her resolve faltered.

Ariana stepped forward hesitantly. "Madison..." she began.

"Stay back!" Madison snapped, wheeling on her. The gun swung wildly in her trembling hands. Ariana froze, eyes wide.

A deafening explosion rocked the chapel, sending shockwaves through the air, splitting the floor and tearing through the structure. The force of the blast threw Lexi, Ariana, and Kana off their feet, their bodies colliding with the cold, hard ground. Flames erupted, casting ominous shadows across the wreckage.

The dust and smoke billowed, obscuring the chaos that unfolded within the shattered remains of the chapel. Panic and urgency filled the air as survivors scrambled to safety, but Lexi's focus was singular – on the spot where the explosion had torn the floor asunder.

"Eric!" Lexi's voice cut through the chaos, carrying a

desperate plea. She staggered to her feet, eyes wide with fear as she searched the debris for any sign of movement.

"We have to get out of here Lexi. This place won't hold for long," Daisuke yelled.

"We have to go mi hija," Catalina said. Lexi's eyes darted between the wreckage, torn between the desperate need to find Eric and the looming danger of the collapsing chapel. The realization that Eric might be buried beneath the debris tightened its grip on her chest, the fear threatening to drown out reason.

12

White Lines

Outside the crumbling chapel, the scene transformed into a spectacle of flashing lights, sirens, and a clamor of voices. Detective Penbrooke, standing among uniformed officers and paramedics, wore a frustrated expression. He knew of the Montalvo family's involvement in the cities underworld, but proving it was another matter entirely.

As Lexi and Catalina emerged from the wreckage, the media swarmed, cameras flashing, and microphones thrust forward. The air buzzed with anticipation, and the townspeople, held at bay by police barricades, strained to catch a glimpse of the unfolding drama.

Catalina, the picture of poise, stepped forward, her voice cutting through the chaos. "Ladies and gentlemen of River Creek, today's tragedy has shaken us all. Our hearts go out to those who have lost loved ones and to the brave first responders who are working tirelessly to ensure everyone's safety."

A wave of sympathetic murmurs washed through the crowd. Lexi felt a surge of revulsion at her mother's ability to spin tragedy into a carefully crafted narrative.

Detective Penbrooke approached, a stern look on his face, determined to pierce through the facade. "Catalina, don't play games with me. I know the Montalvos have their hands in more than just charity work. I'm not buying your act."

Catalina's eyes flashed with a mix of defiance and feigned innocence. "Detective, you and I both know that rumors and old wives' tales have no place in a police investigation. The Montalvos are victims here, just like everyone else. This tragedy has no connection to our family's legitimate businesses."

Detective Penbrooke narrowed his eyes, unconvinced. "Legitimate businesses? I've been digging into your family for years, Catalina. I know the darkness that lurks beneath the surface. Don't think you can fool me with your polished words."

Catalina's lips curled into a sly smile, her demeanor shifting to a more confrontational tone. "Detective, your imagination is quite impressive, but fabricating stories won't get you anywhere. Perhaps you should focus on finding the real culprits instead of chasing shadows."

Detective Penbrooke clenched his jaw, frustrated by Catalina's slick evasion tactics. He knew she was hiding something, but in the public eye, she maintained a veneer of innocence.

As the media continued to barrage Catalina with questions,

Lexi's eyes drifted to the wreckage of the chapel. The realization that Eric and Madison might be lost in the debris gnawed at her, a cold emptiness settling in her chest. She couldn't comprehend how her mother could navigate this moment so effortlessly while daughter's world crumbled.

As Catalina continued to address the crowd, spouting carefully chosen words, the police department had managed to apprehend a few members of the La Concha cartel who were responsible for the fire. They were currently in custody, their faces hidden from the media's relentless gaze.

Detective Penbrooke, aware that the town was hungry for answers, stepped forward, his voice cutting through the clamor. "Ladies and gentlemen, we've apprehended individuals connected to the events that unfolded here today. We are working diligently to confirm the extent of casualties and provide you with accurate information. I assure you; justice will be served."

A murmur of anticipation and unease rippled through the crowd as reporters scrambled to capture every word. The tension in the air was palpable, and Lexi, standing beside Catalina, felt a heavy weight on her shoulders.

Catalina, maintaining her composure, subtly shifted the narrative. "Detective Penbrooke, I appreciate your dedication to the truth. We're all eager to see those responsible brought to justice. Let's allow the authorities to conduct a thorough investigation, and in the meantime, we stand united as a community in the face of adversity."

Amidst the chaos that followed the explosion, Ariana fought her way through the debris and the crowd to catch up with her parents. Her eyes were filled with a mix of anger and confusion as she confronted her father, who seemed unfazed by the turmoil.

"Why today?" Ariana's voice cut through the noise, carrying the weight of her emotions. "Why, at Scott's funeral, did you announce your political campaign and with all people Catalina? Do you even realize the danger you've put us in?"

James sighed, his expression a mix of weariness and determination. "Ariana, this town needs change. It needs someone who can lead and protect. The alliance with Catalina provides the strength and support we need to make a difference. I have worked and will continue to work to keep this city safe."

Ariana's frustration deepened. "You're dealing with dangerous people. You're putting Morgan, me, everyone at risk!"

James' gaze hardened. "I'm doing what I believe is right for this town, for our family."

Ariana shook her head, the realization hitting her like a punch to the gut. "No, you're doing what's best for you, and like always it's at the expense of your family. But lately family to you have just been accessories. I bet you didn't even realize your other daughter didn't even come today." She couldn't trust her own family.

Chase, who made his way through the sea of people, led Ariana away from the tumultuous scene involving her family, his grip firm yet gentle. Once they found a momentary refuge away from the chaos, he turned to her, frustration etched on his face.

"Ariana, we can't let this continue. The Montalvos, the La Conchas – they've caused enough pain. We have evidence, documents that can expose them for what they are. We need to submit it to the police, bring them down once and for all."

Ariana's eyes flickered with conflict. The weight of the

decision pressed down on her shoulders. "Chase, I understand what you're saying, but it's not that simple. If we expose the truth, it'll hurt people too."

Chase took a deep breath, his gaze unwavering. "Ariana, I get it. But if we don't act now, more innocent people will suffer. We can't let personal ties blind us to the bigger picture."

Ariana sighed, torn between loyalty and the greater good. "I know, Chase, but it's not just about the bigger picture. It's about the people we care about. We need a plan that protects them while taking down the ones responsible."

Chase nodded, acknowledging the complexity of their situation. "The truth needs to come out, no matter the cost."

Ariana sighed, knowing Chase was right but hating the painful reality of it.

As they stood under the flickering streetlight, she noticed a mysterious figure standing across the street. The figure was cloaked in darkness, his face concealed by the hood of his cloak. Only the faint glint of his eyes could be seen, shining like two orbs in the shadows.

Her breath caught in her throat. "We're being watched," she murmured under her breath.

Chase tensed but didn't turn his head. "You sure?" he asked quietly.

Ariana gave a slight nod. "Black hoodie, by the alley. He's been there since we started talking."

Chase shifted his stance, angling his body between Ariana and the mysterious figure while trying not to alert them that he'd noticed. "I don't like this. We should get out of here."

Ariana's eyes remained fixed on the hooded man. "I'm going

after him," she declared, already stepping off the curb into the street.

"Ariana, wait!" Chase called in alarm, but she broke into a run, dodging down the empty street toward the watching stranger. The figure turned and sprinted into the alleyway just as Ariana reached the sidewalk. She raced after him, Chase on her heels pleading with her to stop.

Ariana pursued the hooded figure down the dim alley, her heels clacking loudly on the cracked pavement. The man was fast, vaulting over trash cans and debris with ease, but Ariana's determination kept her close behind.

As they neared a chain link fence at the end of the alley, the man scrambled up and over in one smooth motion. Ariana leapt and grabbed the top of the fence, struggling for a moment before hauling herself up and dropping down on the other side.

The hooded man glanced back as Ariana landed in a crouch, and she caught a flash of his face in the faded light - young, handsome, and strangely familiar. He turned and continued running through the abandoned lot beyond the fence, but Ariana could tell she was closing the gap.

With a burst of speed, she launched herself and tackled the man to the ground. He struggled beneath her, still concealing his face with one hand.

"Stop fighting and show yourself!" Ariana growled, pinning his arms down.

The hooded man stopped struggling and slowly lowered his hand from his face. Ariana gasped as she recognized the chiseled features and piercing blue eyes that were so similar to her brother Scott's.

"Scott?" she stammered.

The young man gave a faint, sad smile. "I'm Oliver. Scott was my boyfriend."

Ariana sat back on her heels, stunned. Scott had never mentioned anyone named Oliver or that he was even gay. How little did she even know Scott at all. She opened her mouth to speak, but just then Chase came panting up behind them

"What's going on? Are you alright?" Chase asked breathlessly.

Ariana quickly explained how this was someone who knew Scott. Oliver stood up and looked at them solemnly.

"There's a lot I have to tell you about what really happened to Scott," he said. "But we can't talk here. It's not safe."

Their footsteps echoed through the cavernous gallery space, dust motes swirling in the beams of sunlight streaming through cracks in the walls and boarded up windows. Canvases with ragged tears leaned against the peeling walls, and broken glass crackled under their shoes.

Oliver turned to face Ariana; sadness etched on his face. "Before he died, Scott was hiding here. Let me explain everything."

Ariana nodded, steeling herself for whatever secrets Oliver was about to reveal about her brother and the events leading up to his mysterious death. She knew the truth would be difficult to hear, but she had to know.

Oliver took a shaky breath, his eyes cast downward. "See I didn't really have a great upbringing. I lost both of my parents when I was twelve and the La Conchas took me in. When you're a twelve-year-old kid you don't really question it. They just filled the void of a family and I was grateful." He looked up at Ariana with a pain-stricken expression. "It wasn't until I met your brother that I started to see how messed up everything was," he continued.

Chase crossed his arms over his chest, listening intently to Oliver's story. Oliver noticed the tension in his stance and continued speaking. "Scott found me one day...I was getting my ass kicked by some of our so-called 'brothers' for not following orders or whatever...he stepped in, took a beating for me and managed to get me out of there. Saved my life... literally". He looked away, shame in his eyes. "I owed him my life...I still do," he added quietly.

Ariana placed a comforting hand on Oliver's shoulder. "It's not your fault Oliver, they manipulated you, you were young" she told him firmly. Oliver gave a sad smile and nodded in thanks.

"Right before he died, Scott started asking questions...didn't like the direction things were going in the gang anymore." Oliver explained, shifting uncomfortably on his feet. "He knew too much...about the drugs, the guns, everything".

A sudden realization dawned on Ariana. "He was going to turn state's evidence" she whispered to herself as it all started to click into place. Oliver nodded. "He wasn't the only one either," he added ominously.

"Diego," Chase whispered.

Oliver nodded gravely. "Yeah, and some others too. People higher up who were getting tired of the way things were being run. But the moment word got out, the walls started closing in."

Ariana's mind raced as the pieces fell into a disturbing puzzle. The danger her brother faced, the risks he took to protect Oliver.

Chase's jaw tightened, a simmering anger in his eyes. "That's why they went after Scott. To silence him."

Oliver lowered his eyes, looking pained. "Scott was desperate. He knew he was marked. That's why he came to me that night." Oliver paused, taking a shaky breath. "He talked about you a lot, Ariana. How you were the only one he could really trust."

Ariana blinked in surprise. She had no idea her brother confided in Oliver about her.

"The night he died, after he got the warning, you were the only person he thought to run to. But they caught up to him before he could get here." Oliver's voice broke.

Ariana felt like she'd been punched in the gut. Her brother's last moments were spent trying to reach her for help. Guilt and sorrow crushed down on her. If only she had known, she could've done something, saved him somehow.

Chase put a steadying hand on her shoulder. "It's not your fault. You couldn't have known." His reassurance only provided small comfort.

Ariana attempting to steel herself. "We have to stop them, all of them." Her voice rang with conviction. "We have to bring them down before anyone else gets hurt."

Oliver and Chase exchanged resolute glances. "Where do we start?" Chase asked.

Ariana's eyes narrowed, jaw set. "Victor. We start with him."

✳ ✳ ✳

Inside Catalina's house, the tension was palpable. The air hung heavy with unspoken words and repressed feelings. Lexi tried to focus on her salad at the dining table, but her mind was a chaotic storm of conflicting thoughts. Kana and Daisuke shared concerned looks, but neither spoke up, not wanting to add to Lexi's inner turmoil.

Catalina continued to move around the kitchen with a cold and calculated precision, unfazed by the tense atmosphere. Lexi's frustration boiled inside of her, threatening to overflow as she sat at the table, weighed down by the recent events and burdened by the heavy weight on her shoulders.

Unable to contain her emotions any longer, Lexi pushed her plate away forcefully and locked her piercing gaze on her mother. "Aren't you going to acknowledge what happened at the funeral? About Eric?" Her voice crackled with a volatile mix of anger and hurt, shaking with unbridled intensity.

Catalina looked up, her expression unreadable. "Lexi, mi amor, you know I have to be careful with what I say. The world is watching, and appearances matter more than ever."

Lexi scoffed, her frustration boiling over. "Appearances? Eric could be dead, and all you care about is the silly game you're playing with Ariana's father. You're more concerned about some stupid game of thrones you're playing with the La Concha's than the people who actually matter in your life!"

Kana and Daisuke exchanged uncomfortable glances, sensing the tension in the room. Lexi's chest heaved with each breath as she struggled to convey the depth of her emotions.

Catalina maintained her composure, her eyes steady on Lexi. "You're upset, Lexi, and rightfully so. But you must understand that there are forces at play that go beyond what you see."

Lexi slammed her hand on the table, her frustration breaking through. "I don't care about your political games or your secrets, mother! I was actually born with a fucking heart. I care about the people I love, and right now, I don't even know if Eric is alive or dead!" Catalina's expression remained stoic, and Lexi felt a surge of anger. "Do you even care? Do you care about anything other than your own ambitions?"

Catalina sighed; her tone measured. "Lexi, I've always done what I believed was necessary to protect our family. Sometimes sacrifices are required for the greater good. Eat your food now, be a good girl."

Lexi's eyes narrowed, her voice cutting through the air like a blade. "Sacrifices? Is that what you call it? I won't be a part of this anymore. I won't sacrifice the people I love for your version of the greater good that somehow only satisfies you."

Lexi's frustration erupted into a boiling rage, and she couldn't hold back the torrent of words any longer. "You listen to me, mother," she spat, her voice cutting through the air. "If you know what's good for you, you better pray that Eric is still alive. Because if anything has happened to him, I won't stop until I expose every secret, every twisted game you've played. You will know nothing but fire because I will burn everything down that you touch."

Catalina's expression remained composed, but there was a flicker of uncertainty in her eyes. Lexi didn't wait for a response. She turned on her heel and stormed out of the house, Kana and Daisuke following closely behind.

Kana and Daisuke hurried after Lexi as she strode down the sidewalk, her steps fueled by rage.

"Lexi, wait!" Kana called out, rushing to catch up with her. "Just take a breath, let's talk this through."

Lexi whirled around, eyes ablaze. "Talk? There's nothing left to say." Her voice broke. "I can't let her hurt anyone else I love."

Daisuke gently grasped Lexi's shoulders. "I know you're scared for Eric, we are too. But we need a plan, not rash action." He searched her eyes, willing her to calm down.

Lexi's chest heaved, adrenaline still flooding her system. But she gave a short nod, the red haze of anger receding slightly.

"Daisuke's right," Kana said gently. "Losing your temper won't help Eric. We need to work together on this."

Lexi took a shaky breath. "You're right. I'm sorry, I just..."

"We know," Daisuke said. "But now we need to focus. Let's go somewhere we can talk safely."

Lexi nodded, the fight going out of her as her shoulders slumped in defeat. "I just feel so powerless. I wish we had more resources, more help."

Daisuke grimaced, knowing what he had to suggest but dreading Lexi's reaction. "Well, there might be an organization we could ally with," he began cautiously. "One with extensive resources and insider information."

"I've already tried The Hawks, they made it clear they plan to remain neutral," Lexi sighed out frustrated.

"Well we have to try something!" Kana insisted. "Eric's life is on the line. If The Hawks are our only shot at getting information, we have to take it."

"It's risky," Daisuke said slowly. "If the La Concha's find out we're sniffing around..."

"I know it's dangerous," Lexi cut in, "but we're out of options." She set her jaw stubbornly. "I'm going to talk to them, with or without you."

Kana and Daisuke exchanged a resigned look. Once Lexi set her mind on something, there was no stopping her.

"Okay," Kana relented with a sigh. "We'll go with you," she said unsheathing a throwing star.

Lexi nodded, some of the tension easing from her shoulders now that they had the beginnings of a plan. "Let's go now, before it gets too late. We can take the back alleys, avoid being seen."

The three set off, sticking to the shadows as they wound their way through the urban maze. An electric anticipation hummed through them, tinged with fear. If this gamble didn't pay off, the consequences could be dire. But it was a risk they had to take. For Eric.

13

Resilience

Detective Penbrooke studied the gathered evidence with a furrowed brow, nodding appreciatively at the thoroughness of Ariana, Chase, and Oliver's work. The wall of his office was adorned with photos and strings, creating a chaotic but organized display of interconnected crimes.

"You've managed to dig deeper than most," he remarked, tapping his pen against the edge of his desk. "But, I need to be clear – if I use this information, if I bring it to light, I can't guarantee your safety. These people," he gestured at the web of connections on the wall, "they play dirty, and they have long-reaching arms."

Ariana exchanged a glance with Chase and Oliver, acknowledging the gravity of the situation. Chase leaned forward, his voice steady. "Detective, we know the risks. But we can't let them continue to operate in the shadows. Innocent lives are at stake."

"While the evidence is impressive; I need to know – how did you get your hands on it?" Detective Penbrooke's tone was firm, his eyes probing for answers.

Ariana hesitated, caught off guard by the direct question.

"We... gathered information from various sources. Some of it was public record, and some required a bit more digging."

Penbrooke leaned back in his chair, a deep frown etching lines on his forehead. "You're playing a dangerous game, Ariana. The FBI is already breathing down our necks because of the mess in River Creek. And now, with you and your friends tangled in this web, it's become a national issue."

A chill ran down Ariana's spine. The implications of her actions were sinking in. She exchanged a glance with Chase and Oliver, both equally uneasy.

"You have three powerful families involved – Montalvos, La Conchas, and your own. The FBI won't buy a story where all three girls are innocent. It's a narrative that doesn't sit well in the optics," Detective Penbrooke explained, his expression grim. "You need a villain, someone to take the fall, or the FBI will turn this into a bloodbath. They're not known for their subtlety."

Ariana's mind raced. Sacrificing one of her friends for the greater good felt like a betrayal, but the alternative was a storm that could engulf them all.

"I'll give you 24 hours to decide," Penbrooke declared, his voice heavy with the weight of the decision. "After that, I turn this over to the DEA. They won't be as concerned with subtleties."

As Ariana prepared to exit the detective's office, Chase assured her he would follow shortly. Once Chase quietly shut the door, Ariana found herself alone with Oliver in the waiting room. Her gaze shifted to Oliver; her expression filled with worry. "Are you alright?" she inquired gently, recognizing the weight of the toll on him.

Oliver sighed; his gaze distant. "As okay as I can be, given everything. I just want to see justice for Scott. I want those responsible to pay."

Ariana nodded, her determination matching his. "We'll make sure they do, Oliver. Scott deserves that much."

As they waited for Chase to return, Ariana's phone buzzed with an incoming call. The name "Diane Fanburg" flashed on the screen, and a sense of unease settled in her stomach. She answered the call as she stepped a few feet away, holding the phone to her ear.

"Diane, what's going on?" Ariana asked, her voice tight.

Diane's voice came through the phone, urgent and concerned. "Ariana, the FBI just executed a search warrant at the house. They discovered evidence linking Jason's death to organized crime. They're treating it as a major case."

Ariana's heart pounded in her chest. The implications of the FBI's involvement were staggering. "Organized crime? What evidence did they find?"

"His truck. They said they found it at a chop shop marked by the Montalvo's." Ariana felt the pit in her stomach grow deeper. She could still see the bright red brake lights if she tried hard enough.

"Where are you now? Are you okay?" Ariana asked Diane, concern etching her voice.

"I'm still at the house. The FBI is combing through everything. I'm a bit shaken up, but I'm alright," Diane replied, a tinge of anxiety detectable behind her steady tone.

Ariana knew she had to get over there. "I'm on my way. Don't say anything to them until I get there," she instructed before quickly hanging up.

She turned to Oliver; her expression grim. "That was Diane. The FBI found evidence linking Jason's murder to organized crime. They're searching the house now. I need to get over there. Make sure they don't do anything stupid until I get back."

Ariana sped towards Diane's house, her mind racing. The FBI's involvement complicated things tremendously. She knew she had to tread carefully to protect her friends.

As she pulled up to the house, two black SUVs were parked out front. Ariana took a deep breath before getting out of her car and striding towards the front door. Two agents stood guard, giving her scrutinizing looks.

"Ariana Bennett, Diane's lawyer," Ariana stated firmly. "I'm here to advise my client."

The agents nodded and allowed her inside. The house was swarming with agents collecting evidence. Diane stood in the corner of the living room, her arms wrapped around herself, looking small and afraid.

Ariana went to her immediately. "Are you okay?" she asked gently. Diane nodded, her eyes glistening.

A severe-looking agent approached them. "Ms. Bennett, I'm Agent Fowler. We have reason to believe Mr. Fanburg's death is linked to organized crime. I assume you'll advise your client to cooperate fully?" His tone made it clear there was only one acceptable answer.

Ariana met his gaze steadily. "Of course. But you understand my duty is to protect my client's rights."

Agent Fowler gave a curt nod before continuing his inspection of the house. Ariana turned to Diane, speaking low. "Don't say anything until we can confer privately. They're on a fishing expedition right now."

Diane nodded, looking relieved to have Ariana by her side. As the agents finished their search, Ariana pulled Agent Fowler aside. "I'd like to review your findings and understand the basis for this warrant."

Fowler's lip curled slightly. "In due time, Counselor. For now, we've discovered Mr. Fanburg's truck at a known Montalvo chop shop. We have reason to believe his death was an organized hit."

Ariana's heart raced, her mind spinning with dread. If Jason's truck was discovered at a Montalvo chop shop, it meant more than just a connection to organized crime. The evidence inside could potentially implicate her or her friend's in Jason's death.

"I'll need to see that vehicle immediately," Ariana stated, holding Agent Fowler's gaze. "As Mrs. Fanburg's counsel, any evidence related to this case must be made available to me without delay."

Fowler's eyes narrowed slightly, but he nodded. "We're having it transferred to the evidence warehouse now. I can allow you a brief examination."

Ariana maintained her composure, despite the urgency pounding through her veins. "Thank you. I'd like to accompany your team to inspect it."

The car ride over was tense, Ariana's mind racing. She had to find a way to get access to Jason's truck alone, even just for a few minutes.

Arriving at the warehouse, Ariana's demeanor underwent a subtle transformation. The warmth that typically radiated from her was replaced by a steely resolve that shimmered in her dark eyes, hinting at the depth of determination within her. With each step towards Agent Fowler, she exuded a calculated grace, her movements purposeful and deliberate.

"Agent Fowler," Ariana began, her voice smooth yet commanding, "I understand protocol, but this private inspection is crucial for our investigation. We need to uncover every detail to piece together the puzzle of Jason's death."

Agent Fowler's initial resistance hesitated under the unwavering gaze of Ariana. The atmosphere crackled with tension as she deftly guided the conversation, her words like threads weaving a tapestry of persuasion around them.

"It's not just about following procedure," Ariana continued, her tone laced with conviction. "It's about justice for Jason and closure for his family. You can help us bring those responsible to light."

As their exchange unfolded, Agent Fowler found himself slowly succumbing to Ariana's persuasive prowess. Reluctance gave way to grudging admiration for her tenacity as she skillfully led him towards granting her request.

In the end, as respect colored Agent Fowler's features, he finally relented with a nod. "Alright, Ms. Bennett," he conceded, "I'll allow for the private review of the truck as you've requested." Agent Fowler signaled for one of his agents to lead Ariana into the laboratory where the car was being held.

Alone now, Ariana moved quickly, scouring the interior. Under the passenger seat, she found it - her lost cell phone. Hands shaking, she slipped it into her purse just as Fowler returned.

"Well? Anything pertinent?" he asked crisply.

Ariana met his gaze. "Nothing yet. But I'd like our forensic team to go over it as well."

Beautiful Lies

Fowler nodded reluctantly. As they left, Ariana exhaled slowly. The phone was safely in her possession once more.

Ariana's heels clicked sharply against the concrete floor as she strode down the hallway of the federal building, Agent Fowler matching her brisk pace. The fluorescent lights hummed overhead, their sterile glow reflecting off the polished floors.

"I appreciate you allowing me to review the vehicle personally," Ariana said smoothly as they walked. "I know that's not standard protocol."

Fowler nodded; his expression unreadable. "Yes, well, these are extraordinary circumstances. And you've proven yourself trustworthy."

They turned a corner, heading toward the exit. Ariana could almost taste the freedom awaiting her outside these walls. Ariana suppressed a smile. Her lost phone was safely tucked away now, its secrets still her own.

"I'm glad I could be of assistance," she replied modestly.

As they stepped outside into the brightness of day, Fowler turned to her. "You're wasted working for that two-bit lawyer Chase Smith," he remarked bluntly.

Ariana arched an eyebrow. "Is that so?"

"I've done my research. With your skills and instincts, you could be a real asset to an organization like the DEA," Fowler continued. "Especially with our new River Creek field office opening soon

He held her gaze steadily. "Think about it. The offer stands if you want it."

Ariana paused, surprise flickering across her face. She had not expected this.

"I'm flattered," she said carefully. "I'll give your offer serious consideration."

Fowler nodded, seeming satisfied. They parted ways outside the building, the sound of traffic filling the air.

Ariana blinked against the sun, her mind spinning. The DEA's arrival in River Creek could change everything. She had difficult choices ahead. With determined steps, she set off down the sidewalk. The dance was not over yet.

✳ ✳ ✳

Madison stepped into the eerie depths of the La Concha's hideout, a forgotten aquarium that once teemed with life but now lay in ruins. The walls were adorned with remnants of aquatic murals, faded and peeling, as if the sea creatures trapped within them were trying to escape their painted prisons. Water-stained tanks loomed ominously, their glass murky and cracked, casting distorted reflections across the room.

The air inside carried a musty scent of decay mixed with a hint of saltwater, a haunting reminder of what once thrived in this desolate place. Shadows danced eerily in the dim light filtering through shattered skylights, creating an atmosphere of foreboding uncertainty.

Amidst this macabre setting, Eric's anguished cries reverberated off the algae-covered walls, adding to the sense of unease that permeated the space. Victor, a sinister presence cloaked in shadows, fixed his piercing gaze on Madison, his intentions as murky as the waters surrounding them. It was as though he could see into her very soul, waiting for her next move with chilling anticipation.

Beautiful Lies

As the memories of the fiery chaos at the funeral surged through her mind like a relentless inferno, Madison felt the searing heat of the flames licking at her skin once more. The deafening explosion echoed in her ears, leaving a ringing sensation that reverberated through her very core. Each flicker of fire painted vivid images of destruction, searing pain, and shattered glass that mirrored the fractures in her own conflicted soul.

Amidst this harrowing mental landscape, Victor's ominous figure loomed before her, holding out a small vial of pills like a sinister offering. His voice cut through the cacophony of memories with a chilling undertone, "These will help calm your mind, Madison. We can't have you losing focus," his words dripping with a calculated menace that sent shivers down her spine. The weight of her past decisions bore down on her like a heavy burden, leaving both physical and emotional scars that refused to fade.

Madison's gaze lingered on the pills, her mind a whirlwind of conflicting emotions. The allure of temporary escape from the haunting memories and relentless chaos gnawed at her resolve. Despite the warning bells ringing in her head, a part of her craved the numbing bliss promised by those tiny capsules. With trembling hands betraying her inner turmoil, she hesitantly reached for the vial, her thoughts consumed by the desperate hunger for relief that only the drugs could momentarily satisfy. Deep down, amidst the tumultuous storm within her, Madison knew she was teetering on the edge, but in that moment of weakness, it felt like the only solace she could grasp onto.

The drugs worked their magic, spreading a numbing sensation throughout Madison's body and mind. The turmoil within her quieted, allowing a semblance of calm to settle over her.

For the first time in what felt like an eternity, she could take a deep breath without feeling like her chest was constricting.

As she gazed at Victor through half-lidded eyes, his face seemed to morph into something almost beautiful - his sharp features softened by the dim light and the hazy effects of the pills. His voice was like a soothing lullaby as he began to speak, weaving a dark tale of ambition and vengeance.

"You see, Madison," he started, stroking his chin thoughtfully, "the Montalvos have held too much power for too long. It is time for us to rise up and claim what is rightfully ours." He paused, letting his words sink in before continuing.

"Their wealth and influence have blinded them to the suffering of those beneath them. But we see it, don't we?" he asked, gesturing towards Eric who stood silently behind him. "We see the poverty and injustice that plagues our beloved town."

Madison's mind was still clouded by the drugs, but her thoughts were slowly clearing as Victor spoke. She knew what he was saying had some truth to it – she had seen firsthand the struggles faced by the less fortunate in River Creek. And yet, there was something sinister about Victor's words that made her uneasy.

Victor's voice oozed manipulation as he drew closer, his eyes gleaming with avarice. "I have a grand scheme," he began, his tone laced with cunning. "Our path to dominance lies in outwitting the Montalvos, gaining control of their territory, and establishing our rule over River Creek. We don't have to rely on living in the shadows soon. In a few days everything is going to fall into place ," he disclosed, causing a chill to run down Madison's spine.

"You, Madison, will play a crucial role in this symphony of chaos," Victor declared, his eyes gleaming with a fanatical zeal.

"You will be my princess, a symbol of our ascendancy. Together, we will bring the Montalvos to their knees."

Madison listened, a mixture of horror and fascination gripping her. The twisted beliefs of the La Conchas unfolded before her – a distorted vision of power and vengeance that left no room for mercy or redemption.

As Victor spoke, Madison discerned a flicker of hesitation in his demeanor, a subtle hint that not all was as it seemed. She probed cautiously, "You talk of a partner. Who is this ally of yours?"

A cryptic smile played on Victor's lips. "Patience, my princess. All will be revealed in due time. For now, focus on your role in the grand design. We are on the precipice of something extraordinary."

Eric sat bound to a chair, his face bruised and bloodied from the relentless beatings of Victor and his men. His once vibrant blue eyes were sunken and devoid of their usual spark, but he refused to let them break him.

Madison's heart ached as she looked on helplessly, her mind struggling to process the events unfolding before her. She had been brought here by Victor with promises of power and purpose, but now she saw only cruelty and violence.

Victor paced back and forth in front of Eric, a sadistic grin on his face. "You see this?" he taunted, gesturing towards Eric's battered form. "This is what happens when you cross me."

Eric spat blood onto the ground at Victor's feet, his voice hoarse from screaming. "Go to hell," he snarled defiantly.

Victor chuckled darkly and signaled for one of his lackeys to bring over a table filled with various weapons – knives, guns, chains – all meant for causing pain. He ran his fingers lovingly over each item before finally settling on a leather bullwhip.

"Such defiance," Victor observed mockingly as he cracked the whip in the air. "But I think it's time we teach you a lesson."

Madison watched in horror as Victor began lashing Eric with the whip, each strike eliciting agonizing screams from her friend. She wanted to look away but couldn't tear her eyes from the scene unfolding before her.

Eric gritted his teeth through the pain but refused to give in. He knew that any sign of weakness would only fuel Victor's sadistic pleasure. Instead, he focused on his memories of Lexi.

Through gritted teeth and clenched fists, Eric turned his gaze toward Madison. "Madison, don't let them break you," he rasped, his voice strained but defiant. "You're not like them. You don't belong here." Madison met Eric's eyes, a mix of pain and determination reflected in his gaze. "They've taken everything from me," Eric continued, his voice a low growl. "But this – all this violence and death – it won't fix anything. It'll only create more pain, more suffering. You don't have to be a part of this, Madison."

Madison's hands trembled as she clutched the edge of her seat. The weight of the choices she faced pressed down on her, the consequences looming like a shadow.

"I'm angry, Madison," Eric confessed, his gaze never wavering. "Angry at the Montalvos, at this twisted world we're trapped in. But revenge won't heal the wounds. It won't bring back what's lost."

Madison's mind raced as she took in Eric's words. She wanted to believe him, to find the strength he seemed to possess even now.

But the cold tendrils of fear wrapped tighter around her heart.

She thought of the pills Victor had given her, how they had brought a blissful numbness. But their effects were fading now, leaving her raw and exposed once more.

Madison turned to Victor, searching his face for any sign of mercy or compassion. But his dark eyes remained calculating, assessing her like a predator waiting to strike.

"Come now, my princess. Don't let his foolish talk sway you," Victor purred, his voice sickeningly smooth. "He knows nothing of our ways, our code of honor. The La Conchas protect their own."

Victor moved closer, placing a hand on Madison's shoulder. She recoiled at his touch even as her mind whispered that he held her fate in his hands now.

"I can give you purpose, a new family," Victor continued. "All I ask is your loyalty. Your complete and utter devotion." His grip on her shoulder tightened painfully.

Madison's pulse raced, her thoughts scattering like leaves in a storm. She thought of her real family, the people she had lost. Were they truly gone forever now?

The pills' haze still clouded her mind, making it impossible to think clearly. But she knew she had to make a choice now or lose herself completely.

"Tick tock, princess," Victor sneered. "Time to decide where your loyalties lie."

Madison turned once more to Eric, taking in his battered face and unwavering eyes. She wanted to believe they could both still walk away from this, find redemption somehow.

But the cold truth settled upon her that if she refused Victor now, neither of them would make it out alive. Her only chance was to pledge herself to him fully and hope his promises held true.

With a shuddering breath, Madison lowered her head in deference. "I'm with you, Victor," she whispered, sealing her fate.

Victor's mouth curled into a satisfied grin. He reached into his pocket and produced a small white pill, placing it on the tip of his tongue. Gripping Madison's chin, he pulled her into a forceful kiss, pushing the pill into her mouth with his tongue. She recoiled at first, then surrendered, letting the drug dissolve as their lips tangled.

When Victor finally pulled away, his eyes flashed with dark triumph. "Now you are truly one of us, princess," he purred, caressing her hair. "But your loyalty must be proven."

Madison's pulse thrummed as the new drug seeped through her veins, filling her with cold purpose. She met Victor's expectant gaze unflinchingly.

"I know what their going to do next," she said, her voice steady despite the toxic haze in her mind. "If I am to take my place by your side, there can be no doubt where my allegiance lies."

Victor's smile widened, relishing her submission. "Go on," he purred.

Madison straightened, the drugs and Victor's influence wiping all hesitation from her thoughts.

"We will dismantle the Montalvos, bit by bit," Madison suggested with a chilling edge to her voice. "And the most effective way to halt Lexi and Ariana is by tearing them apart."

14

Shattered

The rhythmic knocks echoed through the hallway as Lexi, flanked by Kana and Daisuke, waited anxiously outside Emily's apartment. The tension in the air was palpable, and every passing second felt like an eternity.

When the door swung open, revealing Emily's worried face, Lexi wasted no time. "Get us inside, Em," she urged, her tone urgent. "We need to talk, and it's not safe out here."

Emily's eyes widened at the sense of urgency in Lexi's voice. Without a word, she ushered them into her apartment, glancing cautiously down the hallway before shutting the door firmly.

Once inside the relative safety of Emily's living room, Emily turned to Lexi with a mix of concern and confusion. "Okay, spill it. What the hell is going on? Why do you look like you've just escaped a war zone?" Emily paused for a second. "You were at the church… it's been all over the internet. There's rumors that some people got stuck in there."

"Emily. We don't have much time," Lexi whispered, her eyes darting around the room as if expecting danger to burst through the walls. "What you heard is true. I need you to keep this between us. I'm in deep trouble, Em. There's a bounty on my head, and both the Montalvos and the La Conchas are after me."

Emily's expression shifted from confusion to disbelief. "See I can't leave you alone for one minute before starting a whole gang war."

Lexi gave Emily a solemn look. "I didn't start this, Em. But I aim to finish it."

Lexi began pacing the room as she recounted the events leading up to their desperate visit. "That deal at the church was sacrilegious. Both sides have shown they will stop at nothing to best the other. They're playing some twisted game, and innocent people become the inconvenient link between them."

"You've officially out-crazed every soap opera plot I've ever seen. What's the plan, then? How can I help you, Lex?"

Lexi stopped pacing and turned to Emily; her expression deadly serious. "I need access to your gun safe. And a car - something nondescript that can't be traced back to you."

Emily looked between the three of them, uncertainty etched on her face. She cared deeply for Lexi, but getting involved in a mob war was insanity. Still, the determination in their eyes gave her pause.

Finally, she sighed. "I have an old Civic I was planning to sell. It's parked two blocks over. We can take that." She moved to the bookshelf, sliding it aside to reveal a wall safe. With trembling hands, she opened it and retrieved two handguns and ammo.

"Em, it's too dangerous. I don't want to involve you anymore that I already have."

Emily took a deep breath and met Lexi's gaze steadily. "I'm already involved. I care about you, and I want to help. We're in this together now."

She turned to Kana and Daisuke. "I don't know you two, but it's clear you're important to Lexi. That's enough for me to offer my trust."

Kana gave a slight bow of acknowledgment. Daisuke simply nodded; his expression unreadable.

Emily chewed her lip thoughtfully. "If you need information on this Hawks organization, I might have an idea. I volunteer at the museum downtown, in the archives. They have all kinds of old records and documents. It's possible there could be something there that would give you a lead."

Lexi considered this and then nodded. "It's worth a shot. Better than anything we've come up with so far." She checked her watch. "The museum should still be open. Let's go."

The group headed downstairs to the small parking area behind Emily's building. The old Civic sat waiting, anonymous and nondescript. Emily slid into the driver's seat, Lexi in the passenger side, while Kana and Daisuke took the back. Emily's knuckles were white on the steering wheel as they pulled out into the street. This wasn't at all how she had envisioned her day going. But one glance at Lexi's determined face strengthened her resolve. She would do whatever it took to help her friend.

The group pulled up a block from the museum's rear entrance and parked in the shadows. As they approached on foot, Daisuke's sharp eyes noticed the back door was ajar. He put a hand on Kana's arm, halting her.

"Something's not right," Kana murmured.

Lexi scanned the area. The loading dock was empty, the security lights dark. Too quiet. She caught Emily's frightened gaze and gave a slight shake of her head, signaling caution.

Moving cautiously, they approached the employee entrance Emily had described. The heavy metal door swung open with an ominous creak. One by one, they slipped inside, eyes rapidly adjusting to the dim lighting. Their footsteps echoed through the cavernous halls lined with display cases. At the archive's door, Emily pulled out her keycard, swiping it with a shaking hand. The light blinked red - access denied.

"That can't be right," she whispered. "I was just here yesterday."

A faint shuffling sound came from their left. Daisuke and Kana spun, hands on their weapons. A floor-to-ceiling glass case at the end of the hall now lay shattered, its contents missing. Then, the shriek of the alarm split the air.

The Montalvos had come for the same reason - looking for the Hawks. But this wasn't intelligence gathering. This was an ambush.

Lexi's jaw tightened as she surveyed the scene through the glass wall. The archives had been ransacked; display cases smashed.

"We need to move, now!" she barked.

They sprinted down the corridor, the wail of the alarm at their backs. Skidding around a corner, they stumbled into a group of figures clad in black, faces obscured by balaclavas. Lexi's heart sank. The Montalvos.

"Well, well," purred a woman's voice. "If it isn't little Lexi."

Lexi squared her shoulders. "Let us pass, Carla. We don't want trouble."

"Oh, but troubles already found you, niña." Knives glinted in the muted light.

"Stand down," Lexi growled. "They're with me and there's still time to turn around. Attacking the hawks, when they've vowed nothing but tradition and neutrality? Who even are we anymore? "

Carla laughed, cold and mirthless. "How ironic. You, protecting anyone? Don't make me laugh. You're one of us, Lexi, but you find yourself unfocused always hanging with the lower stock. You're ruining your own legacy."

Lexi met her glare evenly. "I don't care about your twisted idea of legacies. Stand down or you will go through me."

For a long moment, no one moved. Then Carla nodded and the Montalvos attacked.

Lexi moved with lethal grace. She swept the legs out from under the first attacker, following through with an elbow to the throat as he fell. Spinning, she snatched a knife from the belt of another and slammed the hilt into his temple. He dropped like a stone.

Kana was a blur of movement, her fists and feet striking with brutal efficiency. Each blow found its mark, and soon a pile of groaning Montalvos lay at her feet. Daisuke fought at her side, his powerful form barreling through their opponents.

But the Montalvos kept coming, wave after wave descending upon them. Lexi cried out as a knife slashed her arm, warm blood soaking her sleeve. She staggered back, struggling to keep her footing.

"Lexi!" Kana shoved another man away and was at her side in an instant. "Are you alright?"

Lexi nodded grimly. "I'm fine. We need to end this."

With a fierce yell, she launched herself back into the fray. The fighting was brutal, the hallway echoing with grunts of pain and the sickening sound of fists meeting flesh. But Lexi would not stop, would not yield. This was her stand. Her choice.

As the last man fell, she stood panting amidst the groaning bodies. Carla glared at her with undisguised hatred.

"You'll regret this, Lexi," she hissed. "We're your family. Your blood."

Lexi stepped closer, eyes hard as flint. "No. My family is right here." She gestured to Kana and Daisuke. "And you'll never touch them again."

Carla's lip curled in a sneer. But she motioned for her people to stand down.

"For now," she spat. "But this isn't over."

Lexi watched as they retreated, tension coiled in every muscle. Finally, she let out a long breath and turned to her friends.

Lexi, Kana, Daisuke, and Emily moved cautiously through the dimly lit museum halls, stepping over the bodies of fallen Hawk members branded with a serial of six numbers on their limp arms. The fighting had been brutal, but they had managed to push forward into the center of the museum.

As they entered the central atrium, the sight before them made Lexi gasp. More bodies lay strewn across the floor, blood pooling around them. But these were not just Hawk members - they were civilians unbranded. Men, women and children lay where they had been gunned down, expressions of terror frozen on their faces.

Lexi's stomach churned. This was her family's doing. The people she had tried so hard to save had still ended up doing so much harm.

"How could anyone do such a thing," Emily whimpered, clutching at her stomach.

"It doesn't matter, we have to finish this," Kana said through gritted teeth. They had no time for sentimentality, not when the fate of an entire city hung in the balance.

The group pressed on, their steps echoing in the silent halls. The closer they came to their destination, the thicker the air became with tension. They knew they were getting closer to the endgame - and with it, whatever dark secret lay atop the museum spire.

For a brief moment, Lexi wish she could turn back time - before she ever got involved in this mess, before innocents had died because of her actions... or inaction. But there was no changing the past. All she could do now was try to make it right.

A nearby door creaked open, and they froze. The Observer's body sprawled on the ground, a canvas of bullet holes painting a grim picture. Yet, amidst the wreckage of flesh and bone, his eyes shimmered with an unsettling fervor.

Lexi, Kana, Daisuke, and Emily gathered around him, their expressions a mix of shock and concern. The Observer coughed, blood staining his lips, but a twisted grin played on his face.

"I knew you'd come," he rasped, his voice weak yet strangely triumphant.

Lexi knelt beside him, her eyes searching his face. "What happened here? Who did this to you?"

The Observer chuckled, a pained sound that sent shivers down their spines. "It was meant to be. The city's fate... your fate. It's all intertwined."

Kana frowned. "What do you mean?"

The dying man's eyes bore into Lexi's. "You think you understand the game, but you're just a piece on the board. The true players... they're still hidden."

Lexi felt a chill run down her spine. "Tell me who's behind all this. Why is the city in chaos?"

The Observer's laughter turned into coughs, his body convulsing with the effort. "There are forces at play beyond your understanding. The Montalvos, the La Conchas, they're just puppets in a much larger game. And you, Lexi Montalvo, you're the key."

Emily exchanged a puzzled glance with the others. "The key to what?"

The dying man's gaze shifted to the ceiling, as if glimpsing something beyond their view. "The city's destiny. Your destiny. The awakening is inevitable."

Lexi's brow furrowed in frustration. "I need answers, not cryptic riddles. Who's pulling the strings?"

The Observer's strength waned, his breaths becoming shallower. "You'll find the answers in the depths of the city. Beneath the surface, where shadows dance. But beware, for not everything is as it seems. The true enemy wears many faces."

His eyes glazed over, and his body went limp. The Observer, once a powerful figure, had succumbed to the inevitability of death. Lexi, still kneeling beside him, felt a mix of confusion and determination.

"We need to find out what he meant or we might as well lay with him," she declared, rising to her feet.

Kana nodded, her hand resting on the hilt of her sword. "We

cannot let his words be in vain. There's a deeper conspiracy at play."

Daisuke surveyed their surroundings, his senses on high alert. "Whatever lies beneath the city, we must approach with caution. This could be the key to unraveling the entire mystery."

Lexi's phone buzzed in her pocket. She pulled it out to see a text from Ariana.

"Need to meet NOW. It's urgent."

"On my way," Lexi typed back quickly.

She looked up at Kana and Daisuke. "I have to go see Ariana. You three track down any information you can about what's going on with this election. It can't be a coincidence that all of this took place around my mother's run for deputy mayor."

Kana nodded. "Be careful. We'll wait to hear your call."

Lexi pulled her leather jacket tighter and headed for the door. As she stepped outside, the busy sounds of the city flooded her ears. Cars honking, sirens wailing, the rumble of the elevated train. But the urban noise faded away as her mind raced with possibilities.

Something big was happening in the city. Dark secrets long buried were clawing their way to the surface.

* * *

Ariana sat at her desk; her gaze fixed on the old phone she had found in Jason's car. The weight of the device felt heavier than ever in her hands. She traced the edges, the memories of finding it flooding back – memories she couldn't quite piece together.

With a deep breath, she attempted to power on the phone, only to be met with a black screen. The battery was dead, and the frustration welled up within her. What secrets could that phone hold? Why was it in his car?

Her thoughts spiraled into a labyrinth of confusion when the office door creaked open. Chase stepped in, his expression a mix of concern and determination. Ariana quickly covered up the phone, her mind racing to keep her composure.

"Hey," Chase greeted, his eyes narrowing slightly as he noticed Ariana's guarded expression. "You okay?"

Ariana forced a smile, tucking the phone away in a drawer. "Yeah, just dealing with some work stress. What's up?"

Chase crossed his arms, his gaze never leaving hers. "We're at a critical point, Ariana. The evidence we've gathered – are you ready to hand it over? Once we do this, there's no turning back. It's all or nothing."

She met Chase's gaze, a determined glint in her eyes. "We have to do this. We can't let them continue their reign of terror. If the FBI can take down the Montalvos and the La Conchas, it'll be worth it."

Chase nodded, the weight of their choices pressing on them. "Alright, we go through with it. But Ariana, be prepared for what comes next. The FBI isn't known for subtlety. They'll dig into everything, and our lives won't be the same."

Ariana took a deep breath, her gaze fixed on Chase. The weight of her revelations hung heavy in the air. "Chase, maybe I don't want things to go back to normal. Maybe I wasn't happy before. Maybe it took everything falling apart for me to realize that."

Chase's brow furrowed in concern. "Ariana, what are you saying? You love your job, you love this firm. We can rebuild, and—"

But Ariana interrupted, her frustration bubbling to the surface. "Chase, I don't want to be just a divorce lawyer. There's more to life than billing hours and navigating messy breakups. I want something more meaningful."

Chase's worry deepened. "Ariana, I'm not just your boyfriend; I'm your boss. If you decide to walk away, it's not just our relationship on the line – it's the firm. We've built this together."

Ariana sighed, the weight of her decisions pressing down on her. "I know, Chase. But right now, I'm not ready for more. I need to figure out what I want, who I want to be. And..."

Her voice trailed off as she hesitated, conflicted by what she was about to reveal. "Agent Fowler from the FBI seems to think differently. He offered me a position, Chase. A chance to make a real difference."

Chase's eyes widened in surprise. "The FBI? Ariana, you can't just—"

"Chase," Ariana's voice quivered, her eyes darting to the window before meeting his gaze. "We can pick this up later, but Lexi... she's here now. ."

Chase's concern deepened, sensing the gravity of the situation. As Ariana moved towards the door, he called after her, "Ariana, whatever you decide, we face it together. Don't forget that."

Ariana took a deep breath as she entered the room where Lexi was waiting, her heart heavy with the weight of the conversation she was about to have. She approached Lexi cautiously, trying to gauge her friend's state of mind after the tumultuous events of recent days.

"Hey, Lexi," Ariana began softly, her voice tinged with

concern. "How are you holding up after everything that happened at the church?"

Lexi's expression was guarded, her eyes betraying a mixture of exhaustion and determination. "I'm trying to put an end to all of this," she replied tersely, her tone clipped.

Ariana nodded, sensing the tension in the air. She hesitated for a moment before broaching the topic that weighed heavily on both their minds. "Have you heard anything about Madison and Eric? Do you think they made it out okay?"

The mention of Madison and Eric was like a knife to Lexi's heart, reopening wounds that had barely begun to heal. She swallowed hard, her voice tight with emotion. "I don't know," she admitted, her words barely above a whisper. "I'm trying not to think about it."

Lexi turned away, struggling to maintain her composure. Ariana's heart ached for her friend, knowing the torment she must be going through.

"We'll find them, Lexi," Ariana said gently. "Madison and Eric are resourceful. If anyone could escape and stay hidden, it's them."

Lexi crossed her arms, staring blankly ahead. "I wish I shared your optimism.

"Lexi, there's something you need to know," she began, her voice steady but filled with urgency. "I've been working with the police department and the FBI to stop all of this. We have enough evidence to bring down both the La Conchas and the Montalvos."

Lexi's eyes widened in shock, her defenses rising like a wall between them. "Why didn't you tell me this before?" she demanded, her voice tinged with betrayal. Lexi stared at Ariana, her body rigid with tension. She couldn't believe what she was hearing.

"How could you go behind my back like this?" Lexi said accusingly. "Do you have any idea what you've done?"

Ariana held her hands up imploringly. "Lexi, please try to understand. I had to make this call. Too many innocent lives have been destroyed by the violence between the Montalvos and La Conchas."

Lexi's eyes flashed dangerously. "You think I don't know that? I've seen the damage firsthand. But taking them down is not as simple as you seem to think." She began pacing agitatedly. "Once the FBI makes their move, all hell will break loose. There will be retaliation, bloodshed. My family - your family - we'll all be caught in the crossfire."

Lexi stopped and looked at Ariana beseechingly. "Please, you have to call this off before it's too late. We can find another way, a way to make peace between the families."

Ariana sighed heavily. "I wanted to protect you, Lexi. But you have to understand, bringing them down means..." her voice trailed off, the unspoken implication hanging heavily in the air.

Lexi's jaw clenched, her fists balling at her sides. "It means I go down too," she finished for her, her voice laced with bitterness.

Ariana's eyes welled with tears as the weight of her betrayal sunk in. She had hoped to shield Lexi from the harsh realities of what was to come, but now there was no going back.

"Lexi, I'm so sorry," she said, her voice cracking. "I never wanted this for you. But the FBI gave me no choice - it was to cooperate or become a target myself."

Lexi's shoulders slumped in defeat, the fight draining from

her body. She sank into a chair, dropping her head into her hands.

"So that's it then," Lexi said dully. "How could I have not seen this coming? You've always looked down on me, Ariana. Like you're better than me."

Lexi stared at the floor, her mind racing as she processed Ariana's revelation. She had trusted Ariana, considered her a true friend - perhaps the only person outside of her family that she could rely on completely. And now that trust was shattered.

"I never judged you, Lexi," Ariana said gently. "I know you got caught up in things you can't control. But this violence has to end."

Lexi's head snapped up, her eyes flashing. "Don't pretend you know anything about my life," she said sharply. "You've always seen us as criminals. Thugs. Admit it - you think we deserve this."

Ariana flinched at the accusation. "That's not true," she protested. But even as she spoke the words, doubt crept into her mind. Had she seen Lexi that way, deep down? Is that why she had gone behind her back?

"Save it," Lexi said bitterly. She stood up and paced to the window, staring out at the city lights. "So what happens now?" she asked quietly.

Ariana hesitated. "Witness protection, maybe. I know someone at the FBI. We can negotiate something for you, for your friends..."

Lexi whirled around, her eyes flashing. "Witness protection? You want me to abandon everything - my family, my life - and go into hiding?" Her voice rose in anger.

"Lexi, please, it's the only way," Ariana pleaded. "I'm trying to help you."

Beautiful Lies

"Help me? You're destroying me!" Lexi shouted. She advanced on Ariana, jabbing a finger toward her. "I will never turn against my family. If you think I'll testify or cooperate in any way, you're dead wrong."

Ariana shrank back, stung by the venom in Lexi's voice. This was not her friend - this was a stranger, hardened by anger and betrayal.

"I won't give up on you, Lexi," Ariana said softly. "When this is over, I hope you'll understand."

Lexi shook her head bitterly. "Don't you get it? It'll never be over. My family and The La Concha's will never stop looking for me, or for revenge. You should have stayed out of this, Ariana. Now we all have to face the consequences."

She turned away, signaling an end to the conversation. Ariana stood motionless, riddled with doubt over what she had set in motion. Had she destroyed the lives of those closest to her? And could their friendship ever be repaired? With a heavy heart, she left the room, the weight of Lexi's words lingering.

Josiyah Martin

15

Machinations

Madison stood beneath the lukewarm water of the employee shower in the abandoned aquarium, her mind a tempest of conflicting thoughts. The high from the pills Victor had given her was starting to fade, leaving a hollow feeling in its wake. What was she doing here? What had she become?

The sound of water droplets hitting the tiled floor echoed in the empty room as Madison turned off the shower. She wrapped herself in a threadbare towel, a sense of vulnerability creeping over her. She hadn't felt this lost in a long time.

Dressed in borrowed clothes that hung loosely on her slender frame, Madison ventured out into the dimly lit corridors of the aquarium. The once vibrant and bustling place now felt like a hollow shell of its former self.

As she roamed the deserted hallways, Madison couldn't shake the feeling of being watched. Faint echoes of La Concha men's voices reverberated through the empty spaces, signaling their presence. Curiosity sparked within her, and she found herself drawn towards the source of the sounds.

Madison watched with a mixture of fear and fascination as the La Concha men trained in the makeshift area. Their movements were fluid and calculated, each strike executed with lethal intent. The sound of fists hitting punching bags and feet hitting mats filled the room, creating an atmosphere charged with tension.

As she observed, Madison couldn't help but feel a shiver run down her spine. These were not mere thugs or petty criminals. They were skilled fighters, trained to kill without hesitation. She wondered how Victor had managed to gather such a ruthless team.

One man in particular caught her eye. He was tall and lean, his muscles rippling with every movement. His dark hair was slicked back, revealing sharp cheekbones and piercing green eyes. He moved with a grace that was almost intimidating.

Madison found herself unable to tear her gaze away from him, intrigued by the fierce intensity in his eyes as he sparred with his partner. It was as if he was in a world of his own, completely consumed by his training.

The sound of approaching footsteps snapped Madison out of her trance-like state. She quickly ducked behind a nearby pillar, peering out to see who it was.

To her surprise, it was Victor himself, accompanied by two other men who seemed to be high-ranking members of La Concha. They spoke in hushed tones before turning their attention towards the training area.

"He's getting stronger," one of them remarked, nodding towards the man Madison had been observing.

Victor nodded in agreement. "He has potential."

The other man scoffed. "Potential? He's already surpassed most of our best fighters."

Madison, hidden in the shadows, trailed behind Victor and his men as they navigated the eerie corridors of the deserted aquarium gallery. The sound of their steps reverberated off the worn tiles, blending with the haunting groans of corroded metal fixtures in the distance. Abruptly, Victor stopped in his tracks, pivoting to confront them with a calculated speed, his piercing green eyes locking onto theirs and amplifying the dim reflections filtering through the shattered skylights above. From her concealed vantage point, Madison observed every move with a mix of trepidation and intrigue, her presence unnoticed as she absorbed the unfolding scene.

"Tomorrow is the day we have been waiting for, my friends," he began, his voice low but powerful. "Years of patience and preparation have led us here, to this pivotal moment."

The men listened intently, transfixed by his commanding presence.

"The time has come for the La Concha family to regain our rightful place in this city," Victor continued. "For too long we have lurked in the shadows while corrupt politicians and businessmen have grown fat and lazy from our labor."

His words were met with murmurs of agreement from the crowd. Victor allowed himself a thin smile.

"Tomorrow night, at the Masquerade Ball, we will make our move. Our associates on the inside have already set the trap perfectly." He paused for effect. "By the end of the night, the Mayor, the Police Chief, and every other crooked official in attendance will be in our hands."

The warehouse erupted into chaotic shouts and applause. The men were riled up, eager for vengeance. Victor raised his hands to quiet them.

Beautiful Lies

"Patience, my friends. The time for action will come. For now, rest up and prepare yourselves. When the clock strikes midnight tomorrow, the tides of war will turn, and the La Concha family will finally rise to reclaim our power!"

His proclamation was met with roars of approval. As the men filed out, thrilling in anticipation of the following night, Madison clung to the shadows, her mind racing over what she had just heard.

Madison stood in the shadows, fear and uncertainty etched on her face as Victor suddenly approached her with a sly smile. In his hand was another small pill.

"Looks like you could use this," he said, offering it to her.

Madison hesitated, glancing between the pill and Victor before reluctantly taking it and swallowing it with a resigned sigh.

"Do you trust me?" Victor asked, his eyes piercing into hers.

"I don't trust anyone anymore," Madison replied defiantly.

Victor chuckled, admiring her honesty. "I can respect that. But sometimes, trust is necessary. Let's try something."

He revealed a blindfold and held it out to Madison. Skeptical, she asked, "What's the blindfold for?"

"It's a test of trust," Victor explained. "Put it on."

Madison was hesitant but the effects of the pill made her feel powerless. With a defeated sigh, she allowed Victor to blindfold her.

"Now follow me," he instructed as they walked through another section of the aquarium.

As they moved, he spoke again, "I want to show you something."

He gently placed a soft black cloth over her eyes, taking care not to disturb her hair. After guiding her through the towering tanks that used to hold exotic fish, he brought her to a secluded corner of the aquarium. There, he unveiled three ornate display cases, revealing masquerade costumes fit for a dream. The first was his own, a fallen angel with intricate feathered wings and glistening silver adornments. The second was hers, a shimmering garment made of celestial fabric and topped with a delicate porcelain mask. And the third was a majestic swan, its regal white feathers cascading down its elegant form. Madison couldn't help but reach out and caress the velvet lining and sparkling beads, as Victor described each enchanting costume in detail.

"Whose is the swan?" she asked.

Victor glanced at her, the corner of his mouth turning up slightly. "That one belongs to my silent partner. She prefers subtlety and mystery over flashy theatrics."

Madison narrowed her eye's sensing Victor was still withholding information. She chose her next words carefully. "This partner of yours must be someone important for you to keep her identity so secret."

"All will be revealed soon enough," Victor said smoothly. His voice dropped to a hushed whisper. "Tomorrow at the mayor's masquerade ball, everything will come to light. Our true destinies will be revealed under the veil of these masks."

Madison feels lightheaded, unsure if it's from the pill or Victor's words. She sways slightly and he catches her, his strong hands gripping her arms.

"It's alright, just breathe," he murmurs. "I know it's a lot to take in. But you must trust me now. Your role in all of this is crucial."

Beautiful Lies

Madison's mind swims with questions but the effects of the drug make it hard to think clearly. Victor's touch and close proximity make her pulse quicken.

"What...what is my role?" she finally manages to ask.

Victor traces a finger down her cheek. "In time, my dear. For now, know that you are special. You have a power within you that must be harnessed."

His lips graze her ear as he whispers, "And I will teach you how to use it."

Madison shivers, unsure if it's from fear or desire. The secrets lurking behind Victor's words excite and terrify her. She feels as though she's on the edge of a great abyss, preparing to fall into the unknown.

Madison, her mind still swimming with the images of the masquerade costumes, gathered her courage and turned to Victor.

"I need to see Ethan," she said, her voice steady.

Victor studied her for a moment, a faint smile playing on his lips. "Even in the midst of all this, you're still concerned about him. A true La Concha, always protecting those you care about."

Madison didn't let his comment faze her. "Ethan is innocent in all of this. He has nothing to do with your plans or the Montalvos. He's just a guy caught up in something much bigger than him."

Victor chuckled, amused by Madison's loyalty. "Very well, princess. You may see Ethan, but be careful – there are people after you. The city is a dangerous place for someone in your position. But remember, you're not a prisoner here, we are your people."

Madison left the aquarium and made her way across the city.

She kept her head down, avoiding eye contact with passersby. The night air was cold and damp, matching the unease in her chest. What would she say to Ethan? How could she explain that his life was in danger without revealing too much?

She arrived at Ethan's small, dimly lit apartment. Taking a deep breath, she knocked softly, listening for any movement inside. After a few moments, she heard footsteps approaching and the door opened halfway, stopped by the chain lock. Ethan's face appeared in the crack, his expression shifting from confusion to shock as he registered her presence.

"Madison? What are you doing here? I thought you were..." His voice was hushed, eyes darting side to side as if checking they were unobserved.

"I know, I owe you an explanation but I don't have time. I needed to see you, to warn you," Madison replied.

"Ethan, let her in," Lexi's voice, cold and unwavering, cut through the silence.

Ethan opened the door wider, and Madison cautiously stepped inside, her eyes meeting Lexi's icy gaze. The atmosphere in the room became tense, the unspoken history between the two women lingering in the air.

"I guess you haven't completely changed, after all," Lexi remarked, her tone cutting. "I knew if you were still breathing, you'd find your way here eventually."

Madison tried to speak, to apologize and explain, but Lexi interrupted with a glance that spoke volumes.

"Don't even bother," Lexi said sharply. "You literally betrayed your friends for someone who would kill his own brother in cold blood." Lexi's piercing gaze bore into Madison as she asked the question that hung heavy between them. "Is Eric even still alive?"

Madison nodded, a sense of relief and worry mingling on her face. "Yes, he's alive. But, Lexi, you need to get out of the middle of this. Victor will stop at nothing to bring your family down. I don't want you hurt."

"What about everyone else Maddie? You think every Montalvo is like my mother? There are innocent people on both sides being slaughtered."

"Don't you think I know that? My whole family is gone thanks to yours, and the last person I have you want me to turn my back on?" Madison's plea hung in the air, the weight of their shared history and the current chaos in River Creek pressing down on them. Lexi's expression remained stoic, a mask that hid the conflict within.

Lexi scoffed, bitterness tainting her words. "Your family? The La Conchas? They're criminals, Madison. Don't try to paint them as victims."

Madison's eyes flashed with frustration. "I'm not defending them, Lexi. I'm trying to prevent more bloodshed just like you. Victor is playing a dangerous game, and he's not just a threat to the Montalvos anymore. He's a threat to the entire city. We need to stop him together."

Lexi's gaze hardened. "I don't need your help, Madison. I can handle Victor and anyone else who comes my way."

Ethan, who had been silent during the exchange, finally spoke up. "Lexi, whether you like it or not, we're all involved in this now. Madison came here to warn me, to warn us. We need to find a way to deal with Victor, not tear each other apart."

Madison took a deep breath, the gravity of her revelation weighing on her shoulders. She looked at Ethan and Lexi, knowing that what she was about to say would change everything.

"There's something you both need to know," Madison began, her voice steady. "Victor has a silent partner, someone operating in the shadows, and they've gone to great lengths to conceal their identity. Tomorrow night, during the Mayor's Masquerade ball, Victor plans to execute a significant move. If we can intercept his plan, not only can we stop Victor, but we have a chance to unveil the identity of the person working with him."

Ethan and Lexi exchanged glances, a mix of surprise and concern etched on their faces. Lexi's eyes narrowed as she processed the information. "A silent partner? Do you have any idea who it might be?"

Madison shook her head. "No, that's the tricky part. Victor has kept this person well-hidden, and they're using the masquerade ball as a cover. The only clue I have is that they'll be wearing a swan costume. It's their way of blending in while maintaining anonymity."

Ethan furrowed his brow. "A swan costume? That's not exactly subtle."

Madison nodded. "Exactly. It's a deliberate choice, probably meant to throw off suspicion. But if we act strategically, we might be able to expose them without Victor knowing."

Lexi crossed her arms, deep in thought. "So, we stop Victor, unveil the silent partner, and put an end to this mess. Easier said than done."

Madison agreed. "It won't be easy, but it's our best shot. We need to work together, pool our resources, and be one step ahead of them. The fate of River Creek hangs in the balance."

Ethan took a moment before nodding. "We're in this together, then. Let's stop Victor and expose this silent partner. But remember, Madison, this doesn't absolve you of your past actions. We're doing this for the city and the innocent people caught in the crossfire."

Madison met their determined gazes, understanding the significance of their reluctant alliance. "I know, Ethan. And I'm ready to face the consequences of my choices. Let's make sure Victor and his silent partner don't get away with whatever they have planned."

* * *

Ariana sat in the cold, sterile conference room, her heart pounding in her chest. The weight of the decision she was about to make pressed heavily on her shoulders. She was surrounded by Chase, Officer Penbrooke, and Agent Fowler, all waiting for her to begin her testimony. But Ariana couldn't shake the images of Madison and Lexi being hurt, their lives ruined by the truth she held.

She cleared her throat, attempting to steady her nerves, but the words caught in her throat. The room was filled with an awkward silence, broken only by Officer Penbrooke's impatient tapping of a pen on the table.

"Ms. Bennett, we need you to start your testimony," Officer Penbrooke urged, irritation evident in his voice.

Ariana hesitated, her mind racing. She knew the information she held could bring down Catalina and Victor, but it would also implicate Madison and Lexi. She couldn't let her friends pay for the sins of their families.

"I... I can't do this without some assurances," Ariana finally spoke up, her voice shaky but determined.

Chase frowned, exchanging a concerned glance with Officer Penbrooke. Agent Fowler remained stoic, studying Ariana with a keen intensity.

"What kind of assurances are you asking for, Ms. Bennett?" Agent Fowler inquired, his tone measured.

Ariana took a deep breath. "I want immunity. Not just for me, but for my friends—Madison and Lexi. I'll give you everything you need to bring down Catalina and Victor, but you leave them out of it."

Officer Penbrooke scoffed, a disbelieving smile playing on his lips. "You think we're going to let you dictate terms here? This is a serious investigation, not some negotiation."

Chase shot Ariana a concerned look, but Agent Fowler raised his hand, silencing Officer Penbrooke. He studied Ariana, her expression unreadable.

"Immunity for you and your friends, in exchange for information on Catalina and Victor?" Agent Fowler mused. "It's an interesting proposal. But why should we believe you? What makes your information so valuable?"

Ariana met Agent Fowler's gaze, her eyes reflecting a mix of desperation and sincerity. "Because I'm willing to risk everything to bring them down. I've seen the devastation caused by both the Montalvos and the La Conchas, and I want to end it. My loyalty is to justice, not to the criminals who have destroyed the lives of those I care about."

Agent Fowler leaned back, considering Ariana's words. After

a tense moment, she nodded. "I appreciate your candor, Ms. Bennett. Loyalty to justice is a rare commodity in this city. I'm willing to entertain the idea of immunity, provided the information you provide is substantial and actionable."

Chase's phone buzzed abruptly, and he quickly glanced at the screen. A solemn expression crossed his face before he spoke up.

"Guys, we have a problem. There's been a massacre at the museum. Over a hundred dead."

The room fell silent, the weight of the news sinking in. Ariana's eyes widened in shock, realizing the magnitude of the tragedy that had just unfolded.

Agent Fowler's phone buzzed next, and he read the message with a furrowed brow. He stood up abruptly, his chair scraping against the floor.

"This changes things. We need to wrap this up. Penbrooke, we have work to do," Agent Fowler declared, his tone brisk and businesslike.

Officer Penbrooke nodded, his features hardening. "We'll reconvene later, Ms. Bennett. Don't think this changes the gravity of your situation."

As they left the room, Agent Fowler turned to Ariana, his expression intense. "If you can help us take these sons of bitches down, I'll make sure you and your friends get immunity. But we need actionable intel, and we need it fast."

Ariana nodded, a steely determination in her eyes. "You'll get what you need. I want them to pay for what they've done."

Chase took a deep breath, the air heavy with the weight of the recent revelations and the chaos that had unfolded. With the room now empty, he turned to Ariana, his eyes searching hers.

"Ariana, I know things have been rocky between us lately, and the last few weeks have been chaotic, to say the least," he began, his voice sincere. "I need you to know that what I said to you the last time we talked was out of fear. My instinct is to protect you, but I've come to realize that, instead of protecting you, I've been holding back your potential. I'm sorry."

Ariana met his gaze, a mixture of emotions playing on her face. The sincerity in Chase's words began to soften the edges of the tension that had built between them.

"I've been just as guilty of pushing you away as you have been. I've always been the one with my head buried in books, trying to escape my past. I should've confided in you sooner," Ariana admitted, her voice shaking slightly.

"I think it's safe to say we've been a mess. But I can't imagine a world without you in it," Chase admitted, his voice genuine. He took a step closer, reaching for her hand. "In fact, Ariana Bennett, will you—"

Before Chase could finish his sentence, there was an urgent knock on the door. Rachel, Ariana's assistant, entered the room with a panicked expression.

"Ariana, Chase, I'm sorry to interrupt, but there's someone in your office. I think you both want to see this," Rachel explained.

Ariana's heart raced as she and Chase followed Rachel into her office, only to be met with the shocking sight of Brayden on the couch, a gunshot wound staining his clothes. Without a second thought, Ariana called out for Rachel to call an ambulance, her instincts kicking in to help.

"Wait, don't!" Chase interjected urgently, his eyes locking onto Brayden. "Rachel, leave us. Now!"

Rachel hesitated for a moment, glancing between the wounded Brayden and Ariana's pleading eyes. Eventually, she nodded and left the room, closing the door behind her.

Alone in the room, tension hung in the air as Ariana and Chase focused on Brayden, whose face contorted in pain.

"I was at the museum," Brayden confessed, his voice strained. "The Montalvos... they were targeting the Hawks."

Ariana furrowed her brow, confusion evident on her face. "The Hawks? Who are they?"

Chase stepped forward, his expression grave. "The Hawks are information keepers, historically a neutral party. But it seems things have changed."

Ariana's mind raced, trying to process the information. Brayden's bullet wound was severe, and she knew they needed to act quickly. She grabbed a nearby cloth and pressed it against the wound, attempting to slow the bleeding.

"The La Conchas are planning something big at the mayor's masquerade ball," Brayden revealed, his words punctuated by pained breaths. "Catalina will be there, and the mayor plans to officially back James and Catalina's campaign."

Ariana felt the room sway dangerously around her. The implications were terrifying; if the Montalvo's had the mayor's endorsement, their power would be virtually unchallenged.

Ariana turned to Chase, her eyes wide. "We need to stop them, Chase. Whatever they're planning... it's going to be worse than the museum."

Chase nodded; his jaw set in grim determination. "I know. But first we need to get you somewhere safe," he said, turning to Brayden. "Can you walk?"

Brayden grunted in pain but nodded, doing his best to push himself off the couch. Ariana and Chase quickly moved to support him on either side.

As they helped Brayden out of the office and into the elevator that led down to the building's private parking garage, Ariana couldn't help but let her thoughts race ahead. The mayor's masquerade ball is tomorrow night - there will be hundreds of people there, all potential victims of the La Conchas' plot.

Beside her, Brayden had gone pale and was sweating profusely from the pain of his wound and blood loss. Ariana knew they had only one chance at stopping both Catalina and Victor - she would have to attend the ball herself.

Once they had successfully loaded Brayden into the backseat of Ariana's sleek black sedan parked in the garage, Chase turned to Ariana. His eyes were filled with concern.

"Ariana, this is insane," he argued. "You can't seriously be considering going to that ball tomorrow night."

Ariana took a deep breath, meeting Chase's gaze head-on. "I have to, Chase," she insisted firmly. "You heard what Brayden said – the mayor is going to officially back James and Catalina's campaign tomorrow night."

"But you could get hurt," Chase protested, his worry evident in his voice.

Ariana shook her head stubbornly. "I know what I'm walking into, Chase," she said determinedly. "And I can take care of myself. Besides – as long as my father and Catalina are in power, this war won't end. Come on, Chase," Ariana called out, her voice firm yet tinged with urgency. "We need to go now." She swiftly settled into the driver's seat, the engine humming to life as she glanced expectantly at him.

Chase hesitated for a moment, his expression conflicted, before nodding in silent agreement. "You're right," he finally conceded, determination flashing in his eyes. "I'm not letting you face this alone." With resolve in his voice, he stepped towards the car and slid into the passenger seat beside Ariana as they sped away from the looming building.

As they merged into the traffic-choked streets of River Creek, a sense of foreboding enveloped them both, each lost in their own thoughts about the mysterious events that awaited them at the mayor's holiday masquerade ball.

The next twenty-four hours would decide the fate of her city, possibly even her country. And she was right in the thick of it. But as scary as that thought was, Ariana knew she wouldn't have it any other way – she was born to fight, to stand up against those who sought to inflict harm on others.

And tomorrow night at the mayor's masquerade ball, she would do exactly that. With Chase by her side and a city relying on her, Ariana knew one thing for certain: Catalina and Victor were going down.

16

Recompense

Ariana and Chase walked into the doors of the masquerade ball, held at the Sandino mansion nestled within the lush expanse of the River Creek Botanical Gardens. Anxious tendrils of anticipation coiled around Ariana's heart as she entered the grand hall, her steps faltering slightly beneath the weight of her midnight-blue gown. The dress was embellished with intricate silver lace that shimmered like elusive starlight against the darkness of its fabric.

Ariana's dark brown locks cascaded down her back in elegant waves, intertwining with delicate silver threads woven into her hair, creating an ethereal halo around her sharp features. Her eyes, usually guarded behind a veil of composure, now flickered with a hint of unease as they scanned the room filled with masked strangers.

As they ventured further into the opulent venue, each step felt like a dance on a tightrope between elegance and apprehension as Ariana grappled with the weight of their hidden identities. The ornate masks adorning each guest veiled their true selves in layers of secrecy, turning every interaction into a delicate game of perception and deception.

Beautiful Lies

The ambient glow from above painted an otherworldly sheen over the guests, illuminating their elaborate costumes that whispered tales of forgotten realms and forbidden desires. Every figure seemed plucked from a dark fairy tale spun from moonlit dreams amidst the botanical wonders that encased them in an embrace both beautiful and foreboding.

Chase, sensing Ariana's unease, leaned in and whispered, "Stick to the plan, Ari. We've got this."

She nodded, appreciating the reassurance. The plan was carefully crafted, relying on their ability to blend into the crowd, gather information, and, if necessary, intercept whatever scheme the La Conchas had in motion.

With a shared understanding, they split up, seamlessly blending into the crowd. Ariana moved gracefully through the sea of masks and costumes, her eyes sharp and observant.

Ariana spotted her father, James, near the bar, engaged in animated conversation with influential figures from the city. Taking a deep breath, she approached him.

"Father," she said, her voice muffled by the mask. James turned to her with a nod, acknowledging her presence.

"Enjoying the festivities, my dear?" he asked, a glimmer of pride in his eyes. Ariana bit her lip, urgency weighing on her.

"Doesn't this all seem a bit careless," she pleaded, her eyes searching his for a flicker of understanding. "The violence around the city has gotten worse. A crowd like this, don't you think it's just inciting trouble?"

James regarded Ariana with a measured gaze, his expression unreadable behind his own ornate mask. "My dear, this is a celebration of unity and progress," he replied, his voice carrying the weight of authority. "The city must move forward; despite the challenges we face."

"Wow dad, you really do sound like a politician. Self-serving in the name of the people." Ariana's words cut through the air like a knife, her frustration palpable beneath the veneer of civility. James's gaze hardened, a flicker of irritation crossing his features before he composed himself.

"I understand your concerns, Ariana," he said, his tone firm. "But sometimes progress requires sacrifice. We must show strength in the face of adversity, for the greater good of our city."

Ariana clenched her jaw, resisting the urge to argue further. She knew she wouldn't sway her father's convictions tonight. With a curt nod, she stepped back, her disappointment simmering beneath the surface.

"Of course, Father," she said, her voice tinged with resignation. "I hope you're right."

As James turned away, Ariana's gaze lingered on him for a moment longer, a mixture of resentment and determination burning in her chest. She may not be able to change his mind tonight, but she refused to stand idly by while the city plunged further into chaos. With a deep breath, she turned her attention back to the task at hand.

Exiting the grand ballroom, Ariana made her way through a side corridor and found herself in a quieter corner of the mansion. It was here, away from the buzz of the masquerade, that she stumbled upon a familiar face.

"Is that Ariana Bennett I spot?" The voice came from behind her, accompanied by the soft rustling of fabric. She turned around to see a figure stepping out from the shadows. The woman was

Beautiful Lies

wearing a peacock mask, but Ariana didn't need to see her face to recognize the voice.

"Evelyn," Ariana replied, her surprise quickly replaced with relief at seeing a friendly face. Evelyn had been her confidante during her years at Columbia Law School and now worked as a reporter for River Creek News.

Evelyn pulled off her mask to reveal her bright smile. "It's been so long, Ari." She looked Ariana up and down before adding playfully, "And you look as ravishing as ever in that gown."

Ignoring the compliment, Ariana quickly steered the conversation towards Evelyn's occupation. "I guess as a reporter, you're here to cover the masquerade. Any juicy story on your radar?"

"Well," Evelyn began thoughtfully, leaning against the wall beside them. Her eyes turned sly under the soft light, showing an unmistakable spark of journalistic curiosity. "There's one about your father's campaign..."

A knot of tension formed in Ariana's stomach as she remembered their earlier confrontation. "What is it?"

Evelyn paused for a moment, then leaning closer she whispered, "There's word going around that James isn't exactly playing by the rules."

A wave of unease washed over Ariana. Her father's campaign had been shrouded in a cloud of mystery and rumors ever since he linked himself to Catalina.

"I'll need to verify it," Evelyn continued, "But I thought you should know."

"Thank you," Ariana said sincerely, grateful for the tip-off. "I'll keep an eye out for any developments." As Ariana processed

Evelyn's revelation about her father's campaign, Evelyn's next question caught her off guard."By the way, Ari, are you still working at Smith & Associates?" Evelyn inquired, her tone casual but with a hint of concern.

Ariana hesitated, her mind racing to make sense of the unexpected inquiry. "Yes, why do you ask?"

Evelyn's expression softened, her concern evident as she spoke. "I heard some rumors circulating in legal circles. Seems like Smith & Associates might be on the verge of closing down."

Panic surged through her, catching her off guard. Amidst the whirlwind of personal and family worries consuming her thoughts, the idea of financial troubles at work hadn't crossed her mind. The question lingered: Why hadn't Chase mentioned this to her if it was true?

"That's... news to me," Ariana admitted, her voice tight with worry. "I had no idea things were that dire."

Evelyn nodded sympathetically, her eyes reflecting understanding. "I'm sorry to be the bearer of bad news, Ari. But I thought you should know, especially if you're still with the firm."

"Thank you again, Evelyn," Ariana replied, her gratitude mixed with a sense of unease. The revelation added another layer of uncertainty to an already tumultuous evening.

Evelyn flashed her a knowing smile before putting her mask back on. "Just doing my job, Ari. And speaking of which, I have a feeling tonight's festivities might just give us the scoop we've been waiting for."

With a nod of farewell, Evelyn disappeared back into the throng of masked guests, leaving Ariana alone with her thoughts.

The grand ballroom was alive with the sound of music and

Beautiful Lies

chatter as Lexi, Daisuke, Kana, and Emily made their entrance. All eyes turned to them as they walked in, a striking quartet amidst the sea of elegantly clad guests.

Lexi commanded attention in her fiery red dress, the fabric swirling around her as she moved. The intricate lace detailing and flowing train added a touch of old-world elegance to her modern ensemble. Her lion mask, adorned with glittering jewels, only added to her fierce aura.

As they made their way through the grand entrance, they were stopped by a vigilant security guard, his stern expression softened only slightly by the elaborate mask concealing his features.

"Excuse me, but I don't believe you're on the Mayor's invite list for tonight's event," the guard stated, his tone firm but not unkind.

Lexi exchanged a glance with her companions, a hint of defiance flickering in her eyes. Before she could respond, however, a figure approached from the crowd, drawing the guard's attention.

It was the Professor, his presence commanding respect as he moved with a quiet confidence through the throng of guests. He leaned in close to the guard, whispering something into his ear in hushed tones.

Whatever words passed between them seemed to carry weight, for the guard's demeanor shifted almost immediately. With a nod of understanding, he stepped aside, allowing Lexi and her group to pass without further protest.

After the guard let Lexi's group through, the Professor gestured for them to step aside, his expression grave beneath the mask. As they moved out of the flow of guests, he leaned in close, his voice low and urgent.

"I know you have a plan for tonight," he began, his eyes scanning the room for any prying ears. "But you need to be careful. This place is swarming with Montalvos and police."

Lexi nodded, her dark eyes intense as she scanned the room. She had expected this to a certain extent - it was an Montalvo's nature to be present where power dwelt.

Daisuke, standing beside Lexi, wore an unreadable expression. His long hair was pulled back into a tight ponytail, highlighting the stern lines of his face. Beneath his bird mask, his eyes were hard and alert.

"We'll stay cautious," he assured the Professor, his voice deep and steady. "Thank you for your warning."

The Professor gave them a curt nod before disappearing back into the crowd, leaving the group with a sense of heightened tension that echoed through the noise of the party.

The four of them stood in silence for a moment, each absorbed in their own thoughts. The grandeur of the ballroom seemed to mock their grim situation, the opulence only serving to highlight the sinister undercurrent flowing beneath the surface.

The grand doors of the ballroom swung open, revealing a scene that crackled with an electric intensity. The air hummed with a mix of excitement and tension as guests, their faces hidden behind elaborate masks, mingled under the soft glow of crystal chandeliers. Shadows danced across the opulent setting, adding a mysterious edge to the atmosphere.

In the center of it all loomed the mayor, a commanding presence in his shimmering ceremonial attire that caught and reflected the golden light like shards of glass. His stern gaze swept over the crowd, silencing even the faintest whispers with its sharpness. As he stepped forward, his voice sliced through the murmurs like a thunderclap, drawing every eye towards him in a mix of fear and respect. The anticipation in the room was palpable, each guest on edge as they awaited his next words.

"Ladies and gentlemen," he began, his words resonating throughout the grand hall. "Tonight marks a new chapter in the history of River Creek. A chapter of progress, prosperity, and unity."

Lexi stood amidst the throng of masked figures, her eyes fixed on the mayor as he spoke. Beside her, Daisuke and Kana exchanged concerned glances, their instincts on high alert.

As the mayor continued his speech, his words took an unexpected turn. "And it is with great pleasure that I announce my support for the future of our city," he declared, his gaze sweeping across the room. "I stand behind James Bennett and Catalina Montalvo as they step forward to lead River Creek into a new era of greatness."

A hush fell over the crowd as James Bennett and Catalina Montalvo stepped forward, their faces hidden behind ornate masks. Lexi couldn't help but feel a prickle of unease at the sight of them standing side by side, their presence exuding an almost palpable aura of power.

The mayor's eyes gleamed with satisfaction as he announced their alliance to the assembled guests. The tension in the room seemed to dissolve into a collective murmur of surprise and curiosity.

As if on cue, James Bennett removed his mask, revealing his

rugged features and sharp green eyes. He smirked confidently at the crowd before turning to face Catalina Montalvo.

Catalina kept her mask on, her dark hair cascading down her back like a midnight waterfall. But even without seeing her face, Lexi could sense the steely determination emanating from her.

"We are honored to have your support," James said with a slight bow towards the mayor. "Together, we will lead River Creek into a new era of prosperity."

The crowd erupted into applause, seemingly won over by James' charismatic tone and Catalina's enigmatic presence.

The announcement sent ripples of shock and speculation through the crowd, but Lexi's attention was drawn elsewhere. She noticed shadowy figures moving with purpose along the balconies on the second floor, their movements furtive and suspicious.

Sensing trouble, Lexi turned to Kana and Daisuke. "Check it out," she instructed quietly, her voice laced with urgency. "Something's not right."

Without hesitation, Kana and Daisuke nodded in understanding before slipping away into the crowd, their masks blending seamlessly with the sea of faces as they set out to investigate the ominous presence lurking above.

As the mayor's speech concluded, the grand hall erupted into a flurry of activity, the strains of music filling the air as the masquerade dance commenced. Dancers, their elaborate costumes swirling around them, flooded the center of the room, moving in perfect harmony to the rhythm of the music.

Lexi watched as guests began to join the dancers, swept up in the enchantment of the evening. Amidst the swirling mass of masks and costumes, she felt a gentle touch on her hand, a silent invitation to join the dance.

Lexi hesitated for a moment before giving in to the temptation of the dance. Lexi accepted, allowing herself to be swept into the graceful movements of her masked partner. As they danced, she couldn't shake the feeling of familiarity in the touch of their hands, the way their steps seemed to sync effortlessly.

It was only when her partner dipped her low, their faces mere inches apart, that the truth hit her like a bolt of lightning. Beneath the mask, she recognized the eyes that met hers, the voice that whispered urgently in her ear.

"Lexi," he rasped, his voice strained from the ordeal, his bruises stark against his pallid skin, a grimace flickering across his face as he spoke. "Victor's here," Eric urgently gasped, locking eyes with her, the weight of impending danger heavy in the air. "You need to get out of here," he implored, each word laced with urgency and desperation, the tension of the moment palpable as they stood on the brink of a harrowing climax.

In that moment, everything clicked into place. It was Eric, alive and standing before her, risking everything to deliver a warning.

As Ariana navigated through the sea of masked figures, her senses heightened by the urgency of the situation, she couldn't shake the feeling of being watched. A chill ran down her spine as she locked eyes with a figure clad in a swan mask, their gaze piercing through the intricate feathers adorning their disguise.

Before Ariana could react, the figure turned and swiftly made their way through the crowd, disappearing into the throng of masquerade revelers. Instinct took over as Ariana bolted after them, her determination overriding any sense of caution.

As she pursued the mysterious figure, Ariana found herself drawn deeper into the heart of the botanical gardens, where the labyrinthine maze loomed before her like a maze of tangled secrets. With each twist and turn, the foliage seemed to close in around her, casting eerie shadows that danced in the moonlight.

The sound of her own heartbeat echoed in her ears as Ariana pressed on, her footsteps echoing against the cobblestone path. But despite her best efforts, the elusive figure remained just out of reach, slipping through her fingers like smoke on the wind.

Lost in the maze, Ariana's sense of urgency turned to mounting unease. The darkness seemed to press in on her from all sides, disorienting her with its shifting shadows and whispered secrets.

Ariana fumbled for her phone, her fingers trembling with urgency as she attempted to dial Chase's number. But as she held the device to her ear, all she was met with was silence. No signal. Panic surged within her as she frantically searched for any semblance of connection, but the stubborn reality remained — she was alone in the heart of the maze.

Inside the opulent ballroom, the air heavy with the scent of perfume and intrigue, Lexi's hand tightly clasped in Eric's, navigates through a maze of costumes. The soft glow of chandeliers overhead casts a warm light on their determined faces as they push towards the exit, their path a dance through a sea of swirling gowns and whispered conversations.

As they approached the door a familiar voice sliced through the air like a blade, freezing her in her tracks. "Going so soon?"

The words sent a shiver down her spine as she slowly turned to face the source. Victor, adorned in the costume of a fallen angel, stood before her, a sinister smirk playing at the corners of his lips. Beside him, Madison stood like a specter, her expression unreadable behind the porcelain mask that obscured her features.

Lexi's heart pounded in her chest as she stared at the two figures before her, a sense of dread settling like a heavy weight in the pit of her stomach. She had hoped to slip away unnoticed, to rescue Eric and make her escape. But now, faced with the embodiment of her worst nightmares, she knew that escape would not come easy.

"Victor," Lexi spat his name like a curse, her voice laced with defiance despite the fear that coiled within her. "What do you want?"

Victor's smirk widened into a predatory grin as he took a step closer, his gaze piercing through her like daggers. "Isn't it obvious, my dear?" he replied, his voice smooth as silk. "I want what's rightfully ours."

Madison remained silent at his side, her presence a haunting reminder of the tangled web of betrayal and deceit that had ensnared them all. Lexi's mind raced with a thousand questions, each one more urgent than the last. But she knew that now was not the time for answers. Now was the time for action.

Amidst the glittering chaos of the masquerade ball, chaos erupted in a violent crescendo. Victor's men, the dreaded La Conchas, emerged from the shadows like specters of death, their weapons flashing in the dim light as they unleashed a barrage of gunfire upon the unsuspecting security and police officers.

Panic swept through the room like wildfire as screams pierced the air, mingling with the staccato rhythm of gunfire. Guests scattered in all directions, their elaborate costumes billowing behind them as they sought refuge from the onslaught of violence that had descended upon them.

The once-elegant ballroom transformed into a slaughterhouse, its opulent decor now stained with blood and shattered glass. Bodies littered the floor, a grim tableau of carnage and chaos that bore witness to the brutality of Victor's men.

Amidst the chaos and carnage, Lexi stepped forward, her voice cutting through the cacophony of violence like a clarion call. "Victor, stop this madness! There are innocent people here," she cried out, her words echoing with a desperate plea for reason amidst the chaos of destruction.

Victor turned to face her, his expression twisted with rage and pain. "You dare to speak to me of innocence?" he spat, his voice laced with venom. "You, who stand as a beacon of the very corruption that has plagued this city for generations?"

Lexi's jaw tightened, her resolve steeling against Victor's accusations. "I'm not my mother," she retorted fiercely, her eyes blazing with defiance. "I won't let you drag River Creek down with your vendetta."

With a roar of fury, Victor lunged forward, his movements swift and brutal. Lexi met his onslaught with skill and determination, trading blows with the ferocity of a lioness defending her pride. Each strike reverberated through the room, a symphony of violence born from the clash of wills and ideologies.

For a brief moment, it seemed as though victory hung in the balance, teetering on the edge of possibility. Lexi's agility and speed matched Victor's strength and ferocity blow for blow, each combatant locked in a deadly dance of survival.

But then, with a sudden surge of power, Victor seized the

upper hand, his grip like iron as he wrenched Lexi off balance. With a swift motion, he delivered a devastating blow that sent her crashing into a nearby beam, the impact reverberating through her body like a thunderclap.

Lexi gritted her teeth against the pain, her vision swimming as she struggled to rise. But before she could regain her footing, Victor was upon her, his fists raining down upon her with merciless force.

With each blow, Lexi felt her strength wane, her resolve faltering against the relentless onslaught. She fought valiantly, every fiber of her being screaming for survival, but in the end, it was not enough.

Just as the edge of consciousness threatened to claim her, a loud, shattering noise echoed through the room. Victor paused, momentarily distracted by the sound of breaking glass. Using that moment to her advantage, Lexi drove her elbow into his abdomen, stunning him with the unexpected counterattack. But it was not enough to keep him off.

Victor retaliated with a savage backhand that sent Lexi sprawling on the cold marble floor. As stars exploded in her vision, she could see another figure entering the fray. It was Eric, his face set with determination and anger. His entrance was as unexpected as it was timely.

Eric launched himself at Victor with a roar, his fists flying like pistons. Victor was caught off guard, barely having time to block Eric's first punch before another hit him square in the jaw. Fierce determination fueled Eric's assault; each blow landed with an intensity that betrayed his protective instincts.

Victor staggered under the ferocious attack, but quickly

recovered. He lashed out at Eric with a vicious swipe of his arm, catching Eric off guard and knocking him aside. But Eric was undeterred. He surged back onto his feet and lunged at Victor once again.

All the while, Madison watched from a distance, her gaze shifting between Lexi and Victor. The uncertainty etched on her face suggested an internal struggle - a battle between loyalty and fear.

Lexi fought to regain her bearings, blood pounding in her ears as she watched Eric grapple with Victor. Her body screamed in pain, but she pushed it aside for now. Determination steeled her resolve as she started to pick herself up off the ground.

The world around them faded into a blur of movement and noise, all that mattered was what happened next in this deadly confrontation within the maze of high society.

The La Concha men swiftly moved to restrain Lexi and Eric, their movements methodical and precise. Bound and helpless, they could now only watch in horror as Victor advanced towards the mayor and Catalina, his intent clear and chilling.

"I have to admit, your commitment to family is honorable. But do you really know who you're fighting for Lexi," Victor laughed. "You're fighting for the same woman who burned down your bar and blamed it on the La Concha's. The same woman who put a bounty on her own daughter"

Lexi's breath caught in her throat as Victor's words cut through the chaos like a knife. Memories of past betrayals and deceptions surged to the forefront of her mind, each revelation adding another layer of complexity to the tangled web of lies and manipulation that had defined her life.

Beautiful Lies

As Victor taunted her with the truth, Lexi's hands clenched into fists at her sides, her nails digging into her palms until they drew blood. Anger and resentment boiled within her, fueling her determination to stand her ground against the man who had brought so much pain and suffering into her life.

"You think you know everything, don't you?" Lexi retorted; her voice laced with defiance. "But you don't know me, Victor. You don't know what I'm capable of."

With a surge of strength born from desperation, Lexi fought against her restraints, every muscle in her body straining against the iron grip of the La Concha men. She refused to let fear dictate her actions, refused to let Victor's words undermine her resolve.

But even as she struggled against her captors, a seed of doubt began to take root in Lexi's mind. What if Victor was right? What if everything she had believed about her mother, about her family, was nothing but a carefully constructed lie?

As the weight of uncertainty threatened to overwhelm her, Lexi's gaze locked with Madison's across the room. In that fleeting moment of connection, she saw a reflection of her own inner turmoil mirrored in Madison's eyes.

With a malevolent gleam in his eyes, Victor seized the mayor and Catalina, dragging them towards the center of the room where a makeshift altar had been arranged. The air crackled with tension as he raised a dagger high above his head, the blade glinting ominously in the dim light of the masquerade ball.

A collective gasp swept through the room as the guests recoiled in horror, their masked faces twisted with fear and disbelief. The mayor and Catalina struggled against their captors, their voices rising in desperate pleas for mercy.

But Victor remained unmoved, his expression cold and unyielding as he prepared to enact his twisted vision of retribution. With a cruel smirk, he raised the dagger high, ready to strike the final blow that would seal their fate.

As the tension reached its breaking point, a sudden commotion erupted from the shadows, drawing Victor's attention away from his intended victims. The sound of approaching footsteps echoed through the room, accompanied by the unmistakable ring of gunfire.

With lightning speed, Kana and Daisuke emerged from the darkness, their faces grim and resolute. Kana's blade sliced through the air like a deadly whisper while Daisuke's bullets lacerated the silence with deafening roars, tearing into Victor's men who had congregated near the altar.

Victor snarled and spun around, his cold eyes flashing dangerously as he took in the sight of the unexpected resistance. His men fell, one after another, under Kana's formidable onslaught and Daisuke's unerring aim. The room echoed with cries of pain and fear, but the two warriors remained undeterred, their focus solely on reaching Victor before he could harm the mayor or Catalina.

But Victor was not a man to be underestimated. With a snarl of rage, he lunged at Daisuke, closing the gap between them in an instant. Daisuke's eyes widened slightly but he didn't falter, quickly raising his gun and firing off several rapid shots at Victor.

Victor weaved around the bullets with an eerie grace unbecoming of a man his size. His body moved like water, defying gravity and logic as he made his way towards Daisuke with alarming speed.

A shot rang out, this time not from Daisuke's gun but from Victor's own weapon which he had drawn out almost supernaturally fast. With wide eyes and a grimace of pain distorting his features, Daisuke collapsed onto the floor. A burst of red blooming on his forehead where Victor's bullet found its mark.

"No!" Kana's scream split the air as she watched her companion fall. Her expression horrified yet hardening into a seething fury as she turned her attention back towards Victor, her blade gleaming ominously under the dim light.

Without a moment's hesitation, she flung herself at Victor, echoing Daisuke's earlier ferocity and speed, her sword slicing a deadly arc through the air. But Victor was ready for her. He parried her attack effortlessly, his own weapon glinting menacingly. Yet Kana was just as relentless, her movements fueled by rage and desperation.

Meanwhile, Lexi and Eric found themselves grappling with two of Victor's henchmen. Despite their best efforts, they were losing ground fast. The guards were well-trained and armed to the teeth, their brute strength dwarfing the duo's cunning.

Seeing this from the corner of her eye, Kana made a split-second decision. With a powerful yell that echoed through the grand hall, she pivoted mid-movement and using every ounce of strength in her body, threw her sword like a deadly spear toward the guards.

The weapon whistled through the air as it spun towards its targets with a terrifying accuracy. It struck one guard in the chest with such force that he was thrown backward against the wall where he slumped to the floor, lifeless. The second guard barely had time to react before the boomerang-like action of Kana's sword hit him in his side, sprawling him out onto the floor beside his comrade.

The ballroom fell into silence as everyone stared at Kana with newfound respect...and fear. Unfazed by the sudden hush surrounding her, she turned to face Victor again, her eyes narrowing dangerously as she advanced on him.

Back outside, Ariana stumbled through the labyrinthine maze, each twist and turn leading her deeper into its tangled embrace. With each passing minute, the sense of urgency gnawed at her insides, urging her to find a way out before it was too late.

After what felt like an eternity of wandering, Ariana stumbled upon a secluded corner of the garden maze adorned with a magnificent waterfall. The soothing sound of cascading water filled the air, offering a brief respite from the chaos that surrounded her.

But her moment of tranquility was shattered by a sudden noise, rustling in the bushes nearby. Before she could react, a powerful force slammed into her, sending her tumbling into the pool below the waterfall. The shock of the cold water enveloped her, stealing the breath from her lungs as she struggled to regain her bearings.

Panic gripped her heart as she thrashed against the unseen assailant, but their grip was unyielding, dragging her deeper into the water with each passing second. Desperate gasps for air turned into choked sobs as Ariana's strength began to wane, the darkness closing in around her.

As she felt herself slipping away, fragments of memories flickered through her mind like distant stars in the night sky. Images of Scott, Lexi, Madison, and Chase flashed before her eyes, each one a reminder of the people she held dear.

Just as she felt herself surrendering to the darkness, a sudden gunshot echoed through the maze, jolting her back to consciousness. The force holding her beneath the surface released its grip, allowing Ariana to claw her way to the surface, gasping for precious air.

Collapsing onto the ground, Ariana's senses reeled as she struggled to comprehend what had just happened. Through blurred vision, she saw a figure in a swan costume lying nearby, trembling from a gunshot wound.

Chase emerged from the shadows, his face pale with horror and his handgun still smoking in his hand. His eyes met Ariana's, a silent understanding passing between them. He had not been too late. The relief that washed over her was indescribable, yet it was quickly replaced by a surge of realization. Chase had saved her life.

With all the strength she could muster, Ariana crawled towards the fallen swan figure. As she reached out a shaky hand to remove the mask, her heart pounded against her ribs, anticipation mixed with dread. The mask came away easily revealing a face Ariana knew all too well.

It was Morgan. Ariana could only stare in disbelief at the familiar contours of Morgan's face, distorted now by unfeigned shock and betrayal.

Morgan's eyes fluttered open, meeting Ariana's tear-filled gaze. In them shone an inscrutable mixture of remorse and defiance that left Ariana's heart thumping in her chest. What had driven her sister to such desperate lengths? Was it greed? Jealousy? Or a twisted sense of revenge?

Josiyah Martin

As Ariana grappled with her emotions, Chase lowered his gun slowly, his face etched with deep lines of regret and sorrow. His hands clenched into fists at his sides as he stared down at Morgan's trembling form.

As Ariana's trembling hand reached for the fallen swan mask, a rush of memories flooded her mind, fragments of a night she had long tried to remember. Images flashed before her eyes like shards of broken glass, each one revealing a piece of the truth she had been desperately seeking.

In those fragmented memories, Ariana saw Morgan, her sister, standing beside Diego at Eclipse.

"It was you," she muttered, her voice barely above a whisper. "You were there that night with Victor."

Morgan's gaze shifted between Ariana and Chase, a flicker of guilt passing over her features before being replaced by a cold resolve. "Yes," she admitted, her voice tinged with bitterness. "I was there."

Ariana felt a surge of nausea rising in her throat as the pieces of the puzzle fell into place. The memories flooded back, fragmented and distorted, like shards of glass cutting into her soul. She remembered the fear, the confusion, the desperate struggle to escape a nightmare she couldn't comprehend.

"You worked with Victor," Ariana whispered, her voice hollow with disbelief. "You helped him hurt me."

Morgan's lips curled into a twisted smile, devoid of remorse. "It was never just about hurting you, Ari," she spat, her words dripping with venom. " You just couldn't let it go. There are no heroes here, Ari. It was about freedom and love. Freedom to write my own ending, one where you don't exist."

Beautiful Lies

Ariana's world reeled. The pain of the words was worse than the icy water, worse than the lingering fear of drowning. It seeped into her heart, twisting and turning like a blade. She felt as if she stood at the precipice of an abyss, gazing down into a darkness that threatened to consume her.

"You killed Scott, didn't you?" Ariana demanded. "It was you the whole time. You killed our brother Morgan. You knew exactly what was going to happen at his funeral, that's why you didn't show up."

Morgan didn't speak, her silence telling more than any words could. The twisted smile faded from her face, replaced with a hollow look of resignation. Her eyes, always so full of defiance, now held nothing but emptiness.

Ariana felt Chase's hand on her shoulder, his grip trying to offer some semblance of comfort, but it fell on numb senses. She was drowning again, not in the icy waters of the pond, but in the cold hard truth that her own sister was a murderer.

The garden maze around them seemed to mirror Ariana's turmoil. Thick vines twisted around each other in a chaotic dance, casting eerie shadows under the moonlight— a labyrinth of deception and betrayal.

"She's gone," whispered Chase, his words barely cutting through Ariana's shock. His gaze rested on Morgan's lifeless body which lay next to the shimmering pool, the swan mask lying askew beside her.

Gone... The word echoed in Ariana's mind, reverberating off the walls of her psyche. Her sister was gone... killed by Chase in an act of defense... in an act of love for her. The weight of it all felt unbearable.

Chase helped Ariana up from the ground, his arm wrapping protectively around her as they looked down at Morgan one last time. In death, her sister looked almost peaceful - a stark contrast to the violent life she had led.

As they exchanged a worried glance, Ariana's heart raced with a mix of sorrow and apprehension. The weight of the night pressed down on them, casting long shadows in the moonlit garden. With heavy steps, they approached the locked doors leading back inside the gardens, their minds racing with unanswered questions.

Panic tightened its grip around Ariana's chest as she rattled the handles fruitlessly, realizing they were indeed trapped. The cold metal under her touch sent a shiver down her spine, echoing the chilling realization that danger still lurked nearby.

Just then, Emily emerged from around a corner, her expression mirroring their concern. She waved them over urgently, her voice hushed as she relayed the grim news.

"I've been trying to find a way back inside, but it seems the La Conchas have barricaded the place from the inside," Emily whispered, her eyes darting nervously towards the towering walls surrounding them.

Ariana's heart sank at the realization of their predicament. Trapped outside with danger lurking within, they were running out of options fast.

The tension in the room was palpable as Kana closed in on Victor, her gaze locked onto him with unwavering intensity. Despite the chaos erupting around them, her focus remained solely on the man responsible for her companion's fall.

Victor's expression hardened as he assessed Kana, a flicker of uncertainty dancing in his eyes before he swiftly masked it with a facade of cold confidence. He knew the danger she posed, her determination and skill evident in every calculated movement.

With a predatory grace, Victor shifted his stance, his muscles coiled like a spring ready to unleash its deadly force. He held his weapon poised, a silent challenge to Kana as she closed the distance between them.

As the space between them dwindled, Kana's mind raced, calculating every possible move, every potential outcome. She knew this confrontation could end in bloodshed, but she refused to back down. For Daisuke, for herself, for justice.

In a flurry of motion, Kana launched herself at Victor, her sword a gleaming blur as it sliced through the air with deadly precision. Victor met her attack head-on, his own weapon a blur of steel as they clashed in a symphony of violence.

Their blades collided with a resounding clang, the sound echoing through the room like a battle cry. Kana's muscles burned with exertion as she fought to gain the upper hand, each strike fueled by a burning determination to bring Victor down.

But Victor was no ordinary opponent. His years of training and experience lent him an almost preternatural skill, his movements fluid and precise as he countered Kana's every attack with chilling efficiency.

The two adversaries danced a deadly dance, their weapons flashing in the dim light as they circled each other with lethal intent. Each blow struck with bone-jarring force, sending shockwaves of pain reverberating through their bodies.

Despite the odds stacked against her, Kana refused to yield. With a primal roar, she redoubled her efforts, her attacks coming faster and fiercer than before. She could see the strain in Victor's eyes, the cracks beginning to form in his steely facade.

For a moment, it seemed as though victory was within reach. But then, with a lightning-fast movement, Victor countered Kana's strike, disarming her with a swift twist of his wrist.

Time seemed to slow as Kana watched her sword clatter to the ground, her heart sinking with the weight of defeat. But even as she stood defenseless before her adversary, her spirit remained unbroken.

Madison's voice cut through the chaos like a knife, her words carrying a weight of authority that demanded attention. As she stepped forward, her gaze locked onto Victor with a steely determination, a silent plea hidden within her eyes.

"Victor, we need to stick to the plan," Madison urged, her voice laced with urgency. "This isn't what we came here for. There's too much at stake."

For a moment, Victor hesitated, torn between his desire for vengeance and the logic in Madison's words. He glanced around the room, taking in the death and destruction that surrounded them, his expression darkening with a grim resolve.

With a heavy sigh, Victor nodded, his gaze flickering with a mixture of regret and determination. "You're right," he conceded, his voice low and measured. "We have a mission to complete."

Without hesitation, Victor raised his gun and fired, the shots ringing out in the air like thunderclaps. Kana staggered back, pain flaring through her legs as she collapsed to the ground, her strength draining away with each passing moment.

As Lexi and Eric watched in horror, frozen in place by Victor's warning, Madison stepped forward, her eyes brimming

Beautiful Lies

with conflicted emotions. She spared them a fleeting glance, a silent apology hidden within her gaze, before turning back to Victor.

With a sense of grim determination, Victor resumed his path towards the mayor and Catalina, his resolve unwavering despite the bloodshed that stained his hands. As he disappeared into the crowd, Madison cast a final glance over her shoulder, her heart heavy with the weight of their choices.

Victor's laughter echoed through the room, a chilling symphony of triumph and madness as he reveled in his perceived victory. His words dripped with venomous satisfaction as he explained his twisted ideology, justifying his actions as a means of restoring balance to the city.

"This is justice," he proclaimed, his voice carrying the weight of conviction. "Blood for blood. It's the only language they understand."

Lexi's pleas fell on deaf ears as Madison stood frozen, her mind reeling from the horror unfolding before her. She wanted to do something, anything to stop Victor, but the weight of his words held her captive, a silent witness to the violence consuming them all.

Desperation clouded Lexi's eyes as she turned to Madison, her voice trembling with fear and desperation. "Please, Madison, you have to do something," she implored, her words barely more than a whisper.

But Madison could only stare in numb disbelief as Victor raised his gun and fired, the sound of the gunshot ringing out like a death knell in the silent hall. Time seemed to slow to a crawl as the mayor's lifeless body crumpled to the ground, a final testament to the merciless cruelty of Victor's reign.

In that moment, Madison knew that she had become complicit in the violence that had consumed them all. And as Victor turned his gaze towards her, a twisted smile playing at the corners of his lips, she realized with a sinking dread that there was no going back.

As Victor's men erupted into applause, their cheers echoing through the hall like a macabre symphony, he turned to Madison with a twisted grin, his eyes alight with a manic fervor. "Madison, my dear," he purred, his voice dripping with malice, "it seems you have the honor of delivering the final blow."

Madison recoiled, her heart pounding in her chest as she shook her head in disbelief. "No, Victor, I can't," she pleaded, her voice trembling with fear and desperation. "Please, just do it yourself."

But Victor's patience had worn thin, his facade of calm crumbling away to reveal the ruthless predator beneath. With a savage snarl, he seized Madison by her hair, wrenching her head back with a cruel force that sent a jolt of pain shooting through her skull.

"Enough!" he barked; his voice laced with venom as he thrust the gun into Madison's trembling hand. "Kill the snake, Madison, or I'll have to exterminate your friends and everyone else here."

Tears welled in Madison's eyes as she stared down at the weapon in her hand, her mind racing with terror and indecision. She knew that to refuse would mean condemning those she cared about to a fate worse than death. But to pull the trigger would mean betraying everything she believed in.

With a heavy heart, Madison raised the gun, her hand shaking uncontrollably as she took aim at Catalina. The weight of the moment hung heavy in the air, the silence broken only by the sound of Madison's ragged breaths and the distant echoes of chaos outside.

As she hesitated, torn between duty and conscience, Victor's voice cut through the stillness like a blade. "Do it, Madison," he growled, his eyes blazing with fury. "Or watch them all die."

Despair etched itself upon Madison's face, her gaze darting from Victor's ruthless expression to the terrified woman in front of her. Catalina, despite her fear, managed to hold Madison's gaze, even as the gun pointed toward her. It was a silent plea, or maybe an acceptance of fate; in those fleeting moments, Madison couldn't tell.

Against every instinct, she began to squeeze the trigger. Each millimeter felt like a mile, every second stretched into infinity.

Her finger twitched against the trigger; tears streamed down her face and splattered on the metallic surface of the gun.

"No," she whispered to herself, but Victor heard it too.

His gaze snapped towards her. His lips curled into a monstrous snarl. "Kill her or they die!" he roared.

Madison could see Eric now, engaged in fierce combat with one of Victor's men. She could see Lexi too, helping an injured Kana to her feet. Their lives were in Madison's shaking hands.

A sob ripped from Madison's throat but was drowned by the cacophony of violence around her. She willed herself to pull the trigger—yet something inside held strong against the horror of it all.

And then came the pain—searing and blinding—as Victor's hand closed around hers, forcing pressure onto the trigger.

Catalina's terrified scream pierced through Madison's consciousness just as the deafening roar filled the air—an irreversible decision made real.

Its echo bounced off the ornate walls of the room, a haunting reminder of the dark depths they had been plunged into. Amidst the chaos, Madison stood frozen, the smoking gun still clutched in her hand, while Victor's ruthless laughter echoed around her. At that moment she knew she had started an war.

About the Author

Josiyah Martin is a writer and poet born in Fayetteville, North Carolina. With an interest in law and a passion for storytelling, Josiyah weaves intricate narratives that delve into the complexities of human nature, exploring themes of revenge, deception, and the blurred lines between justice and retribution.

Drawing inspiration from real-world events and a vivid imagination, Josiyah brings to life a world of criminal underworlds, dangerous alliances, and secret identities. Each story is meticulously plotted, offering readers a thrilling journey through dark alleys and high-stakes confrontations.

If you enjoy fast-paced thrillers with multifaceted characters and a touch of noir, Josiyah's books are sure to keep you on the edge of your seat until the final page. Discover the world of Josiyah Martin and immerse yourself in tales of suspense and treachery.

Josiyah Martin

Acknowledgments

I would like to express my deepest gratitude to everyone who contributed to the creation of this novel:

To my family, for their unwavering support and encouragement throughout this journey. Your belief in me fueled my determination to bring this story to life. To my friends and fellow writers, for your invaluable advice, brainstorming sessions, and encouragement during moments of doubt. To the readers, thank you for embarking on this thrilling adventure with me. Your enthusiasm and feedback inspire me to keep writing.

And lastly, to the characters who breathed life into this story, thank you for allowing me to tell your tale.

This book is dedicated to all of you. Thank you for being part of this incredible journey.